Frontier Ruby

TABLE OF CONTENTS

unflinching rule.

It was extraordinarily rare for the master of Humble House ever to frequent the establishment that he legally ruled over, and so he left all such mundanely horrid tasks to Miss Mortimer, for Mr. Graver loathed children and anything to do with the day to day administration of them. To him, children were to grow up into responsible and hard-working adults as soon as was imaginably humanly possible. The small and youthful detestable creatures should surely not be seen nor heard in public until they had full control of themselves in every respect. The frenetic energy of any young person was vexatious to him as was their every illogical verbal outburst. He only could be prevailed upon to come to Humble House in the most extreme of circumstances wherein he must be required to visit for some expressively imperative business. Miss Mortimer was custom-fit for Mr. Graver's purposes and needs, for she seemed precisely born and bred to manage the management of Humble House quite without any help from him whatsoever, and exactingly in line with his credos. Mr. Graver could gratifyingly take any or all credits due to the orphanage, as well as most money earned by his establishment without taking any pains, because Miss Mortimer was only too delighted to constantly rule with an iron hand, and the thrill of such harsh tasks were all the glory she seemed to desire. Such were no pains at all to her. Indeed, dictatorship was her pleasure, and she asked very little pay for it.

It was as a kind of blessing to the children of Humble House that Mr. Graver chose to stay afar off, for his administrative presence or frequent attendance would surely have been intolerable to them, perhaps even more so than their mere existence was a revulsion to him. No, Miss Mortimer was more than enough torture and trials for a small house full of orphans. At least the heavens had smiled upon these poor little souls in that one respect: that the dictatorial terrors were limited to the one tyrant rather than the two.

The other saving grace for the orphans of Humble House, as more often is the case for all children, was the ever-constant blessing of childhood in and of itself. Children are resilient and can survive or even fairly well thrive despite the despots or dire conditions around and weighing down upon them. Add to this divinely-inspired, natural treasured ability of youthful flexibility of spirit; the fact that there was such a vast palette of many children, coming and going, for each child to choose at least one or some allies from amongst, at least for some time being. Even the very reality that Miss Mortimer made herself a constant and enduring enemy to the children, each one and all, made the efforts for friendship amidst themselves all the more crucial and likely. True that there would always be enemies made amongst the children, for this seems a too typical horror of human nature, but, to be sure, there were always a few fraternal souls who could be held and called as friends that could substitute as family, however fleeting those friendships and formed family contacts might be. This was an orphanage, after all. What were the children there for? To find homes and families to call their very own was the supposed purpose. At least this was the enduring hope amongst every one of the children.

Although Ruby had never really known (to her current recollection) other than an unloving and derelict upbringing, she had instinct, intelligence and imagination enough to dream of better things, kinder treatment, true family and loving guidance. Her hopes for a happier future for herself were enough to enable her to focus forward and press ahead. Ruby believed in herself, perhaps in part because nobody else consistently and over-archingly seemed to; and her sense of things, of her part and place on this planet, was such that she felt far above and better than her station and current situation would suggest. Ruby innately sensed that every child deserved better than she had received and while she could not change her circumstances in childhood, she could surely imagine otherwise and did generally subsist in her own dream world of better things as she looked forward to when she could somehow do something to improve her environ and outcomes in her future. Ruby believed in the divine spark. She believed that every person began as if a seed of goodness, and only choices exercised or dominated upon the soul would mar and make less perfect what was meant and intended to be pure and even glorious. She believed in heavenly beginnings and indeed, even celestial endings.

Perhaps it was Ruby's tenacious innate belief that every child was indeed a child of God, that kept her mind firmly set upon forging a future for herself that would help to erase any and every sadness of her childhood once it was eventually past. Even the cheerless church-going that was part and parcel of Humble House orphanage and Mr. Graver's carefully chosen gloomy religious program for the children to attend (for Mr. Graver generally believed in torturing the body to save the soul), did not dissuade Ruby from her soul-deep sense of a gentle God who unconditionally loved little children more than any other beings living on earth. Ruby oft dreamt of heaven and such things of perfection even whilst awake. When Miss Mortimer would punish, Ruby would retreat into her mind and the happy imaginings and hopes that always existed there. When Ruby went hungrier than was usual for all orphans in Humble House, due to some imagined infraction, she could imagine sitting at a table filled with diverse foods to feast upon. Ruby's creative mind was her personally fashioned, tailor-made solace. Ruby's talent to imagine was perhaps her greatest saving grace advantage.

Since Miss Mortimer generally treated all the children at Humble House equally abysmally, Ruby at least did not feel inclined to take the mistreatment personally, and so was all the more able to chalk up all neglect, misuse and abuse to the ever-constant miserable temperament of the mistress of the horrid house. As were other children surrounding her, Ruby was also able to seek out and find some comfort and company amid the mutual misery. Ruby sometimes wondered in creative imaginings what early circumstances might have shaped a woman such as Miss Mortimer. Why had she grown to become so miserable, desiring to spread misery wherever she went?

Miss Mortimer did fancy herself more than the overseer of an orphanage, but also the head school mistress of sorts; for she did make certain that some basic learning was accomplished by the children she ruled over. This was generally desired by her employer for appearance sake at least, though within his mind and heart, he did not truly care how well educated the children under his owned and hired roof might become. The orphanage was a means to differing ends: children could find their way into homes and families, or eventually into factories or other work. It did not matter one whit to Mr. Graver whether or not children who came into and left Humble House found happy circumstances sooner or later. What was of true and real concern to him was that he was paid money wherever and however it could be got, relating to the running of the orphanage. What people round about thought of his own publicly proclaimed and painted picture of his philanthropic benevolence to the community at large also meant something to him (in what it could translate to in other eventual money, more than anything). Many folks thought highly of the widely considered altruistic Mr. Graver, who allowed orphans under one of his roofs. This suited his pomposity and garnered fatness to his pocketbook in various ways. The head of a regular person could spin at the ways and means that Mr. Graver gathered money to his own self-aggrandizing realm. The man had made a sort of art of it.

Though schooling the children in any real learning (that would be desired by parents for their own children in particular, and even townsfolk in general for children at large) was of no true import to Mr. Graver (or Miss Mortimer for that matter), some scanty supplies were provided and there was a sort of schoolroom when need be (especially to prop up appearances, should anyone significant wish to inspect such) by quickly converting the common area where the children always ate their meager meals. Ruby took full advantage of old books (often donated by people in and around the town) that ended up on the few orphanage library book shelves, by reading them voraciously, to herself and to any of the children who were keen to listen. Ruby also enjoyed making full use of chalk and slate (when Miss Mortimer was not chastising her for wasting the whitish drawing sticks to illustrate pointless stories), to put down for sight what she held in her imagination. Sometimes Ruby would tell stories to youngsters around her, repeating or creating tales and by drawing pictures along with her words to illustrate in a far more compelling way to her little audience.

"Ruby? What is that?" one little girl interrupted Ruby's illustrated storytelling one day.

"The *dragon*, of course!" Ruby glanced at her slate to emphasize a few lines that might need clarification with chalk, and then looked back at the girl.

"Oh… is it a *bad* dragon?" a little boy added in query.

"Wait… listen as I continue telling the story… and then you will know if the dragon is good or if it turns out to be bad."

An older boy put in, "It must be bad… *all* dragons are bad."

Ruby playfully instructed a life lesson, "I would think that most dragons surely are bad… but… do you not think that possibly some may be good after all. You never can tell for certain about people and creatures by their appearances on their outsides."

Most of the children sat wide-eyed on the ground around Ruby, anticipating the next drawing and sentence that she would create for them. Though it was summer and all Humble House children had been sent outdoors for a good portion of the day to spare Miss Mortimer from hearing or seeing them, Ruby had claimed a generously sheltering shade tree to offer a storytelling time and place for any of her fellow orphans to partake in.

Ruby spent a good deal of the warmer months running, climbing and chasing about outside like the rest of the children, but sometimes she preferred to initiate some enjoyable learning interludes in amongst the pleasant weather activities. And Ruby had learned that far more pleasurable edification could be garnered with book or slate under a tree (away and out from under Miss Mortimer's glare), than indoors on chairs at tables being instructed amid criticism by the scowling house-madam.

Miss Mortimer knew how to stretch a coin better than anyone before her, and Mr. Graver knew his fortune was well guarded in having procured such a scrimping, miserly housemistress. Mr. Graver was intelligent enough to know that he possessed a kind of hidden treasure in the likes of Miss Mortimer. Her ever-parsimonious skillful efforts lined his pockets well, and she did not seem to think herself ill used or cheated in the least through it all. Her joy was to always find and do things on the cheap. She seemed to possess the frugal knack of buying just enough to keep the children alive, by purchasing just enough of the right kinds of foods. She did also garner extra nourishment for the children by sending them out to gather wild berries in their seasons throughout the summer and autumn months.

Ruby was the sort of child who could find great joy in many ordinary circumstances, such as the finding and picking (and eating) of berries. As a somewhat older orphan, and having been at Humble House longer than any other child there, she would generally lead the charge, gathering any willing children around her, to gather as many berries as may be done in whatever time and distance might be allotted them on each fruit picking adventure. As certain children followed her into woods, over hills, into dales, and throughout fields in search of the wild treats, Ruby would draw upon her imagination to tell tales of all kinds. Many children soon learned to generally prefer to go berry hunting with Ruby, for happy diversions could be counted upon, and fun was often valued highly because of joyous moments being usually so horridly lacking at the orphanage (at least when Miss Mortimer was at hand). One particular reason that berry hunting garnered such joyfully playful spirits amongst the children who especially followed Ruby whilst she followed old otherwise forgotten trails and forged new ones, was that it was so exceedingly easy and quick to get so wonderfully far beyond ear and eyeshot of Miss Mortimer and her scolding tendencies. It was a sort of freedom of flight and fancy: a dreamlike escape to be sure.

Additionally, and most importantly, even as baskets or sacks of sorts were filled to their brims with berries as was expected by the housemistress, Ruby fully encouraged her followers to fill their bellies as well, small or larger, as full as could possibly be done without instantaneous great discomfort; and though such stomachs might well pay in varying discomforts later for the actions of their voracious mouths prior, such was surely disregarded, for to eat until filled (most especially with delicious delights of nature whilst in fully ripened glory of the season) was not a typical delight for the children of Humble House. Though eating while gathering was strictly forbidden, Ruby clandestinely rebelled passionately against at least this one rule of Miss Mortimer, for the redheaded youth deemed it unusually cruel and a true crime against nature to ask or tell hungry children to go berry picking, but to command that not one berry should be eaten amongst them.

Risking punishment for such possibly later discovered thievery (due to any loosened tongue of those innocents or co-conspirators with her), Ruby still proclaimed the near necessity of seizing the opportunity to feast secretly while they could do so, and so they always did. Care was taken to hastily put plenty of fruit into whatever receptacle they each carried, that much bounty at the end of a day's work would help to hide how much succulent sustenance had been taken in unto themselves; as was care taken to eat daintily, that the juice of the berries would not betray what had passed through the teeth of those who had thusly partaken, by showing any brilliant stain of coloration around their mouths.

One such berry picking time on a gloriously lovely day, an especially small and particularly beautiful new little girl queried, "Ruby? Is there any berry juice about my mouth?"

Ruby checked with meticulous care and then pronounced with relieved satisfaction for both and even all their sakes, "Not a drop, my little dear. We are safe! Though... mind that you continue to eat most carefully as you take in your fill of fruits. Berry juice is terribly difficult to remove, without removing some of your lips altogether."

The little darling looked worried until Ruby kissed her tiny forehead and then winked and smiled comfortingly, "Do not be distressed, little one. If you stain your mouth with berry juice, we will find some way to protect you from Miss Mortimer, even if we must hide you until the stains are gone. You are small enough that she rarely notices you anyhow."

A little boy promptly put himself in front of Ruby, "What of my mouth, Ruby? Have I any stain?"

Ruby carefully though quickly checked his mouth and then assured, "You are safe as well. Not a single sign of your berry gobbling, to be sure."

As the little fellow stepped back in relief, more young children came forward, spontaneously forming a line to have their little mouths checked by their dear Ruby.

As Ruby checked their mouths one by one, she laughingly remarked in-between assurances of clean mouths, "I must say that dainty berry-eating is one way to assure good mannered eating in young children… due to a full knowledge of Miss Mortimer and the dire consequences to any and all of us, should she discover any berry juice anywhere but on our fingertips and in our baskets and the like. Remember, children, we will hide our mouths if need be… and no opened mouths until our teeth are no longer stained! But, for now… back to your berry gathering and gobbling, my dears!"

The berry picking and eating resumed, though one of the children paused to inquire, "How many berries should I eat, Ruby?"

"Eat your fill, of course! Only be sure that while you eat, that you fill your sack as well. Miss Mortimer would wonder at empty sacks or baskets, and then we shall all be found out!"

Due to usual chronic emptiness of stomachs all around, it did not take a great deal of berries to fill each of the little shrunken bellies. Hunger was always commonplace at Humble House orphanage, though some children found ways and means to supplement the meager portions that were fed them. Sneaking out to partake from neighboring gardens and fruit trees was resorted to by some of the older children in order to stave off hunger pains, though Ruby did never succumb to such; for partaking additionally from nature's bounty while gathering berries occasionally seemed acceptable under heaven to her, though stealing from gardens of folks round about never did. Ruby held to her inborn conscience.

Also due to Ruby's strongly intuitive feelings regarding right and wrong, she tried her utmost to instill true goodness, kindness and fairness in and amongst the little children all around her, though she fully knew that most of the children would come and go fairly frequently and thus Ruby's influence would usually be more than likely fleeting. A born defender and nurturing sort, Ruby tended to feel a motherly and protective instinct towards those children who were younger or smaller than herself, and she was oft as a mother hen to her little adopted chicks.

Indeed, Ruby's inborn tendency to guard over other children was so very tenacious that she would sometimes intervene in various ways, taking stripes or the strap for her fellows. When berry juice found its way onto articles of clothing of other girls, Ruby would gladly trade frocks or aprons in her bold efforts to protect her peers. If juice might confess of any berry eating, Ruby would stand up to be accused and gladly take the punishment for a friend. Any other time that another child was in line for a scolding or a strapping, Ruby would divert attention to herself, transferring the ire of Miss Mortimer towards her own person, accepting a beating or confinement rather than seeing such inflicted on anyone but herself.

That night, Ruby tucked each of her younger friends into their beds with small stories of happy imaginings, their little bellies having been filled with berries and their minds having been distracted with other delights that day. Some of the stories that Ruby weaved for her many favorite little ones at slumber-time were similar to those tales that she had told them along the trail of gathering berries, for all the little children asked for such stories once more, hoping that they might dream of happy fantastic illusions that often sprung up from bedtime fables they might be told.

Ruby spoke of imaginary mischievous though benevolent pixie-like creatures hidden, watching and sometimes whispering and giggling from behind wispy waving bushes; flying horses of every color imaginable flitting about to and fro beyond the clouds above; an all-knowing distant whilst hot and bright light sun that winks and smiles lovingly at children only whilst they are doing good on any given day; stars in the night sky that are actually giant far-away fire-flies on a mission to light up the universe for all living creatures therein and beneath them on earth and any other inhabited planet whilst not brightened by the sun by day; angels in heaven that prepare happy endings for those deserving souls who were unlucky enough to have suffered any sad beginnings whilst away from the Godly sphere; and most of all, of loving families that would soon make their way to Humble House orphanage to choose a child to become all their own and to love all their lives as if they had been their very own offspring from the very first cry of a newborn babe. Once the youngsters that Ruby felt she must watch over were soundly sleeping, Ruby took herself to her own bed and before getting in under her covers, knelt by her bedside to thank the heavens above for every blessing that she could possibly think of at that moment, and to ask for blessings and happier situations for all the children around her that she loved, and of course also, for herself.

2
Sickly Creature

W hat a sickly creature she is!" snorted Miss Mortimer in a concentrated essence of frustrated anger, as she came out into the small hallway outside the sickroom where Ruby lay in a half-sleeping stupor.

Stopped upon passing, the subservient maid Patsy's only brief, obedient and doting reply was, "Yes, Ma'am."

Miss Mortimer continued her red-faced rant, "I am loath to cater to that lazy thing just because she always has a cold near all winter through. For her constant trouble to me, I have half a mind to put her to extra work as soon as she is recovered a little!"

In Ruby's defense, Patsy roused herself, "But, Ruby does have a fever, Ma'am."

Miss Mortimer shot Patsy down, "Oh, what is a trifling fever? She could get better if she wanted and had the will to. She simply enjoys being sick for want of attention."

Patsy shrunk back, saying nothing, giving a hint of a submissive nod.

Miss Mortimer persisted, still seething, "Why has nobody ever taken her off of my hands... and why was she ever dropped off here in the first place? A hospital would have been better suited to her needs. I am no nurse, I tell you, and playing nursemaid to an invalid was not what I was hired on here for. I loathe that infirmary. I do not belong in a sickroom, even for a moment. I do not have time to wait on the sickly. I am far too busy continually herding and chasing after dozens of healthy spoiled brats around here. Tell me, how do I have time to sit with the sick, with all my endless responsibilities?"

Patsy falteringly shielded Ruby, "But, she is very little trouble, Ma'am. She never asks fer nuthin and hardly ever makes a peep."

Initially baffled, Miss Mortimer swiftly recovered, "Well, I still have to wait on her and beyond all that, she isn't any help around here when she's laid up like that. I tell you that I am sick of the sight of her!"

Trying to smooth rough edges, Patsy offered, "I can take over any sick duties for you. I don't mind caring for the girl. Let me be nursemaid to her."

"Well, if you wish, but, her being sick means one less set of chores getting done because I can't get her to do them, and so I have to pull that work out of other children, or one of the servants like you… or be forced to do it myself." Miss Mortimer audibly harrumphed.

Patsy wasn't in possession of a terribly brilliant mind, but she was bright enough to know not to open her mouth to offer to take on more chores in an effort to relieve Miss Mortimer's current irritation. The girl was already saddled with more work than she could tend to keep up with as it was, and so she only said, "Yes, Ma'am. Well, I should get back to my work." and quickly flitted down the hall towards pressing duties in the kitchen.

It was all too true that Ruby was sick much throughout each winter. Though she did attempt to exercise her will to try to be as much in health, well and strong as she possibly could; the chronically cold conditions and sore lack of food were no help in improving her ever-weakening bodily constitution.

One would not know by looking at her (for she was somehow naturally a very thin and pale sickly-looking woman), but Miss Mortimer never lacked for food nor warmth in her situation at the orphanage. With Mr. Graver commonly never there and she being fully in charge of all things, there was no person to refuse her anything she wished to partake of, including clothing, food and fire. A sadly ironic state of affairs it was, but Miss Mortimer loathed Ruby or any other child under Humble House roof for ever being ill, even all the while she was quite predominantly responsible for any child not generally being healthy. If only the matron of the orphanage had compassion enough to care to some degree for the well-being of the children who were under her dominion, those youngsters would have known full health as a more common state of being.

Alas, it was not to be, for Miss Mortimer was as cold-hearted in reference to others as she was selfishly guarded for her own comforts. Unknown to even Mr. Graver, but the un-motherly guardian of his rotating children had her secret stashes of various types of particularly especial foods in several locked places. The fires in her official room of business as well as in her private quarters were always ready to share heat when she felt in need of some warmth. Though she looked the martyred miserly part, she was very well fed indeed. Miss Mortimer did not ever appear robustly healthy outwardly, and yet, she was never truly ill. Thus, the housemistress guardian was every jot as healthy as the children she ruled over were generally sickly.

For Ruby in particular, years as a neglected orphan in Humble House had caused an exacting result. With all her powers of imagination, Ruby could not seem to imagine her many recurring illnesses away. Proper warmth, food, drink, rest and affectionate love would have certainly minimized Ruby's frequent bouts with sicknesses, but in a place like Humble House, with a mistress like Miss Mortimer in charge of overseeing it all, Ruby was destined to suffer all the chronic sicknesses that nature was frequently inclined to attack her weakened body with. Part and parcel of Ruby's weakened constitution and subsequent near continual sickliness, was surely the many years that she had suffered deprivation, unlike so many of the children around her who rarely stayed in the orphanage for any great lengths of time. And so, as was her all too common and frequent condition of being, Ruby was sick again. She suffered her lot bravely, even as Miss Mortimer complained constantly.

All the while that Ruby tried to keep her spirits up, she sometimes briefly feared inwardly that she might become all the more sickly, until she died quite young (before having fully lived). Her fears did seem quite logical given the fact that, for her, each winter seemed a little worse than the last. Every frigid season, Ruby felt the consequences of the cold more than in the wintery weather the year before. She seemed to take to bed with a severe coughing sort of illness all the sooner with a slower recovery each year. More and more, poor Ruby knew health less and less.

Though winters took a downward spiraling toll on Ruby by sending her to bed far too often and for greater lengths of time for each bout of illness, summers had long been a boon to her. Of course, prior to every summer were always the joys of spring, and Ruby was the sort of person who reveled in buds and flowers of every kind. Even while she did surely adore the miracle of snow, pleasantly crispy cold and even chilly rains, her weakened being could simply not stand up against such rigors of winter for long before she was turning to bed in coughs and chills.

Whilst the world around the orphanage came alive because of the spring season, Ruby also seemed to come alive as her health improved with the warmth that the spring weather brought to their part of the world. Ruby could imagine a beautiful world of spring and summer and even into autumn in its infancy: a fantastical place of warmth where she would always be healthy and strong and would not wile away hours, days and weeks on end, coughing, even as she tried to sleep herself into vigor. Well, at least Ruby had her imagination: a creatively fertile mind full of active and even happy thoughts to busy her inner being with, even as her outer shell suffered in its attempts to better itself each season of sickliness.

All the while Ruby's constitution and wellbeing gathered strength from springs into summers, she seized the moments of energy in time. On the earliest days of sunny warmth each year, when Ruby felt her vitality at all rising, she would gather together any willing children to take in the miracles of the season out of doors. Miss Mortimer did not object to any of the children going outside and thus getting out of her hair, particularly after so many of them having been cooped up near her for the long wintery months; and of course, the children were none too reluctant to escape from the unpleasant housemistress.

Once outside, a sort of suppressed energy of joy would erupt in gleeful dashing about, this way and that, each child frenetically searching for bugs and buds, birds and butterflies; and every child wishing to share their discoveries one with another.

"Look at this small strange brown bug, everyone!" one little boy shouted.

"I found a different, smaller... *better*, greenish bug!" another boy clamored for his own attention from friends.

"There! There is a beautiful orange butterfly!" a small girl delighted.

"I saw another yellow one, over here!" another girl shared.

"I found this green bud that will become a leaf soon!" one boy observed.

"Look! There are more! Many more!" his adjacent friend added.

"I think this bud will become a flower!" one girl thrilled.

"We found more flower buds!" more girls joined.

"What colors will the flowers become, Ruby?" one girl inquired on behalf of the group of them.

"Well, sometimes we do not know until the day the bud first begins to spring forth... but, I do happen to know what colors many of these flowers will be, since I do recall what hues they were last year." Ruby smiled lovingly at her young followers, and then proceeded to recall which flowers might become what colors. The younger girls around her were all happy attention. Nearby, the boys were all distraction.

Like horses out of the racing gates, the Humble House children would first burst forth out of the orphanage doors, ready to run this way or that, and certainly seeming to need a little guidance to focus such a jumble into one general direction, rather than scattering wildly with the spring winds. Ruby would oft collect children around her whilst she taught them of this or that (based on her more years of observations), showing them anything she might find of interest to them as well as herself.

"Look at this terribly strange creature. I have found *this* kind in shades of green, yellow or even brownish, depending on what colors of plants I find them. You see, this green one was on a green plant. Does it not look otherworldly in many respects? " Ruby demonstrated and called the children's minds to deeper thinking.

One studious boy observed, "It seems like it is a stick as well as a bug: a sort of stick bug."

"Yes, it seems designed to hide as a part of the plant." Ruby offered.

One little girl asked in earnest, "Does God make bugs, Ruby?"

Ruby attempted to answer, "I do think that God designed and created them, to be sure."

"Why does God make so many different strange and even ugly bugs?" another girl inquired.

Before Ruby could respond, another girl added, "And cruel bugs that bite and sting us. Why would God make those, Ruby?"

"Well, I can only guess. I suppose you could add those questions to your nightly prayers, and maybe God will give you some ideas and clues to the true answers over time. Life holds many mysteries and we can sometimes only imagine the answers for now." Ruby suggested.

"Why does God make thorns, Ruby?"

"I can imagine some practical ideas, but could only guess the true answer to that and many other questions as well. God, heaven, the universe and many mysteries and miracles are surely still beyond me." Ruby smiled.

One girl suddenly scolded a smaller boy, "Stop *eating* the grass! You will make yourself sick."

The little fellow looked up at Ruby for illumination on the subject and so Ruby interceded, "I suppose if you gorge yourself with grass, as if you were a hungry horse, a famished cow or a gluttonous pig, you may become ill… though, I do know that many children have been just fine having eaten a little of it from time to time. I do not think any harm will come to you for eating some grass, my dear. Perhaps, as in all things, you should simply resist overdoing it."

All was settled: the little boy continued to nibble on grass as if he were a contented grazing beast in a field, even while the larger girl hoveringly looked on, in her own personal disgust of sentiment over the matter.

Spring and summer around Humble House were replete with mostly happy moments amongst the children, especially since Miss Mortimer preferred to keep herself within doors. Her waking hours were usually free of the children that she generally detested; even as the children were free of their cruel guardian. The green seasons generally smiled on all at the orphanage.

Though each spring through summer brought similar expected events, creatures, beauties and the like, Ruby never found any monotony in such seasonal repetitions. She truly found joy and exultation in being healthy enough to bask in sunshine and to breathe in fresh outdoor air in each of the growing seasons. Ruby adored even the simplest of pleasures. Indeed, she would relish every fragment of both warm seasons with every energetic ounce that she could muster, knowing that the first still kindly days of autumn would begin to usher in the sometimes relentlessly unkind, dark cold days of winter (for her in particular). Had Ruby been fed and warmed well enough to give her robust health such as the mistress of the house, perhaps she could have loved winters as much or more than anybody. Every snowflake could have thrilled her like flowers were ever certain to.

Though Ruby never truly forgot how drearily ill she typically spent her winters through, the memory of the seriousness of her sicknesses would generally tend to fade while she was lost in the easy breeziness of spring and summer. Thus, as her two cherished seasons said farewell, Ruby would each year be again taken by an almost sudden surprise that autumn winds and rains would begin to bring heavy fogginess to her lungs and then resultant suppressing weariness to her body. As seems always the case, spring and summer were far too soon turned to autumn and thus winter began to howl its chilly calls. When the bitterly cold winds brought winter, so too, did the air seem to always bring sickness for Ruby. Thus, once more, with every year's season of drizzly wet or flurry white coldness, she faced a length of time battling illness, as the first coughs and chills would come over her, to then haunt her for months on end.

Ruby endured the discomforts of her consumptive type of ailment bravely, almost waiting patiently for health to greet her in the same way that she looked forward to spring. Boredom did not overtake her either, for she could easily fly away in the sky ship of her imagination. When Ruby did not sleep, she dreamed; and when she did not dream in her slumbering state, she dreamt in any lengths of wakefulness. Daydreams were her boon in her sickbed. Oftentimes, other children were also in the infirmary with her and if any of them did not suffer their sicknesses as well as Ruby, she would try to help them.

"Imagine some legendary dragon if you will, and let us say that you are some sort of knight in bloodied armor who has slain many a flying serpent beast before meeting up with one great giant of these giants." Ruby painted with her words.

One little one whimpered, "I think that *far* too scary, Ruby. I do not wish to think of such."

"No, no! If you are the conquering hero, you need not fear! You can overcome this beast just as you did slay all its fiendish friends. With your imagination, you can win every battle you set yourself up against in your daydreams!"

Another youngster questioned in all seriousness, "But what of night dreams, Ruby? What of nightmares?"

"Well, my dear, I do believe that if you truly set your mind to do it, you can win every battle in any nightmare as well. Perhaps with practice, you can do it. Only keep trying, and you may learn how… or, in the least, for now… if you awake to a frightening dream, think up a winning ending. Battle the scary thoughts away from your mind and memory."

In-between coughs and shivers, Ruby would create happy stories to delight her sick-room infirmary mates, as well as weave fantastical tales to amaze them. She also routinely conjured up frightening monsters and violent ways to conquer them. Ruby taught the children around her what she had come to believe within herself throughout her times of illness: that whatever made them ill could be beaten down if they imagined it away hard and long enough. Was Ruby not still living, whilst others had died of similar illnesses? She tended towards sensing that her mind had helped to will her better each winter. Added to all that, Ruby taught her friends to pray for recovery. She believed in such things all the more.

Being older than most of the orphans around her and especially having lived at Humble House the longest, Ruby did tend to mother and comfort those around her far more than any consoling returns that might be offered to her from her housemates. Ruby did have Patsy, though. Kindly, but timid, Patsy was oft times medicine to Ruby in spirit at least. Not ordinarily up to the task of standing tall against any rabid barking from Miss Mortimer, Patsy could find the boldness to rouse herself enough to defend and protect Ruby from the unloving guardian if truly need be.

One cold winter night, Patsy finished a session of dabbing Ruby's forehead with a cold wet cloth during one of the poor child's feverish illnesses. In and out of a slumbering stupor, Ruby smiled at her benefactress before drifting off to sleep once more.

Patsy shook her head before speaking near under her breath and then thinking to herself as she finished up with little tasks round the room of sick sleeping children, "Poor child. If I had a husband or a family, I would surely take Ruby from this place. I'd care for her as my very own. All she needs is more warmth and food. That would do her a deal of good. Ruby has surely suffered the most for being here longest. That Miss Mortimer has God to face for what she's done to these youngins. And Mr. Graver… that greedy… well, he will pay for his crimes too. But, what can I do? I do what I can. I've got my job to keep, I do. I need worry 'bout the roof over my own head. Yes, indeed… I do all I can for these young ones… so I'll be fit for heaven, I will."

Upon leaving the infirmary, Miss Mortimer approached in the hall in time to catch Patsy to scold and complain to her regarding a number of tasks undone in and around the place. The housemistress lamented aloud about things to be done (without exactly yet placing the burden of those chores squarely on Patsy's shoulders). In an effort to save herself being laden with all unpleasant duties on the older woman's mind, Patsy quickly offered to spend all the more time in the infirmary taking care of sick children.

Miss Mortimer answered Patsy's offer, "Yes, well... caring for the sick has never been my own art... and it is in your nature to care for the sick, particularly children..."

"Yes Ma'am."

"I find the sick... morbid... and children tiresome."

Patsy did not quite know what to say to Miss Mortimer's last remark and so simply nodded, staying silent, trying to hide her discomfort.

Miss Mortimer took no notice of any of Patsy's uneasiness at her last sort of speech and continued in inquiry after the young infirmary patients, "Do you think that they will all recover? No deaths on the horizon? What about the redhead?"

Inwardly uneasy, Patsy answered, exercising effort to project an outward calm, "I do think they will all find health soon."

"Truth told, I sometimes wished or prayed that the freckled sickly creature would *die* and be done with it."

Patsy was all shock and could not help reactively saying, "Oh, no... pardon my... pertinence... but that seems so unkind... and a sin... if I may so say."

"That's *im*-pertinence, Patsy... and no... why ever would it be a sin to wish or pray someone to heaven? If a child is always under a fever, some sort of consumption or other, then heaven is around the corner for them anyway... and so wishing or praying them there sooner is just doing them a favor. Would you have them suffer longer?"

"No, but... well, I... though, she is such a dear, sweet thing... and always has been... I would think it kinder to pray for her to get well... Ma'am."

"Well, she's only been a bother to me... and she belonged in a hospital long ago... or some kind of asylum for the sick ... anyhow, she seems overdue for death if you ask me."

Patsy's jaw dropped perceptibly.

"Did you know… did I ever tell you… that I asked Mr. Graver about it once… I was so blasted tired of her being sick all winter that I told Mr. Graver that maybe she should be sent somewhere for the sick. I think I as much as hinted that she was costing him a good deal of money by staying… you know… to appeal to his greedy side…"

"No."

"Yes, and do you know what he told me?"

"I can't imagine."

"Told me he'd as soon as get his money's worth on her by letting her stay until we could get a family for her… get some coin for her… told me to try to push her onto some unsuspecting young couple… you know… in the summer months when she always does well… when her true sickly nature is hidden…"

Patsy was agog.

"Well… he might think himself good with money matters, but, he should-a listened to me… for as much as I tried to put her forward, nobody wanted that red hair and those freckles."

Patsy only nodded slightly.

"Well, enough of Ruby and Mr. Graver. What am I to do about all the undone chores?" Miss Mortimer thought out loud.

Patsy attempted to shirk any new duties before taking her leave and scurrying off towards her bed for the night, "Maybe we can leave that worry 'til tomorrow? You must be as tired as I am. I bid you g'night and call it a day."

3
Ugly Freckled Thing

R uby Redhead! Ruby Redhead!" a number of the children chanted with the large new girl leading them in unison.

Ruby wondered at the way so many children were oft wont to follow near anyone who leads them, and then retorted to the leader of the gang, "Do you even know what a ruby is? Someday I will wear a ruby ring and maybe some ruby earrings too. I feel no shame in being told that my hair looks like rubies! Rubies are beautiful. God puts rubies in the ground for us to find as treasures."

Dorcas stumbled for a fitting reply and then, "Well, your hair doesn't look like rubies then: it looks like carrots. Your hair is practically *orange*. Hair should *never* be orange." And then Dorcas led what children would follow her in a new chant, "Carrots! Carrots!"

Ruby's response was grabbed in haste, "Well, I love carrots."

Dorcas felt confidence in stinging her opponent, "Aha! You love carrots! You eat too many carrots, and that is why your hair is the color of carrots!"

The group of chanting children chanted further, "Carrots! Carrots!"

Ruby rolled her eyes, sighed and then tried to defend herself once more, "My hair is more the color of the beautiful copper bowl in the kitchen than carrots. Your eyes don't work very well, my dear."

Dorcas shot back, "I saw a copper *spittoon* once! Yuck!"

Ruby sparred again, "Well, how many dirty, ugly things are the color of *your* dirt-colored brown hair, Dorcas? My hair is the color of copper bracelets."

Dorcas tried a new track, "What about all those nasty, dirty, brown *spots* on your face? I've never seen so many ugly freckles on one face in my life!"

Ruby was whipped. She felt entirely speechless. Strength was barely in her to defend her red hair, as much as she secretly disliked it; but defending her horrid freckles was well beyond her scope. She detested them and knew not what to say in their defense.

The new chant began, and then started to gain momentum and volume, "Freckles! Freckles! Freckles!"

Suddenly, from beyond the growing, chanting and loudening crowd, a little voice promptly piped up above the din, proud and loud, "My bestest horse ever had freckles on her back. I do so love freckles. My father gave that freckled horse to me and called her Apple Lucy, and I loved her 'til the day she died."

All turned around in shock to see that those words had come from the little girl who had been quietly hiding in corners since her arrival weeks before.

After a few moments of a pause, Dorcas tried to renew her strength, "Then we'll call Ruby *Apple Lucy* or maybe we'll just call her a horse. Her last name is '*Steed*', after all."

Ruby answered swiftly while smiling at the little girl, "Call me a horse. Call me a Steed. Call me Apple Lucy. I'm happy to be compared to a horse with freckles on its back that was the bestest horse ever, and loved 'til the day she died."

Dorcas tried again, "Well… maybe we'll call you…"

Ruby was fatigued with the new big bully, "Call me whatever you like, Dorcas, for I just don't care one jot."

Ruby was done. She took the new little girl by the hand and walked away from the gang of children who had been led by Dorcas. The biggest bully that Ruby had ever known simply stood in dismayed frustration. Dorcas wondered how she could push Ruby around, if she walked away such as that and did not care what was said against her. The new brazen girl began taunting one of her (recent co-conspirator) followers, though Ruby (the usual defender) was already out of earshot and had no present heart and strength to come back and dive into protecting her everyday fellows from any verbal or other blows as she ordinarily would.

It was not all that uncommon at the orphanage for one or more children to lead the charge of bullying from time to time, and though she was not always the largest child, Ruby had always instinctively stood up to defend any downtrodden children around her. When a child of any size decided to belittle or harm anyone, Ruby was always promptly there to fend them off, if she at all could.

Dorcas was older and especially taller than most children who happened to be dropped off at Humble House, and as a self-appointed bully, she thus was prone to throw her size around. She had been picking on child after child since her arrival, and though Ruby was small for her age, after having been the champion of each and every sufferer, Ruby had found herself at the end of the line of those being chosen for abuse by Dorcas. The imposing Dorcas had run out of victims to taunt, and in all their defense, Ruby had become an arch-enemy to Dorcas. Thus, in the lumberingly cruel mind of Dorcas, Ruby had set herself up as a fitting target.

There had seemed to be none brave enough to speak or stand up for Ruby against Dorcas until the one little girl chose to step forward and follow in Ruby's footsteps. This little girl was a child Ruby could truly admire and love instantly. She had lent strength in a time of weakening need.

Ruby humbly offered in query, "Forgive me little one, but I am oft inclined to forget names... there are so many children coming and going around here, you see... and you have been hiding in the shadows since your arrival. I have been reluctant to pry into your private moments in the corners... and cannot seem to recall your name, as I have not heard it spoken enough times for my shabby memory. Could you enlighten me?"

"Scarlet." she smiled.

"Oh, my! Our names seem of a kindred kind, to be sure."

"Oh, yes. I was named for my grandmamma who had red hair like you."

"Were you her favorite and she yours?"

"I never met her. She died afore I was borned."

"Though you know of her… you were told about her?"

"Yes, by my… mamma…" Scarlet at first sniffled, attempting brave composure, but then began to cry.

Ruby dared to ask, "You remember your mamma?"

"Of course I do." Scarlet sniffled, wiping her tears as they scatteringly continued to plummet down her rosy little chubby cheeks.

"Sadly for me, I do not recall mine. I was very young when I first became an orphan and was young even still when I came to live here."

Scarlet looked at Ruby with sincere and heartfelt sympathy.

"You lost your mother fairly lately then?" Ruby gently asked.

Though she had gathered some resolve not to weep further, Scarlet whimpered a little, "Yes. She died of a fever afore she had another baby."

"And your father and other family?"

"My father died away on some trek a while back… and in all their family… not a one said they could keep me… and so I was dropt off here… to become a true orphan." Scarlet lost resolve entirely and began crying in earnest this time.

Ruby embraced Scarlet, stroking her back, calming her. They were now true friends. Ruby determined to watch over and love this darling little orphan, though she felt assured that Scarlet was surely pretty and sweet enough to be snatched up by a loving family very soon.

At day's end, after sending Scarlet and other children to slumberland, Ruby became more contemplative than usual as she made her way to her own corner. Scarlet carried the name of a redhead, though she did not exhibit the other telltale signs of having red hair. She did not appear to harbor a fiery temper in the least, nor was she burdened by any freckles and (most fortunate indeed) her hair was a lovely light sunny golden hue. Ruby thought that red hair was a bad enough curse, but freckles were the worst.

Sometimes Ruby would briefly survey her face and shoulders

in the adequately useful, but scratched and foggy looking glass that hung over the washbasin of the girls' room, to determine if true beauty could ever reside there upon her own visage. She believed that her red hair and freckles were her great barrier to beauty (at least popularly accepted ideals of beauty), and wondered if some day, some place, her seemingly obvious traits of homeliness could ever be considered assets to comeliness. She could clearly see that her features were not of themselves ugly, misshapen, misplaced, deformations or disproportioned, and neither were her shoulders too terribly skinny (all orphanage deprivations considered).

Ruby knew that with more food at her disposal she could surely become more plump and pleasing. She surmised that the features of her countenance could, at some time in the distant future, appear lovely as a whole perhaps, to at least some person or other. Ruby generally determined not to allow anyone to tell or at least convince her that she was ugly, though she did have her own secret doubts of her own visual advantages oftentimes.

Miss Mortimer happened to hear of the altercation between Ruby and Dorcas the following day, and for some reason known only to her, the reigning housemistress chose to side with the imposingly unpleasant Dorcas rather than gently kind Ruby.

That evening, Miss Mortimer clearly took pleasure after the fact, in the already transpired event, "Well, Patsy… I heard that our new formidable Dorcas tore a strip off of the weakling Ruby."

Patsy attempted answering with tact, "It may be as you say, though I hear tell it ended otherwise."

"What do you mean? I thought Dorcas soundly put Ruby in her place." Miss Mortimer leaned forward in her chair.

"Well, Ruby held her own and left Dorcas standing, looking confounded." Patsy put a bucket of firewood down by her superior's fireplace and stayed standing beside it.

"I don't believe it. Ruby could not win against Dorcas." Miss Mortimer harrumphed, leaning back to relax.

Patsy shook her head, "Ruby walked off triumphant-like and Dorcas chose another child to pick on, after all."

"Well… I suppose we will never truly know what happened."

"I suppose not." Patsy stirred the fire and put another log on.

"I would like to see the next time Dorcas comes up against Ruby." Miss Mortimer nibbled on something.

"There will likely be another time; Dorcas does like to bully."

"Well, this is not a world for weaklings, you know." Miss Mortimer sipped from her cup.

"I suppose not." Patsy shifted her weight, wishing she could leave and get off of her feet for the day.

"Ruby is a weakling and there is no room for weaklings."

"Though… she does have many good qualities."

"I can't abide her freckles. I have always hated freckles."

"Well, God created freckles as much as anything." defended Patsy, bravely.

Miss Mortimer snorted, "Oh, I can't believe that. God would not create such a thing as freckles. They are too ugly."

"I cannot think of any child as truly ugly."

"Oh, do be serious! Most children are generally ugly… and a freckled child is one of the *ugliest* creatures of them all."

"I am sorry… but I shan't agree." Patsy was quite disgusted, though she contained her composure.

"I tell you Patsy, if I had that red hair and those freckles, I think that I would pray to die rather than live looking like that."

"That seems a sin… no…"

"Yes… and maybe that is just what the girl has been doing all this time… praying to die."

"Oh, no… I can't think so…" Patsy could no longer abide the distasteful meanderings of Miss Mortimer's mind, and in order to maintain her respectful composure before her mistress, quickly found an excuse to take her leave from the room.

The following day, to partially put Patsy in her place, Miss Mortimer went out of her way to find her earliest opportunity to criticize Ruby's freckles publicly during breakfast-time, to the morbid pleasure of Dorcas and the mortification of Ruby. Many cruel giggles and more astonished breath-drawing was heard round the room by children and servants alike. It was all a very shocking display, in Patsy's estimation, and not in the least befitting a headmistress of an orphanage.

Patsy felt compelled by the event to take Ruby privately aside, as soon as she could manage after the morning meal, to say some consoling words to the offended child, "Don't let Miss Mortimer's unkindness bother you, dear. She is a sour sort."

Ruby visibly held back some tears, though said nothing, only nodding in obedient affirmation.

Patsy soothed, "Anyway, your hair will surely become darker and browner in time."

As one tear escaped down one of her cheeks, Ruby looked up, hoping for further happy thoughts.

"Yes, I have seen it in other redheaded persons. Your hair will seem less and less red as you grow older."

"Truly? Are you certain?"

"Oh yes, and your freckles will fade as you grow older."

"You have seen this?"

"Oh yes, my little dear."

To Ruby, this was a happy thought indeed, "Freckles fade?"

"Especially if you stay out of the sun, like refined ladies. It's the sun that makes 'em… it paints spots on you, you know."

Ruby directly determined to always stay out of the sun and to keep her skin in the protective shade, to prevent further freckling and to help with the fading of them. A little later that day, Ruby's attempts having failed to trade an outdoor chore with an inside one, she turned her back to the sun as she swept the porch and other areas around the orphanage.

That night when it was time for all the children to retire to their beds, and after Ruby was telling stories to many of them, diminutive Scarlet managed to make her way to whisper assuring words into Ruby's ears.

"I still very much like your freckles, Ruby."

"Thank you, dearest Scarlet." Ruby whispered in return.

"And your red hair… I do truly like your red hair."

"Thank you for that too. It eases my mind to know it."

"Sometimes I think I would like to call you apple. It would be fittin'… for tasty red apples, and also in honor of my freckled horse. Do you think she runs in heaven now, Ruby?"

"I truly do believe so. You shall see her again."

"I think so too." Scarlet sighed, faintly smiling.

"Yes, I generally believe that all good creatures do go to heaven."

"Do you think that my parents are caring for my horse in heaven for me, Ruby?"

"Yes, and perhaps enjoying a ride now and then too."

Scarlet's eyes lit up with the thought, "Yes, I think Apple Lucy would like to be ridden by others who have loved her while she and I are apart."

"I am certain of it." Ruby supported with conviction.

Scarlet's mind wandered whilst her eyes traversed around the room somewhat and then she had a sudden thought out loud, though in a hushed voice, "Do you think that you will have freckles in heaven, Ruby?"

Ruby considered at length and then leaned in and whispered her honestly secret reply most quietly, "I think not… I hope not. Do not tell a *soul*, my dearest little Scarlet, but I do despise my freckles and do not wish to keep them in the hereafter. I would love a face as devoid of freckles as yours."

"But I truly do like them."

"Thank you for your kindness, but… would not you like me as much without them?"

"Yes, though… you would not remind me of my freckled Apple Lucy, then… and so… I would wish you to keep your freckles."

"For your sake… and for your dear friendship… perhaps I will… perhaps I will."

Ruby quietly chuckled and thanked Scarlet for that thought as well, knowing full well that it was indeed a true compliment. She clearly saw the droopy eyelids of her little friend in the moonlight that shone through the window and so gently tucked the darling little girl into her bed, comfortably under her covers.

A good deal of the rest of Ruby's following week was spent doing her utmost to ignore Dorcas leading a children's chorus of 'freckles, freckles, freckles…' (in attempts to humiliate the redhead), and creative ways to remain out of the sunshine. By week's end, Ruby could not see that her freckles had faded much for all her troubles of keeping them out of the sun, and thus she decided to think more on other more pleasant things and imaginings, rather than to trouble herself all too much further on the subject of her sun spots (and checking in the looking glass continually to attempt to assess them and their success at fading or otherwise). Ruby tried to learn from the loving sentiments of a little girl who loved her all the more for her freckles and did truly wish that she would learn to like to keep them even in the afterlife if she had the chance to leave them behind altogether. Scarlet surely saw her favorite horse as freckled still, though prancing in heaven above.

4

Orphan Overlooked

A soft blue sky lightly painted with wispy clouds and a shining sun throughout it all spoke of a glorious day. Scarlet awoke to look out the window before hurrying to Ruby's bedside to announce the morning.

"It does not look like rain at all, Ruby. It is a sun shining day!"

Ruby roused herself and rubbed her eyes awake before answering her dear little friend, "You are a bright, shining early bird this morning, Scarlet."

"Yes! You were sleeping when I just got up out of bed."

"I am as if still sleeping even now. I did not sleep so well last night and am still so very tired." Ruby yawned.

"Why did you not sleep so well?" Scarlet's darling little head tilted to one side questioningly.

"I dare say you slept deeply through all the thunder and lightning last night, but it kept me quite awake for hours."

"I did not hear or see any of it."

"Yes, as I say, you slept very soundly through it all."

"When was it, Ruby?"

"The storm as much as began shortly after you reached dreamland, I would think." Ruby swung her feet around, forcing herself towards getting out of bed, though she half wished to stay there a good deal longer.

Scarlet nodded, "I suppose so."

"Well, I suppose we should wash up and get ourselves dressed for the day."

"What will we do today, Ruby?"

"Well, after our share of chores around the place, I suppose we will enjoy some time out of doors..." Ruby leaned forward, lowered her voice and smiled broadly, "away from Miss Mortimer."

Scarlet giggled.

After breakfasting and then finishing up all chores, Scarlet, Ruby and the other children were swiftly sent outside, that Miss Mortimer might relax inside in solitude.

Ruby and Scarlet chose their favorite tree to rest under and Ruby began finishing reading a book aloud to her favorite young friend. The two were so excessively absorbed in their story as it was unfolding towards the end that neither noticed a lovely young couple glancing the girls' way, as they passed, walking into the orphanage.

Almost the instant Ruby read to the end of the book, the Humble House bell was clanging for all orphans to scurry inside for some sort of impromptu inspection. Any of the children who had been living at the orphanage for very long were pretty certain what the ringing of the bell might mean to at least one of them: somebody was inside and looking to adopt a child. Ruby grabbed Scarlet's hand and swept her inside.

Long-past very hopeful for her own salvation from being an orphan, Ruby's sudden and natural instinct was to do what she had done for so many other little children prior to this day. Ruby must present Scarlet properly to give her a fair chance at being chosen. Almost in rote fashion from numberless such events, Ruby was swiftly dusting off Scarlet's clothes, straightening her hair, assuring that her face looked clean and so forth. Scarlet stood in dizzying obedience, scarcely opening her mouth to question the reason why her older benefactress of a friend would be doing such to her.

Ruby whisperingly exhorted, "Now Scarlet, if you wish to be chosen, you must be on your very best behavior… and do not forget to smile… sweetly."

Scarlet looking up inquiringly, and thus Ruby gave a brief explanation, "Somebody is likely here to choose a child. You must do your best at every opportunity to be that child."

Ruby smiled reassuringly to Scarlet as all the children lined up in anticipation throughout the assembly hall. A hush fell on the throng of loosely gathered youngsters. Miss Mortimer could now be heard approaching from down the hall, as her speech was detected though not understood word upon word by any orphan as yet.

The first of Miss Mortimer's words to clearly float in front of the children's ears were, "I have a good deal of *that* kind for you to choose from."

"What kind?" the children's minds wondered.

"I am certain that you will find the *right* one."

"Who will be the right one?" all speculated silently.

Some children hoped, "Will it be me? Will I be chosen this time?"

Ruby did truly hope for Scarlet, though her thoughts had not yet encompassed the reality of losing her new little friend. Her mind was only resting upon a brighter future for the little girl who deserved to be loved and cared for and could surely be swiftly saved from the orphanage.

Anticipatory breaths of children throughout were suddenly held in near gasps as the advancing steps brought Miss Mortimer and her guests before the orphans.

Miss Mortimer pronounced commandingly to the group, "Spread out so that this dear couple can see you all."

The orphanage overseer then turned to the young man and woman, "Take your time. Look them over. If you see any you like, just point them out to me and I will call them forward… and then you may take a closer look… and then speak to any that you please to."

The lovely young couple glanced over the faces before them. There was awkwardness for those choosing, and yet excitement palpably felt amongst those hoping to be chosen. Ruby was not anticipating in the least for herself, though she was truly hoping and inwardly praying for Scarlet. A little oblivious to the full scope of the situation at hand, Scarlet was not joining in on any hoping or praying whatsoever. She had not been an orphan for all too long and she had begun bonding to Ruby, who represented maternal comforts to the little girl. Scarlet was currently happy to be Ruby's little friend and fond shadow.

When the young visiting woman's eyes finally rested on Scarlet's darling little face, she was done glancing around. She whispered to her husband and pointed. Ruby started. Miss Mortimer was informed and so called Scarlet forward. The little orphan looked this way and that as Ruby nudged her forward, whispering a reminder for her to smile. Scarlet did no such thing. Amid a flurry of whispering round about her, Scarlet found herself nudged and pushed forward until she was before Miss Mortimer and the auspicious guests. Scarlet's eyes were round and wet. Fear gripped her. She looked back for her trusted motherly friend.

"Ruby? Ruby?!" Scarlet cried out.

As Ruby was about to step forward to attempt to comfort and explain the situation and possibilities to her little darling orphan kindred, the lovely woman began to speak something similar to Scarlet in her own comforting tones. First asking for Scarlet's name and then sharing her own, the lovely woman was all mothering kindness and angelic softness. Ruby halted and even stepped back. She did not wish to interfere. Ruby chose to let the beautiful woman express herself and convince Scarlet of the happy wisdom of submitting to being chosen. Ruby watched from afar as Scarlet was swept along in an almost magical trance, being quickly converted to the idea of becoming a daughter of this feminine mothering creature.

Before leaving Humble House, Scarlet was of course allowed to retrieve her few precious things from her bed station, and in the midst of it all, found a chance to express a lengthy goodbye to her dear Ruby.

It all started with Scarlet's tears, "Ruby, Ruby?! How can I leave you? Can you not come away with me?"

Forcefully holding back her own eyes from releasing their watery pools, Ruby contained herself bravely in a grand effort to aid her friend, "They have chosen *you*. It is enough. Be happy, my dear one. I am happy for you. Someday, my own day will come. Do not worry for me."

"But I will miss you!"

"And I will miss you... terribly... but I can see that you will be well loved and cared for. They seem such lovely folk."

"She is... she reminds me of... of my mother."

"And so she shall be your new mother."

"She seems so very kind."

"I do believe that she truly is."

"Oh, Ruby..." Scarlet burst into tears again.

"I will think fondly of you always, and pray for you often."

"And I will pray for you." Scarlet spoke amid sobs.

The two girls embraced fondly, generously watering each other's shoulders. At length, Ruby wiped her tears as she pulled back, showing forth a happy smile to Scarlet, in her heartfelt attempt to allow and give each of them the courage to finish their mutual farewell.

Blinking back any weeping as she fully let go, Ruby proclaimed encouragingly, "I am certain that this beginning will be the happiest of endings for you my dear young friend. You will have a wonderful life with your new family, Scarlet."

"I promise to pray nightly for such kind parents for you, Ruby. I will be begging heaven to bless you to be so lucky. I hope you will be chosen too... soon." Scarlet gushed forth tearily, wiping her dripping face over and over again with her little hands, until each were scooped up by her new father and mother as they lovingly stole her away from Ruby.

Still smiling broadly, Ruby suppressed sorrowful sobs as she watched Scarlet wave in continuous leave-taking to her as the little angel faded further and further away, step by step, into the distance.

Ruby kept and hid herself away from all others as much as she was able the rest of the day. She did not allow the hidden melancholy to finally overtake her into true grieving until she had safely put herself under her covers, whilst long drawn-out breaths of children all around her could be heard in the dark, still night.

By morning, Ruby could see better beyond her sorrow for losing her sweet younger friend, and determined to think happily of

Scarlet's future. Ruby was angelic enough to be happy for the little girl's adoption into such a fine family and an exceptionally pleasing prospect, even as Ruby was overlooked once again.

Days passed as Ruby attempted to cheer herself with happy thoughts of Scarlet's new joyful life. Ruby tried to throw herself into mothering other little children, in efforts to divert and distract her own inner lamenting. She was successful in chasing away any self-pity most moments, though she was only still a child herself and quite fully human enough. When night fell and all was quiet, when she was not busying herself by day, haunting thoughts would overtake her. She tried to pray her sorrowful thoughts and feelings away, but she was not quite stoic enough to always succeed. Ruby could not help but think of reasons why she had been passed over again and again, year after year. Why had she not been chosen when she was first come to Humble House? Why could no loving couples commit to love her upon seeing her? Why was she an orphan still? Ruby could not but blame her looks for her disgrace and misfortune in not being adopted after all this time in the orphanage. Ruby truly believed that had she been prettier (with hair other than the color red), she would have been adopted long since and would be even now very much loved by some family. She could be climbing into a bed in her own room, or a room shared with sisters.

One such night of contemplation, Ruby gazed at her candle-lit, though less than crisp reflection at a window and whispered in conversation to herself while all others slept soundly around her, "Oh, Ruby. Are you so very ugly that none can love you? Your reflection in the looking glass, window or pond does not always seem so horrid to me. Some days I do agree that you are indeed ugly… but other days… I would venture to say that you might even be deemed pretty by some. If red hair were no obstacle to beauty in this world, would you then be considered ugly? I think not. Well, at least if your freckles could or would fade. Yes, you must determine to stay fully out of the sun that your freckles may fade more and more, Ruby. Then, maybe, you will not be seen as ugly by others. Perhaps you were too ugly when you were smaller. I do think that you are not so ugly as you once were. Maybe you are not ugly now, but are simply too old to be considered. Yes, that is it… you have grown too old. Well, you are practically growing into a young lady, though you are still so small for your age. Loving young couples always want the little ones. Those parents who have lost babies are looking for a tiny child to replace their lost babe and the couples who have not been blessed with their own, also wish for infants. Who wants an older child like me… a near grown young woman? Likely no family will want me… ever…"

Ruby began to truly despair. She tried to pray the feeling away, but grief and sobbing overtook her for a time. Then, quite abruptly, Ruby took hold of herself, shut off the spout, wiped her tears and resumed conversing to herself, "Ruby, it is true that you have been longest at this orphanage. It is true that many folks deem red hair and freckles as ugly. But, do not despair as yet. Scarlet… little Scarlet is quite likely praying for you still… and there may yet be a family for you… not everyone despises red hair and freckles, for God created such… and… if nobody chooses you… you can be family to yourself. Surely you can believe that angels watch over you and that God loves you? Are they not family enough? If your destiny is such that only heaven has family for you, then so be it: you will be family enough for you. You will believe in you. You will believe that heaven believes in you."

A child whimpered and then cried out nearby. Ruby was torn from her own thoughts to go tend to the nightmare of a little one. She soothed and comforted the little one back to sleep with calming words and embraces. The little dreamer was soon slumbering peacefully once more. Ruby's mind returned to her personal contemplations. It seemed to Ruby that every friend she ever found within the walls of Humble House was soon destined to be taken away from her. Whether by adoptive families, apprentice situations, or even sickness and death: each treasured friendship Ruby nurtured was stolen from her tender and loving grasp.

The hour was becoming terribly late. Ruby took herself to her bed where she climbed in and slept somewhat in a state of sadness that night.

The following day and many thereafter were filled with ups and downs as Ruby attempted to find a semblance of normalcy and contentment in her current situation (relative to her speculations about her future, truly trying to discount any disappointments in her past, in the equation). Ruby could not seem to lift her spirits for long, when she could accomplish such at all. If she lifted herself upwards, she would invariably fall back downwards.

Too many moments did Ruby trust in her perceptions of her reflection. One day she was musing, "What an unkind friend the looking glass has turned out to be. The mirror is not my enemy as yet, but, constant collaboration with it might prove to be a losing battle. Oh, but I have come to despise my freckles in a way that can never be recovered from. My hair... my red hair... sometimes I do not hate you... but, even as I make peace with your color, I am lulled into hating you once more... and then... I can convince myself that red hair is not ugly at all. I can talk myself into almost liking you, my hair... but I cannot ever seem to imagine my spotted face as anything other than... hideous. Oh, curse you... freckles."

One day, during a stolen private moment with a looking glass, Ruby sat staring at herself, or more precisely, she was fixated on her own face and particularly the many freckles scattered about upon it. She dared not try to count all those little spots, for knowing their number, which truly seemed to be somewhat numberless, might possibly pull Ruby's spirits down all the more. Even as Ruby continually tried to help her freckles towards fading by steering clear of the sun, she feared that all her efforts would be in vain and that her freckles would always distract from her true looks behind them. For, behind her freckles and under her red hair was surely a pleasant face: such she could generally and usually believe.

5
Finally Chosen

S pirits were all aflutter the day that the right respectable Mrs. Biggsley arrived at the orphanage (with much in the way of fanfare) to choose a child for adoption. Pleasant enough looking even though not plump in a pleasing way, the rather thin Mrs. Biggsley was all smiles as she thoroughly considered each and every girl. Every boy's heart sunk to realize that it was indeed a girl, and a girl alone, that she was after.

It soon became apparent that Mrs. Biggsley desired an older girl, one who could become as an older sister to her youngsters who each happened to be still just over or under ten years of age. All these factors did not even excite Ruby's anticipation, though the field of choice was narrowing her way; for Ruby had been passed over too many times before, despite having gotten her hopes up those multiple times in the past. Ruby had learned to expect nothing good for herself on such an occasion and only felt interest in the other girls, wondering whom might be chosen today.

As Mrs. Biggsley continued to inquire after every girl who did happen to be around Ruby's age of about twelve years, Ruby determined not to allow herself to hope. She did not want her own hopes dashed and her heart to sink as it had too many times before. Ruby had learned to tell herself to be happy for others rather than to hope for herself in these situations.

When Mrs. Biggsley began inquiring with Miss Mortimer regarding Ruby (for all could see where their eyes were affixed and where Mrs. Biggsley's long spindly finger had pointed several times to assure her hostess of the girl she was considering), astounding thoughts abounded all around. Even as she could not decide whether to talk Mrs. Biggsley into or out of choosing Ruby, Miss Mortimer wondered inwardly what strange attraction any woman of any means would have towards such a freckly redheaded girl. Patsy was nearby, hoping that this would finally be Ruby's day. A few dear friends of Ruby hoped for her release from the orphanage while knowing they would miss her, though, each time any child was adopted out of orphan-hood, it gave all witnessing orphans hope for their own future families to finally foster them. Foes of Ruby may have wished that she would never be removed from Humble House to become part of a family, but, even still, hope for themselves seemed to translate to hope for all, even when they attempted thoughts and wishes otherwise.

To all in observation, Mrs. Biggsley seemed to consult endlessly with Miss Mortimer. Time dragged on for all the gathered children as they awaited the fine lady's decision. She did have many exacting questions to put before Miss Mortimer as Miss Mortimer, pointing around the room, tried to put various girls before Mrs. Biggsley. Ruby was old enough to suppose and imagine that Mrs. Biggsley must have a very particular kind of girl in mind, and the fact that she was considering a freckled redhead amongst the bunch, must mean that spirit, character, personality and all other qualities of those kinds, rather than looks, must be key deciding factors.

When Miss Mortimer was tiring of answering all the many varying questions from her guest, and Mrs. Biggsley had exhausted all inquiries that she could muster, all were indeed surprised to see and hear that Ruby had been chosen. More than any other orphan in the place, Ruby doubted she had heard or seen correctly. It was like a dream where one feels the need to pinch oneself to verify that one is fully awake. Could this truly, finally, be Ruby's day to be chosen out of and from among all the other children? Was Ruby to be an orphan no more? Was she to finally become and be loved as a part of a family? Ruby could not believe her good fortune that blessed day. She felt an elation she had only imagined before, each time one of her dear friends or any of the other children for that matter (or even her foes of a sort), had been plucked out of the obscurity that it was to be an orphan, and had been set apart to become one of a family. *Family*: what a word it was.

It was truly something fantastical to Ruby to be the one to be chosen from amongst all the other children and she held a thrill upon thrill of anticipation of a new wonderful life and happiness, to finally be the lucky one to be plucked from the bunch. Through it all, her feelings were somewhat mixed, though the high notes were predominant. While feeling such transcendent splendid joy for herself, Ruby did even have remembrance and heart to feel a true sadness for all her fellow orphans who would be left to remain at Humble House for the time being.

Ruby was soon all washed up and changed into the best (though still quite shabby) clothes she could muster from amongst the meager things that she had, that currently fit her. A fair sized throng of fellow orphans stood round Ruby near her bedside as she near frantically packed up her belongings (almost as if she must hurry before Mrs. Biggsley might change her mind, come to her senses and choose a more fitting girl). Ruby hardly knew herself nor knew how to manage her feelings. This was all so new and foreign. To be chosen and leaving the orphanage was truly very strange to her and the sort of something that she had all but given up entirely upon ever facing herself.

"Will you remember us *always*, Ruby? *Please* do not forget us." One girl remarked with feeling.

"Of course I will not forget any of you." Ruby answered fondly.

Another begged, "Pray for us… each… that our own turns may come about… soon."

"I will pray for each and *every* one of you… nightly." Ruby shared with great warmth.

"The lady seems rich, Ruby. I think you will have a pampered life." one child observed.

"I hope I will be happy. I hope my new family will love me."

Ruby's wish was simple, yet significant.

Patsy was soon near Ruby's side, hoping, attempting, to be of some assistance, "Let me help you with those."

"Thank you… dear, dear Patsy." Ruby was suddenly teary.

Ruby looked around at her friends, other orphan-mates and then back to Patsy, "How will I do without you all? How will I do without *you*, Patsy? You are… more like a mother to me than anyone I've known as long as I can remember… I never thought that I would grieve to leave this place… but… I truly do feel it. As much as I am overjoyed to join a new and loving family, I do not wish to go… to be gone forever…"

Ruby was all tears. Patsy wished to aid her young protégé in taking her first steps into a new life, "You will find new and better happiness, Ruby. Go… go and think of us often… and… write to me now and then. Let me know of how you are doing. I promise I will write back to you… to tell you of any news from here."

Ruby gained strength and new resolve, "Yes, yes… I will write to you, Patsy. And you will keep me connected to everyone."

Ruby gave Patsy a long and fond embrace. Many children gathered close around to join in the embracing and a goodly number also joined in with tears until all farewells were finished with.

Miss Mortimer was soon distantly near, waving her hand frustratingly, hurrying Ruby away to go with Mrs. Biggsley. Miss Mortimer wished Ruby finally away forevermore, and the gaunt woman only smiled self-satisfactorily when Ruby was out of her sight.

"Well, I finally got some money out of that ugly freckled thing for Mr. Graver." Miss Mortimer snorted distastefully to Patsy.

Patsy only looked briefly at her superior before swiftly looking away (quickly wiping one tear from her cheek) to where Ruby had just vanished from view.

"I dare say he will be pleased… for the woman was rich and I talked a pretty penny out of her in the bargain." Miss Mortimer smiled a sort of crooked smile, as she continued feeling proud of herself for her accomplishment in ridding the place of Ruby whilst garnering some coins for her employer.

Patsy as much as nodded a sort of obedient expected agreement, whilst biting her poor tongue, which had suffered such painful exercise far too many times for too many years due to her own employer.

"I never mentioned her being a sickly creature… only extolled her virtues… you know… as being a hard little worker… and good with children… and a fair bit good with books and such too. Mrs. Biggsley was a good deal impressed for my words. I would have to claim to have made a fair good sale of the girl, for Mr. Graver. I should hope he would be grateful to me for my efforts. I should get some reward for my trouble." Miss Mortimer exhaled with satisfaction, anticipating imagined coming benefits in her favor.

Patsy sighed wearily, "I will sorely miss the little redhead."

With that, Patsy found the fastest excuse she could muster to be away from her housemistress (before biting the scrawny woman's head off in her subservient though justifiable anger).

Riding in the buggy alongside Mrs. Biggsley, Ruby's imaginings of her new future and being part of a loving family flitted about in her active mind. Overcoming some initial shyness, she became cascadingly replete with questions in her excitement about being chosen by the woman she now sat by, whom she felt joyousness in admiring as her new mother.

"Please tell me of your children, Mrs. Biggsley. How many of boys and girls do you have?" Ruby's face was lit up with curiosity as she looked up and beside her.

"Two girls… though Mr. Biggsley and I have only been blessed with one boy, as yet." Mrs. Biggsley continued staring in front of her, quite consistently maintaining her broad smile.

"What are their names and ages?" the young redhead inquired.

"My girls, Verna and Selda, are just younger than you and my son Reginald came a few years after they did."

"I will like meeting Verna and Selda. I'm sure we will be fast friends."

"Yes, quite." Mrs. Biggsley's smile faded just slightly, though only momentarily.

"Are your girls tall for their ages… taller than me, perhaps?" Ruby looked at her new mother inquiringly.

"Yes, I think so… perhaps." Mrs. Biggsley kept up a smile whilst still looking forward steadfastly.

"And your son… is he tall… for his age?"

"I suppose."

"Are your children very… very accomplished… for their ages?"

"I dare say."

"Will I be sharing a room with your daughters?"

Mrs. Biggsley hesitated slightly before answering, "I fancy Verna and Selda would prefer to stay, together, alone, as they are and long have been. You will have your own place for sleeping."

Ruby was curious as to why she could not fit into a bedroom with her new sisters, but despite, found delight in the news, "My own room! I have never had my very own room to myself… as far back as I can recall, anyway. As long as I can remember, since I was dropped off at the orphanage, I have shared a very large room with many, many orphans coming and going, you see."

"Yes, of course."

"I would suppose that Mr. Biggsley is as good and kind as you are. Would you say so?" Ruby was attempting pleasantries more than anything.

"Certainly." Mrs. Biggsley's smile broadened.

Ruby offered further compliments in hopeful query, "I venture that your children are very well-behaved."

"Assuredly."

"Do they have ponies?"

"Ponies?"

"I was simply wondering if each of your children had their own pony or horse, or if perhaps they shared one or two, if they have any riding horses at all."

"None at present… but we do have plans for horses in the next year or so."

"Have they ever ridden… on a pony or a horse?"

"Yes."

"I haven't… not that I can recall, you see."

"Yes, I would suppose not."

"Do your children school at home with you… or a tutor… or do they go to a town school?"

"They have done both… though, I have preferred sending them to the town school."

"I fancy that must be an adventure for them. I have never been to a town school. We only schooled some at the orphanage."

"I see."

"But I have been reading a great deal. I do so love to read."

Mrs. Biggsley nodded, still managing her protracted smile.

"What sort of business does Mr. Biggsley engage in?"

"Oh, this and that."

Ruby paused a little before commenting, "That is quite a gloriously blue sky today, do you not think?"

"I suppose it is."

"The clouds do not mar it whatsoever."

"True."

"How far is your home? Do we have much further to drive?"

"A good deal further."

"Well, it is such a lovely day; the time will continue to pass just as pleasantly as it has thus far." Ruby stayed cheerful.

"Yes."

"Can you tell me about your house… how many rooms and such?"

"I shall let you wait to see it." Mrs. Biggsley relit her dimming smile.

"I am eager with anticipation."

"Of course you are."

"I have waited so long to be loved as a part of a family." Ruby wondered at her candidness.

"Yes, well… you certainly do jabber on." Mrs. Biggsley's smile altered into something of annoyance before rejuvenating itself into a similitude of pleasance.

Ruby felt a little mortified, "Oh, please forgive me. I am not always this talkative. It is just that I am so excited… today."

"Yes, I am sure."

"I will try not to say every last thing in my head."

"Yes, that would ease my ears, my dear." Mrs. Biggsley continued smilingly gazing forward.

As land, sky, houses, horses, and all such things passed by them, Ruby found something to say about most things in her sight, even as she held her tongue a great deal. She was of soaring spirits. As they rode along, Ruby chattered happily. Mrs. Biggsley had little to say beyond the necessary, though she almost continually smiled throughout the rest of the trip towards her home.

Upon arriving at the Biggsley house, Ruby was brought in to meet the Biggsley children. No fanfare was offered, though all was pleasant enough. Mr. Biggsley was kind enough to Ruby at their first introduction. Then the Biggsley children were sent swiftly towards their bedchambers, after brief expressions of 'good night' were managed.

Mrs. Biggsley looked at Ruby in grinning announcement, "Well, my dear. Let us get you off to your little sleeping quarters so that you can get settled in for the night."

Ruby followed her new mother to a tiny cramped back-room behind the kitchen. Even Ruby, an orphan accustomed to belittling uncomfortable treatment since she could remember, was a good deal shocked to see where Mrs. Biggsley was proposing that she would reside her nights. The bed was barely big enough for even a smallish girl like her to curl up on and there was scant space to walk around the bed. One shelf above the bed was to serve as closet storage for her, since the space under the bed was already filled with firewood. Ruby's heart sunk as she fully realized that this place to call her own was some sort of storage closet which she was to be stuffed in to. Her mind quickly swam with wondering incredulousness, briefly pausing on thoughts towards any possible way back to the orphanage. She looked up at Mrs. Biggsley with profoundly heartfelt injury.

Mrs. Biggsley's tiring smile awoke once more, "Oh, you are disappointed, I see."

Ruby said nothing but looked down at her worn shoes.

"Well, well… I would have thought that a mistreated orphan of so many years would have been happy to have her own space, no matter how small and humble…"

Ruby knew not what to say in answer.

Mrs. Biggsley laughed a little and then calmed her energy down into a smile once more, "No matter… this is only temporary, you see… for we are to be moving into a grander, larger house very soon… out west, m'dear… onto the wild frontier."

Ruby feared to dare, though did, "And I will have a larger… room there… then?"

"Oh yes, of course, my dear." Mrs. Biggsley assured.

Ruby's dampened spirits lifted somewhat, even as she contemplated some nights spent in such confined and rustic quarters.

Mrs. Biggsley's smile widened, and her voice lilted, "Well, then, off to bed with you… for it's off to bed with me and mine."

With that sort of farewell, she was gone, off and upstairs to where all the members of her family were engaged in varying stages of bedding down for the night.

Ruby did not sleep well at all that night. She heard scurrying of what she was sure to be mice, feared she had felt more than one spider crawling upon her and was subjected to a stiff and cold wind blowing through some cracks in the walls next to and surrounding her. Ruby never thought she would miss and wish to go back to the orphanage itself and her bed or even the infirmary there, but she surely did, for she had only ever slept on the second floor and had never quite been subjected to the natural horrors she had been forced to acquaint herself with what had turned out to be her very own room (a closet) in the house of what was supposed to be her new family.

She did spend some time (instead of sleeping) trying to conjure up a way back to Humble House, but how could she possibly manage it? Could she walk her way there? She feared greatly that she would surely end up very lost. Who would help a runaway orphan? And what would Miss Mortimer say if Ruby did somehow get back to the orphanage? She could not imagine that there would be welcoming arms from Miss Mortimer (the very woman who was truly so very pleased to get the freckled redhead finally off of her hands). Every way that Ruby thought the thing through, she ended up stuck where she was.

Perhaps if Ruby had not been so very innocently young and naïve as she was, she might have more keenly fathomed how distantly far away, how remote and vast the western frontier was, from where she stood, still in the east. She might also have far more fully realized how permanent a move to the western wilds would turn out to be. Still youthfully full of hope and faith, in her innermost self, Ruby thought or believed that she could always return to the east to try to survive on her own if the worst should happen to her and she was mistreated enough to be finally forced to forage out a living on the frontier.

Pushing all thoughts of frightening possibilities out of her mind, Ruby determined to forge ahead, for she did not see that there was any way to go back to live at the orphanage, even if she believed that she could find her way there. No, she was now a part of this Biggsley family, and though Ruby did not feel embraced as a member of the Biggsley family in any way, as yet; she did force herself to hope and pray towards something better where, and with whom, luck had placed her.

The next day, Ruby did find strength in being hopeful for a gradual improvement in her new situation.

No Biggsley greeted Ruby first thing that morning, for a somewhat unpleasantly unhappy woman was working in the kitchen when Ruby came out of her little bedding space.

"Well, well… and here's the orphan the Missus picked up yesterday then. Not much of a pretty picture, ere ya? Not much of a room she gived ya to sleep in, eh?" the woman spoke to herself more than to Ruby. Ruby did not speak, but only stood sheepishly, wondering what to do or say.

"Well, soon you all will be gone west onto the wildish frontier to a grand house and then you might get a better situation… at least you can only hope for something better. Well… I won't be goin' so I wash my hands of it."

Ruby still stood staring.

"So… why don't you stop gawking and help me here. I gots too much work to do and you might as well pitch in."

Ruby was soon following orders as the woman barked them out to her. She was shortly thereafter sent up the stairs with a large tray covered in breakfast foods in dishes and the like, for all members of the Biggsley family. Doing exactly as according to the instructions she had been given, Ruby stopped at each bedroom door, knocked and waited, breathing heavily under the great difficulty of holding steady the weight of the heavily laden tray which was as if larger than herself. In their turns, Mrs. Biggsley, one of the Biggsley daughters, and then the Biggsley son each opened their doors and took from the tray, offering only sleepy and near reluctant thanks before taking their food and closing their doors. After finishing up at the third door, Ruby took the empty tray down the stairs, glad to be done the task and now carrying a much lighter object. Once in the kitchen, after placing the tray on the table, Ruby looked to the woman there (who was most apparently the cook, and perhaps more to the Biggsley family), for her own breakfast.

"What ere ya gawking at?" the cook demanded impatiently, in-between moving and clanging things around.

Being fairly famished (for not having eaten any morsel since long before she left the orphanage), Ruby dared, "I was just wondering if there was some breakfast for *me*? I have not eaten since midday yesterday."

"Oh, dern… I clean forgot 'bout you. I eat a little here and there while I work on things. Yes… I do suppose I must feed you somethin'."

With that, the woman threw a piece of bread and a slice of bacon on a tin plate, before saying, "There you go, and the water is over there. Here's a tin cup… help yourself."

The contrast between what the cook tossed to Ruby and what had been arrayed on the tray for the Biggsley family was painfully clear to her. She sincerely hoped that such was a stark and glaring oversight. Perhaps the miserable cook was too unkind to feel any generosity towards an orphan just moving in, as she herself was about to move out of the family.

The day moved on. Nothing of significance revealed itself to Ruby. She could not tell how she was to be treated in detail or accepted as a whole by this new family. Beyond Mr. Biggsley, who was off and away on business for the entire day, the rest of Biggsley family was generally busy going through their things in their rooms, for they were packing up for their grand move west (and placing things aside to be given to others, the poor, or whomever). Ruby heard this and that little piece of news or thing of information relating to the great move, but, nothing was truly told directly to her and she did not manage to pick up much in the way of facts of any import. She was, however, requested by the mother, daughters and the cook (or maid or whatever was her title for her remaining short time with the family), to come help with this or that thing. Ruby dashed about, this way and that.

Ruby was kept dizzyingly busy that day and for many days (into a few weeks) to follow, helping with packing things up, preparing some foods, cleaning and so forth. Ruby quickly learned that most meals were to be brought to the family members on the large tray (for there was very little of eating together at family table) and so to be certain of gaining any necessary sustenance, Ruby had to do as the cook did (by eating what she could muster during her assistance in food preparations). Stealing bites here or there, Ruby was able to keep her strength up to a modicum of what one might expect, without drawing the wrath of the cook for eating too much altogether.

When the family did actually eat together at the dining table, the meal was rushed and everyone was soon off and gone before they seemed to have been barely come together. Where was all the family chatter and repartee? Ruby truly hoped that this strange mode of separated life amongst the Biggsleys would alter for the better in familial attachments once the grand move west had been accomplished. She surmised that the scattered lives spent in rooms and more apart, was only a temporary situation whilst the household was in upheaval in preparations to move far away. Once settled, surely the family would seem more as such, eating meals together and making pleasant memories as a happy group.

Mrs. Biggsley was seen beyond her room now and then, coming out to direct what was to be done about all things in rooms other than her own bedchamber. The son went out with his father sometimes, though mostly to be delivered to another house, where he might spend much time with his friend before departing from him for what might possibly turn out to be forever. The sisters fairly kept strictly to their room. Ruby's hopes to become their sister or even friend had not been granted as yet. Had the girls not wished for a sister, having had it thrust upon them? Perhaps they were reluctant to give her a chance to join in on their kinship. Ruby did not allow her hopes to slide by much in measure, for she looked ahead to future opportunities to make friends with her new sisters and to be a happy part of a loving family. Ruby did believe that soon, all would be well and as it should be for her, within her new family.

6

False Face

All was a blur on the way west. Each was only too happy to finally have arrived in the excitingly exotic wilds of the frontier. To arrive at one's final destination was the pinnacle of the trek itself. The new home was certainly larger than the former, though it was slightly more rustic, as was surely the surrounding territory. Mrs. Biggsley's first priority was to set about getting their new place in proper order, particularly before any visitors might be invited to the house. Perhaps Mrs. Biggsley would not have (on her own account), preferred to invite neighbors over, but Mr. Biggsley would want to entertain company in reference to promoting himself and his various business ventures in the area. Thus, Mrs. Biggsley would be forced to be a smiling hostess, in spite of any of her true feelings, and since money was to be had, Mrs. Biggsley could easily be convinced to smile all the while that she visited with her husband's chosen guests in their home.

Verna, Selda, & Reginald were generally sent to their rooms to make their own order out of chaos whilst Ruby was constantly under Mrs. Biggsley's command. As there was no maid, cook or servant of any kind for the moment; Ruby found herself filling all such roles. Though she was still fairly hopeful in her thoughts that her services every waking hour were to be temporary (until such women could be found and hired), Ruby's feelings did suffer at seeing that she was still to be given no true room of her own (upstairs with the rest of the family, even though there were rooms left curiously empty on the second floor), but only a small space: a back quarters of a closet behind the kitchen, once more. Nevertheless, this closet was certainly larger than the last, and she did find comfort for the time being in such a counted blessing.

As Ruby was and had always been a generally cheerful sort of person, even as she worked constantly in her efforts to please her new semblance of a mother whose demands of the poor orphan were seemingly endless, Ruby did labor her days away in a spirit of happy thoughts for the future, even whilst she sang as she toiled. Ruby held fast to a faint wish that as she served the Biggsley family, perhaps they would grow to love her for her many generous gifts of efforts towards them. However, for the time being, as much as Ruby exerted herself for Mrs. Biggsley and her family, so was Ruby equally neglected and ignored.

The father was near always gone, and when the mother, daughters and son were not gone to town, they all generally kept to their rooms, save when Mrs. Biggsley opened her door to call out orders to Ruby. Thus far, Ruby had only been treated as if a hired servant, but still she clung to thoughts that she could more than earn and would eventually find the place that she so deserved amongst the family that had chosen her. She believed that she should finally be treated as their own. Ruby chose to exercise patience with the Biggsleys. She looked forward with cheerful hopes.

One light in the darkness of dreary week upon weeks of toil for Ruby was the singularly unusual event of going to church altogether as a family, as they all did every Sunday. Perhaps Sundays had become the light of each week to Ruby, in that it was Sundays that helped her to believe that someday, each day of the week could be more like Sundays with respect to the Biggsleys feeling far more to Ruby like a family and even as one to call her own.

Early on in their arrival out west, when in church on Sunday, Ruby chanced to perk her ears enough to thoroughly hear the speech of the pastor, relating to keeping the Sabbath day holy. There was one scripture that spoke of no living being working on the Lord's Day, and this thought was comprehensively impressed upon her mind at once in a completely saddening and delightful way (causing a mix of diverse emotions), since she was only too keenly aware of how hard she had been working these many Sundays since having been taken from the orphanage.

When later, the family was home again from church and Mrs. Biggsley habitually ordered, "Ruby, bring the tray to our rooms with some food, as I mentioned before, you know. Quickly now, for there is much work to be done before the sun sets. Stop your dilly dallying: you must get yourself back to your everyday chores."

Ruby did cleverly seize the moment and bravely rouse herself enough to gently mention in return, "I would prefer to follow the pastor's suggestion today in obeying the scriptures that commanded all not to work on any Sabbath day."

Mrs. Biggsley tried, "Well, I do not think that he truly meant… that… *every* person should not work at all… all the daylong… each Sunday."

"Please do forgive me and my impertinence, but, I listened intently to his speech and did distinctly hear him say that no living creature in your house or your fields… not even the beasts… should be required to work on the Sabbath day. I am quite certain that I could find the passage in your family Bible, if you would like me to look it up for you."

Mrs. Biggsley stood all aghast: her face in shock. She did not know what, as yet, to say in response to Ruby's sudden bold rebellion. Her mind was in a fury of thought. How could a woman as she, trying to maintain an image of piety and good Sunday church-going behavior, find a way to make the redheaded girl work on the Sabbath? Oh, that cursed pastor! How could he spoil Sundays so thoroughly for her in this way, by repeating that set of scriptures for Ruby to hear? Oh, that the redhead had not been there that day. If only the orphan had been too sick to go to church!

Ruby took her chance to set a precedent forevermore, "Oh, do not worry about going hungry today. Of course there are some foods I prepared yesterday, and you are all very welcome to them. And as to my chores… they will certainly wait for the morrow. Do not fear, for I will surely work on them tomorrow."

With that, Ruby was off and away from the Biggsley household (that she had so much waited upon), for a delightful afternoon walk in the fields. On her way out, she snatched a little food for her own sustenance.

Sundays became a day for Ruby to look forward to with great happy zeal. She had been given an honest way to rest one day a week. Thanks be to the pastor for mentioning such and the Bible for holding those words. Ruby took the opportunity before and after church, to get away from the Biggsley house, and more especially from Mrs. Biggsley, whose endless commands had become such drudgery and even a sort of horror to Ruby.

Sundays also had become the day to truly see Mrs. Biggsley's false face in full action. All smiles it was. Over a space of time, Ruby had gradually noticed that Mrs. Biggsley's pleasant looks had faded immensely in her own eyes, as the woman's actions showed more and more of her true nature. Mrs. Biggsley's once seeming pleasant smile, now appeared almost as if a sneer or a sort of frightening staring glare and all Ruby could seem to see were Mrs. Biggsley's many lines on her pinkish hued face, a color which caused Ruby to recall the diluted watery beet soup that she had often eaten at the orphanage. Though she had detested her time at that place, she found herself often wishing to return there, where she was one of many overlooked orphans instead of the one and only lonely virtual slave to the Biggsley family.

When Ruby had first seen Mrs. Biggsley, on her very best smiling behavior, with her best face forward, Ruby had thought the woman pleasant looking on all accounts. It was not until Mrs. Biggsley's true face and nature became more and more apparent, that Ruby began to think her new fostering mother rather ill looking, from her dire thinness to her prunishly wrinkled skin. Mrs. Biggsley still smiled a great deal, particularly when they were in company at church, but Ruby seemed more and more able to see past Mrs. Biggsley's false smile that fronted her face like some sort of veil.

Ruby's thoughts often instinctually explored her wish that she could return to the orphanage, but of course she fully realized that she could not find any way or means to go back (especially now that she was way out west, far away from her origins). She knew that she must force herself forward. Before the traverse to the frontier, Ruby had wondered if she should plan an escape, before it was too late to find her way back home to the orphanage (at least to what had been as if a home to her), but she did not now berate herself nor lament much for not having tried *something* to get away from the Biggsely family back then when she was still out east, for she did not know how she could have managed it.

Mrs. Biggsley did now fully appear other than what she had first seemed. Ruby could see that this woman had not the makings of a loving adoptive mother but an overbearing foster figure, servant overseer or even slave driver. Surely Mrs. Biggsley must be better than Miss Mortimer, at least in her outward temperament, but, she did not begin to show herself as the sort of woman a girl would choose to become beholding to and ruled by. Mrs. Biggsley was fast being revealed as a mother Ruby would not desire as her own. No matter to Ruby, for Mrs. Biggsley showed no signs of desiring another daughter: it was clear now that the falsely smiling woman had only wanted a servant when she had gone to the orphanage to choose a girl that day. Ruby was treated as a mere servant or even more as a slave, for she did not receive pay for her work. She began to see very clearly why she had been chosen to be a part of this family. Ruby was picked by Mrs. Biggsley for servitude, and for no other reason.

Ruby consoled herself to a very small degree that amongst her new brother and sisters she might still find friends and even a true sense of family: if not instantly, perhaps in time. If they would ever leave their rooms, she believed that she could win them over. Indeed, as an orphan, Ruby had practiced the art of winning friends for many years, and so held out hopes and confidence that at least her new sisters would warm to her eventually, later if not sooner. However, it was not to be, for Verna, Selda, & Reginald were each spoiled, lazy and predisposed to be unkind, even to each other, but more especially to the outsider who had been brought in without any consultation of theirs whatsoever.

Generally, when Mrs. Biggsley would take her daughters and son out in the wagon to go to town or to visit neighbors, Ruby was glaringly left alone at home to try to keep up with the many chores and much work to be done. The orphan girl was still only an appearing part of the family at church on Sundays. On one occasion, however, due to the pastor requesting Mrs. Biggsley and her children to drop by for a short visit with him, his wife and children, Mrs. Biggsley was forced to also bring Ruby (whom he mistakenly included as a full member of that family). Since the pastor was fully expecting Ruby to come along as one of the family party and as such referred to her by name in that context, Mrs. Biggsley could ill afford to refuse him. Ruby had come to know Mrs. Biggsley's outward countenance enough to see that she was much displeased about feeling obliged to bring Ruby along on this outing, on other than a Sunday to church. Indeed, in the woman's own mind, it was unpleasant enough that she must take the girl to church with them and feign as if she were a true part of their family, but now she was bid by the pastor even on a weekday to bring Ruby along with them for neighborhood visits!

Ruby enjoyed their somewhat brief visit with the pastor's family. Indeed, Ruby had become fairly fond of the pastor, if only because he had opened a door to her claiming Sunday respites from her foreboding daylong weekday labors. Once gone from the pastor's place, Ruby found that they did soon stop in on a near neighbor to his. Mrs. Biggsley climbed down from the wagon, went to and knocked on the door and then shortly thereafter, waved her children to her (calling to Ruby to stay in the wagon). Promptly, the Biggsleys all went inside the house, coming out shortly afterwards with their arms laden with some foods such as cheese, bread and milk. Ruby had seen no sight of anyone within who would have let the Biggsleys inside, nor did she see anyone at the door when they came out from the home. All this seemed very curious to Ruby.

After loading all these things into the wagon, Mrs. Biggsley instructed her children, "Run to the chicken coop and fetch some eggs, for I found none in the pantry. Now, hurry, each of you!"

The woman looked around whilst climbing aboard her wagon, as Ruby sat in awe at the seeming strangeness of this event. Had this neighbor previously invited Mrs. Biggsley to help herself to foods in their pantry? Why would this be so? Was it some sort of trade or a gift? The Biggsleys were one of the richest families in these parts. Why on the green earth would she need such a kind of charity of sorts? Ruby's mind spun in the wonderment of it all. She wished to beg questions, but feared to tread there for the moment.

Soon, Verna, Selda, & Reginald scrambled into the wagon, each bearing handfuls of eggs, which were promptly put into the back of the wagon with the other foods, all such foodstuffs apparently being gotten from the pantry of this other family.

Mrs. Biggsley as much as barked over her shoulder, "Verna, put that blanket over everything, and be quick about it. I see what's-her-name coming. I cannot be found out."

As Mrs. Biggsley was driving her brood and their booty out of the property, the woman of the place drove up and hallooed a happy greeting, "Well! Fancy you coming to see me today! I was just at the pastor's for a very short stop and he told me that you had just been there. How was I to know that you were to grace me with a visit as well?"

Mrs. Biggsley was all smiles, "Oh, dear me! How sad that you were not here when I called! I am so sorry that I cannot stay… now. Something pressing calls me home. Yes, I was to offer you a short visit, since I was in the area, but now I really must take my children home this instant."

"Oh, dear… I was too late then?" the woman seemed truly disappointed to lose out on her guest.

"Yes, but, there will be other times, my dear… many other times… and very soon, I dare say." Mrs. Biggsley flashed her broadest smile and then held it with a strength of force only she seemed capable of.

Smiling and waving was exchanged between the two women as their wagons proceeded to finish their passing. The Biggsleys were on their way towards their home even as the woman drove herself to her own.

Mrs. Biggsley expressed with a laugh, "Well, children! Was that not a close one? My heart was in my throat over that escapade! How dare the woman sneak up on me in such a way! I was doing just fine, not fearing for a moment… until she came into sight! Well, well… I will remember this adventure for many a day!"

Ruby looked around her as Mrs. Biggsley and her children were all laughing. Ruby's mind could not at first comprehend what had just transpired. As she rode along in uncomfortable silence for her part, even as the Biggsleys thrilled aloud somewhat in exchanges about their exploit, all began to unfold around Ruby and she could not believe what was as clear as the day before her. Mrs. Biggsley and her children had robbed that woman of many foods, and smilingly rode away with not one whit of regret about what they had done. Obviously the woman had not given Mrs. Biggsley leave to do such a thing, and was even now ignorant of the fact of what had just happened in reference to her kitchen pantry and chicken coop. Instead of being ashamed of their gross crime, the Biggsleys were reveling in it. Ruby had half a mind to call them each and all to repentance instantly, but then where would she be? Ruby was truly an orphan, in the middle of the frontier nowhere, with nobody to turn to. Perhaps she could call upon the pastor for help or charity or even worthy work? Ruby dared to think upon it.

Even as Ruby pondered on what she might say to the pastor about what she had just witnessed, Mrs. Biggsley turned to her and with a face not smiling as usual but ardently sour, rather; and eyes as cold as the darkest night in winter, spoke acidly, "And don't you be getting any wild thoughts about turning us in, you freckled little turncoat. If you tell anyone about our little neighborhood visits, I will convince them all that it was *you*, and you shall be branded a thief, and then… our redheaded orphan… you will be hung."

Reginald put in gleefully, "Hung by your neck… until you are dead."

Ruby was truly inwardly horrified, as she attempted complete composure without.

Verna scolded, "No need to be so morbid, Reginald. I'm sure Ruby understands the seriousness of her future words or actions, without such horrid detail from you. You will be wise and silent, will you not, Ruby?"

Selda added, "Yes, you will not tell a soul of what we have done, will you Ruby? You know how quickly supposed thieves are hung… out here on the frontier."

Ruby suppressed tears, fearing even to blink, that the watery droplets might escape out to cool her hot cheeks.

Mrs. Biggsley clarified, "You do us no harm, and we'll do you none, Ruby. Just remember, that folks will believe me over an orphan, any day of the week… even your beloved Sunday. You have no true friends out here in the wilds of the west, Ruby. None at all, I assure you. Even the dear pastor would as soon throw you over as not. Mark my words well… do as I say… and you will avoid the gallows."

Ruby kept her gaze affixed in a glancing stare along the horizon off beside her. She did not wish to meet the gaze of any of the Biggsleys who she rode along with. How could she look them in the eyes without contempt showing in her own looks? The Biggsley chatter turned to other subjects for a time, before dancing upon some of their other, previous neighborhood exploits. Ruby did not wish to hear of the other things that they had stolen from unsuspecting surrounding neighbors and supposed friends. She could not believe her ears, but knew that she must. She felt the certain burden of knowing of a crime whilst not having any power to right the wrongs that had been done to others. What must other folks around about think to find foods and other such things gone missing? How could Mrs. Biggsley do such things? How could she justify such actions to herself? And to teach her children to do such as well? It was all so terribly wrong (and strange as wel). Not only was it all unconscionable (and that was surely enough to make a reasonable person with a conscience stare in confusion), but it was unreasonably illogical. Mr. Biggsley made enough money and to spare for his family. Why under heaven would they feel the need to steal?

Did Mr. Biggsley know of all this? Why would Mrs. Biggsley

take the risk of being caught? She seemed to believe herself above the fray somehow: that she could not be caught and could weasel her way out of trouble and public guilt if she were to be found out. Ruby could imagine Mrs. Biggsley's smiles and explanations, and the thought of such a woman (who appeared so respectable and amiable outwardly) doing such a horrible thing was so unbelievable, that people would tend to want to believe almost anything else. They would be open to her explanations and fooled by her smiling ways. Yes, they would of course be far more inclined to be persuaded to believe that such as Ruby had done it. She was an orphan, freckled and a redhead. Yes, Ruby could easily be blamed. If caught in a pinch, Ruby could imagine how Mrs. Biggsley could twist and turn the truth to make almost anyone believe that all was Ruby's fault.

All the way home, Ruby was as quiet as those surrounding her were raucous. Once arrived at the Biggsley house, Ruby took to her chores with a fervor and vengeance, doing her utmost to avoid every family member. She did not wish to face any of them, to look them in the eyes, to speak to them, to be seen by them, or to even breathe the very air near them. Ruby's head was spinning and the little world around her was whirring wildly. She did not know what to do, or what she could do. In her prayers that night, she begged heaven to aid her in knowing what course to take. The only answer she seemed to receive in the coming days was to cope in the situation that she had found herself lost in.

As days and weeks passed, Ruby had thoroughly become the lowly servant, who kept her head low, said as little as possible and kept herself to herself and her work. Ruby became suddenly happy that this family all generally kept to their rooms and that she need not partake in much of their discourse when they were out amongst each other. Even still, when the family was seemingly as a family, Ruby still kept apart from them, whether physically or only mentally. Her work was her comfort, for keeping to her duties at least helped her to keep a distance from the Biggsleys. On their rides to church each Sunday, Ruby would draw herself within and stare off and away, that she need not interact with any of this family.

As a short space of time passed, Mr. Biggsley began to intently desire that Mrs. Biggsley begin to exert herself a little more with neighbors, to help him in furthering any of his business pursuits that might need a little coaxing or tugging by the benefit of having friends round about. Mrs. Biggsley seemed to do her part in this, though she would oft come home with a tendency towards vicious verbal attacks against this or that woman that she had been visiting with that day. She did not seem to truly like anyone. Though she smiled and complemented generously whilst with other women; beyond their hearing, she could turn venomous against them in an instant. Ruby saw enough of all this to begin to see more and more clearly into the many facets of Mrs. Biggsley's character and person. The woman was all confusion, but Ruby could see this true picture of her.

From afar and from her close vantage point at church every Sunday, Ruby seemed to perceive that just as Mrs. Biggsley did not generally like any woman that she openly called friend (mostly for what she and her husband could make in money of the relationship), neighboring women around about did not typically like Mrs. Biggsley either. Mrs. Biggsley also seemed to begin to perceive that her popularity in the neighborhood was sliding downward. Early on after recognizing such, Mrs. Biggsley began her own personal crusade in efforts to redeem her reputation and to thwart any alliances that might be forming against her. As Mr. Biggsley was near always off and gone in the business of making money, Mrs. Biggsley was oft gone, busy making trouble betwixt and amongst other women.

Mrs. Biggsley knew full well that a character can be ruined easily enough. Seeds of doubt can be simply sewn; someone's die can be cast effortlessly. All that was needed was a disparaging word or a look here and there, now and then. Suspicions, speculations, rumors: all such hearsay was planted without difficulty into the willing minds of the many. She could manipulate and connive to her own advantage whenever she so chose to. Pointing any blame in this or that direction was an easy thing. Dividing loyalties and sewing contentions round about was seeming play to her.

It became increasingly clear that it was in Mrs. Biggsley's very nature to expect and even demand exclusivity. She jealously guarded each friend towards herself and against each other, even though she did not actually care for any friend. Her greed and gluttony surpassed her needs, endless wants or desires for foods, apparels, fine shelter and many other luxuries. Indeed, she wanted all things at her disposal and all people she met to be at her beck and call, to love or adore her, and her alone. She fancied herself a sort of queen on earth: higher than all but the angels themselves. All persons must bow to her, and if this did not come naturally to them, she would orchestrate such to come about.

7

Rigors Out West

Mr. Biggsley announced to his wife in their room, whilst they were both readying themselves to retire one night, "It is high time we got a real cook here. We need to be hosting some dinner parties… you know… to help get my business plans going… and that little orphan will not do for such. She might be adequate for the likes of us… but not for the folks I plan to bring over here on occasion."

"All right then, if you wish, my dear." His wife answered obediently, knowing full well that they could surely afford a cook and that Ruby's crude cooking skills were not up to the task of entertaining any guests, to be sure.

Mr. Biggsley curtly suggested, "Just post an advertisement at the general store and I'm sure many applicants will appear for you to choose from."

"Yes, certainly, m'dear."

"And be quick about it. We have been here far too long, not having hosted any party. What must people think of us? We are looking badly. You know what appearances may do." he was a little impatient and cross in his address.

Mrs. Biggsley rolled her eyes but moderated her tone even as she spoke, "Forgive me, my dear… I will get us a cook as soon as may be."

"Good then." Mr. Biggsley was now mollified.

Promptly the following day, Mrs. Biggsley took her little advertisement to the general store and posted it inside on the board that was provided to customers for that purpose. Before leaving, she made some smiling inquiries with the owners of the store, just to add some advantage to her search for the perfect cook who would come cheap in the bargain.

Later that day, Mrs. Biggsley suddenly felt inclined to sardonically berate Ruby for being an amateurish cook, though Ruby was not inwardly mortified in the least, for she knew that she had been doing very well in the kitchen for not having much true experience at all as a cook. And Heaven knew that she was still so very young. When she later took herself out to the barn to milk the cow, she contrarily told herself within that she was doing marvelously. Was she not managing all manner of chores in, out and around the place? As the Biggsley mother and children leisured their days away mostly in their rooms, did not Ruby do all the work that must be done? Did she not keep their clothes and household clean? Did she not conjure up all kinds of foods to keep the family fed? During the brief period that she had observed the former Biggsley family cook out east (relative to her required duties helping that woman in the kitchen), Ruby had swiftly learned some basic skills that she had built upon and continued teaching herself from. Ruby had always been a quick study. She was prompt to learn any new thing and was sharp-minded enough to think on her feet even as she worked. Her rich creative mind had helped her to become an adequate cook indeed. Thus she firmly believed and could not be scorned or beaten into thinking otherwise.

As Ruby milked the cow that day, the growing number of barnyard cats gathered round her, waiting for the milk that they knew she would give them. As had become her habit of late, Ruby began talking in a soliloquy of sorts to the cats (that had become quite her own), "And how are you all today, my dears? Come to beg an ounce of milk apiece off of me, have you? Well, you are in luck for I am in a generous mood today... as you dear darling cats are my only friends in the entire world... out here, out west, at least... and I do mean to share a great deal of milk with each of you. Please do not tell me that your little bellies are full of mice... for my feelings and heart shall be hurt a great deal if you do not lick up every extra drop of milk that I shall give you to drink. I have half a mind to give less milk to that family of undeserving people that I now milk for... though any excuse I give... such as that some of the milk was spilled... kicked over by Bessy the cow... or that Bessy was unusually ungenerous today... well... nothing would go over very well with the house mistress... and I might bring ill down upon myself for my rebellion... but... a few drops more of milk will be greatly appreciated by each of you... and none in the house will be any the wiser for the loss of an ounce or two of milk gone missing, to be sure."

The cluster of cats generally stared at Ruby, some of their heads cocked to this or that side. The felines were so very attentive to her speech that they behaved somewhat even as dogs in their alert attention to her words, tone and movements. Ruby then almost instinctively began making cat sounds to her patiently waiting whiskered barn companions, so much so, that more cats gathered round her, coming out of the haystack and even from surrounding territory from beyond the barn. Ruby suddenly burst out laughing at the grand audience that she had generated, and promptly poured milk into tin plates that were still lying about from the most recent feline feast of white liquid. Ruby thought the chorus of cat sounds that erupted quietly deafening, but in a most pleasing way (despite a few hisses and snarls that continually established an hierarchical order amongst the ranks). She left the cats generally scratching and fighting over their plentiful creamy bounty, as she took her adequately filled bucket into the back of the house.

Ruby had noticed quite recently, at least by virtue of her small looking glass, that she had filled and rounded out somewhat of late. Being able to eat adequate portions even as she cooked, Ruby was generally well fed for the first time in her memory, and not only did she know that she was no longer the skinny creature she once was, but that she was fairly assured that she was a good deal taller as well. Where once she was as short as or shorter than the Biggsley girls, Ruby was now taller, she was quite certain. At least once in recent weeks as they all went to church together, she happened to steal a glance of comparison and was at first shocked to realize that she had surely grown faster than the Biggsley girls were doing. She was older, it was true, but Ruby had always been so very short for her age, and now she thought that she was caught up to at least a normal height. Ruby had always surmised that with a modicum of food and warmth, she would be a healthier size and of stronger constitution, and now she could see the results of such a welcome change.

As to warmth, it was true that Ruby still roomed in a cramped closet of sorts behind the kitchen, and that she had no fireplace as the family members each enjoyed (and which Ruby was required to stock firewood by and light for them each chilly night before the Biggsley family retired), but she was sharp-minded enough to realize right off that she could get away with stoking the kitchen stove fire enough most nights to give her a good deal of radiant warmth while she slept, at least through the first part of those nights. All in all, Ruby still believed she was generally warmer than she usually had been in the orphanage.

Beyond growing taller and filling out so nicely, Ruby also was generally in health compared to her former days at Humble House. She did not know for certain all the reasons why, but wondered if the dryer climate that they had moved to out on the frontier, and simply becoming a little older in years had mainly done the trick for her; though Ruby first concluded that much food and a little warmth had also been very beneficial, contributing to her greater general robustness.

Though Ruby was at work all the days long, tired as death every night when retiring, and sometimes becoming truly cold to the bones as any chilly night did progress towards the dawn; her greatest lament was the true coldness of the Biggsley family. If only they could have tried to love her just a little. That little would have gone such a lengthy way. At least her heart could have been warmed whenever her body was not.

The fakery of the Biggsley family on Sundays only exacerbated Ruby's feeling of loneliness, loss of friends and want for family.

Seeing how they pretended to be familial and kindly towards her in the public church-going eye, hinted of the way that life could have been for her with them, if only the Biggsley family attempted to live as well as they cared to appear to be. Ruby could not understand these folks: this family who went to such great lengths to appear to be loving, kind, friendly and yet despised everyone (and even each other in many ways, oftentimes). Ruby had seen how Mrs. Biggsley had taught her children to put up a solid front of false friendliness, always smiling to even people they secretly detested. Mr. Biggsley was not around the household and family enough for Ruby to truly know if he was exactly as counterfeit as the rest of his family. She did know, however, that money was his truest friend and beloved joy, and if smiling all around was a way to get more in the way of coin, he would surely do it.

From time to time, Ruby would be given to some despair. Too often did she feel downtrodden, discouraged and terribly lowly. Not even a servant who could expect some pay and respect, she was only a slave without coin or supposed due. There was not a penny to be paid to Ruby for her endless unceasing work. At least Ruby still held fast to Sundays as rest to her weary body and soul. Enough time and sad events had elapsed that Ruby was not given to thoughts of her first wish to become a beloved daughter and sister within the Biggsley family. She knew she would not know familial love or even friendship, but only critical scorn from amongst them. If there had been any love, she could have endured giving endlessly.

The hard labors that Ruby was chained to by the falsely smiling Mrs. Biggsley, caused the redhead to longingly pine again and again for the ease of Humble House. The entire void and lack of true kindness from any of the Biggsley family sent Ruby's mind back to the orphanage in fond remembrances and lamenting for her current sad and sorry situation. Her prayers always seemed to turn to tears and she did tend to begin to lose faith in heaven (at least in reference to herself and her own wellbeing). She did often fear to pray at all because she knew that she would end and even oftentimes begin in weeping. Though not ever entirely unbelieving, Ruby often generally felt abandoned entirely by the heavens above.

Mrs. Biggsley's wish of a good cook on the cheap was fairly quickly and easily realized. After the new cook did come, Ruby was now relegated to helping her out in the kitchen as a cook's assistant rather than being the only cook of the household. Of course, still owning all other meager tasks, Ruby was at least relieved to have a large burden lifted from her shoulders to be shared with this new cook: namely a Mrs. Eliza Hanratty, who was quite thoroughly amiable. Ruby could not feel complaint for the new situation. Indeed, she was most grateful that this cook was obviously kindlier than the last one (at the Biggsley's out east). Promptly Ruby's ally (at least in spirit, for she was not a woman to stand up against her employers on almost any count), Mrs. Hanratty was jolly enough when the two worked together. Ruby was soon fondly calling her Eliza, as was the older woman's wish for the young woman to do in addressing her.

Mrs. Hanratty was given a main floor room as her own sleeping quarters, which was larger and of more comfort than Ruby's dire little so-called (closet-of-a) room, though it was not anything like unto the family and spare (empty) bedrooms upstairs.

Feeling quite badly about Ruby's tiny closet space called her room, early on, Mrs. Hanratty did once timidly inquire of Mrs. Biggsley on behalf and for the sake of her new young friend, "Yes'm, though I was jist wundrin 'bout one'o them empty rooms upstairs. Couldn'a Ruby have one'o them to be her very own?"

Mrs. Biggsley's answer was instant, curt and commanding, "Ruby stays where she is."

"But… 'tis such cramped quarters…"

"Ruby stays where she is, I say, and I don't wish to hear another word on the subject." Mrs. Biggsley's smile had quickly faded.

Mrs. Hanratty hesitated a breath's length, but then proceeded, "Yes'm, please forgive me… but I was just wund'rin why there were all them empty rooms upstairs."

"Those rooms are for guests. We will be furnishing them in due course."

"Ah, yes'm… I understand." Mrs. Hanratty inwardly wondered

if these supposed guests would ever come to claim their rooms, or if they would be left glaringly empty as a reminder to Ruby of her lowly place amongst the Biggsley family.

That evening, Eliza was all the more generous in her efforts (than before or even afterwards), in making certain that Ruby consumed plenty of goodly foods and that the kitchen stove fire was most thoroughly stoked and hot before she retired to her own room, that Ruby would have warmth in her belly and round about her throughout that night.

Though Ruby no longer needed to sample her own cooking before serving it up to the Biggsley family, Eliza continued to give Ruby plenty of opportunity to stay thoroughly fed by sharing in the sampling of her own cooking. Ruby did not hunger. And though Mrs. Biggsley preferred to jealously guard the many foods that entered her household, since she did not cook or work in the kitchen herself, she could not keep a close enough accounting of every morsel to prevent Ruby from being very well fed.

Beyond internally wishing that she could (and even sometimes trying to) control into who's belly any morsel of food was destined to inhabit, it was also true that Mrs. Biggsley had long commanded that there were particularly expensive special foods that were only ordained for the mouths of herself and her husband (as they had long insisted be so, for in their minds, there was such as adequate food for the children and then there were the grander foods for themselves) and only regular fare for their offspring, but since the parents and children generally ate separately, this separation of lowly standard rations versus lofty epicurean foods was accomplished without much notice from the lower family ranks. Ruby and Eliza at least generally ate as well as the Biggsley children.

Ruby thanked the heavens above often for the likes of Eliza Hanratty living at the Biggsley household. Indeed, the two were firm friends from the very beginning of their acquaintance. Here was a woman that Ruby could laugh with daily as they worked side by side in the kitchen. There was an instant kinship between them that Ruby cherished beyond expression. In her own gentle, subtle and even clandestine way, Eliza looked out for Ruby as much or more than Patsy ever had been able to do at the orphanage. As a matter of personal principled duty, Eliza continually determined to watch over her younger helper. Any of Ruby's occasional dream-like thoughts of escaping back east to the orphanage swiftly faded away, as her life, even as it was (working so very hard, day in and out); with Eliza as her friend, Ruby could see clear to counting her blessings, as meager though they may be. Eliza had brought needed light and joyfulness into the lower and back rooms of the Biggsley house. Ruby's burdensome efforts to stay cheerful on her own were daily eased by Eliza's typically happy presence.

As some time passed, Ruby and Eliza worked together to keep the Biggsleys as content as was possible, all the while the two generally endeavored to avoid much interaction with any members of the family. The two workers of the house enjoyed each other's mutually beneficial company even as the family members tended to avoid time spent with one other. Eliza had soon learned what Ruby had fairly rapidly garnered from being amongst the Biggsleys: that they were as falsely pleasant publicly as they were full of true defects individually.

After Verna and Selda had each been granted their own separate rooms in the new house, their previous general peace as sisters had lessoned almost exactingly in tandem with every passing month. The viewpoints and desires of the two sisters had become increasingly divided. They were at odds and even rivals over nearly every imaginable thing. This growing unpleasantness in temperaments did nothing to enhance their lacking beauty, which was contrasted with escalating depiction by Ruby's ever-present pleasing qualities of character and rising beauty.

The more lovely Ruby seemed to become (the reality of which was often noticed by young men at church, and these pleasing attentions or attractions to Ruby were certainly noticed by at least the Biggsley females), the more Mrs. Biggsley wished to work Ruby like unto an oxen as an effort to demean and diminish the redhead (for the greedy old baggage hid a secret growing jealousy against the orphan for fast becoming so much more than her own daughters). Ruby was everything quick-witted, hardworking, lovely and delightsome that the slothfully plain Biggsley girls were not, though Mrs. Biggsley's envy more specifically focused on Ruby's outward beauty versus the lack thereof in her own girls. The more Mrs. Biggsley attempted to suppress Ruby's beauty through toil, the more beautiful Ruby became. Her cheeks glowed rosily, her eyes were bright due to exercise and her bodily structure was lean and fit, though still visually pleasing and healthily rounded.

Beyond Mrs. Biggsley's futile attempts to work the redhead into ugliness, the harsh woman purposely kept Ruby shabby in dress to diminish her outward attractions; but (though some women might scorn her for her apparent poor and humble appearance) young men did not generally care what the young beauty was wearing. As is the prevailing case in such instances, her natural beauty shone through to most men (from under her shabby clothing), even though many females and dandies preferred to be impressed by more outward appearances of fashion and wealth.

As time wore on, the Biggsley girls again found something to agree upon. They found delight in scorning Ruby when they saw any opportunity to do so. Mrs. Biggsley's daughters were following in her own footsteps. The more that Mrs. Biggsley jibed and sneered at Ruby over this or that fault (manufactured excuses), the more Verna and Selda followed suit. The Biggsley girls were not entirely unaware of Ruby's growing beauty and other attractions, and though they were slightly younger and barely beginning in the way of caring what any young man might think, their jealousy did start to bud as they did commence growing towards becoming young women.

The belittling of Ruby by the Biggsley females did catch on somewhat by the males, as if a sort of disease. Though he really knew not why, Reginald began taunting Ruby more than ever before, perhaps only just because the thing was in the air. Mr. Biggsley began to instinctually treat Ruby with real disdain and condescension whereas he had only tended to ignore her existence before. Ruby tried to take little notice of this new habitual mocking and mistreatment, even whilst Eliza attempted to lessen their ill effects upon her younger lovely friend by whatever means she could. The more Eliza Hanratty noticed the growing malevolence of her youthful friend by the Biggsleys (since there seemed to be very little she could do or say to halt the cruel family practice), the more she did endeavor to lift Ruby's spirits as an antidote to such an evil.

When Ruby had first come amongst the Biggsleys, she had very briefly tried the family name on for size (when she still thought or hoped that she might eventually be properly treated as their daughter and sister). Mrs. Biggsley laughed at the thought, and the unkind woman quickly found every occasion to tell near all within hearing that Ruby was 'a no account orphan'. 'Ruby Nobody', Mrs. Biggsley had too often said. In subtle defiance of the label, Ruby stood tall and represented herself as 'Ruby Steed', though she knew not of her origins further. She would not allow her own person to be labeled a nothing on any count by any person (even her supposed surrogate mother). Ruby would not allow herself to be repressed (in her own view, at least). Miss Mortimer had never done it, with all her efforts, and neither would Mrs. Biggsley (or would all her family combined manage it). The new efforts of the Biggsleys against Ruby were only another mountain to climb to her. She faced the maliciousness with determined fortitude.

As Mrs. Biggsley saw that her daughters were beginning to become young women, she began to teach them well (as she thought), to set their sights on men with money. She was prone to give little lectures on the subject, as (no doubt) her mother had done before her. Verna and Selda were willing students, for they did indeed like money, and more especially, all the treasures that money could buy. Mrs. Biggsley taught her girls the fine arts in being as pleasing as possible to anyone who may assist in throwing them in the path of any marriages that would bring money. The Mother thought it not too early to begin proper habits for her daughters to put into practice.

Verna and Selda did not care to recognize their grand hypocrisy in mocking Ruby for trying to better herself (by working and learning to increase her skills), when their own mother was teaching them to better themselves as she had done (by marrying for more money than she had ever known in her growing up years). To be sure, Mrs. Biggsley had begun very low indeed, had risen greatly by marrying Mr. Biggsley, and had profited all the more so by encouraging and fostering his greed for ever more money. Indeed, one of Mrs. Biggsley's favored speeches was this: 'The more money I spend, the more my husband will need learn to make'. For comfort and security sake, the Biggsley daughters needed not be taught to reach for young men any higher in riches than below what their father had attained, though Mrs. Biggsley desired ever greater fortunes to befall their family by every means possibly within her reach.

Mr. Biggsley's good fortune increased by leaps and bounds in an incredibly short space of time. Indeed, it was as if a gargantuan waterfall of money was descending upon him and as if with buckets filled and emptied, he and his wife could not spend the cash fast enough to keep up with the rapid and continual flow of coins, for they surely had a great deal more wealth than they knew what to do with. And throughout it all, Mrs. Biggsley did puff herself up in the pride of thinking that it was she alone who had truly caused all such wealth to pour unto her through her husband.

Ruby's situation in life was surely not improved by the Biggsley family's growing riches, and quite to the contrary, she was treated with more proud contempt and disparagements than ever, by especially Mrs. Biggsley and her daughters. As far as the Biggsley family was concerned, Ruby was no friend, no sister (not an adopted daughter as she had claim to expect to be considered) nor even a maid (since she was never paid one jot for all or any of her work); for Ruby was relegated to that of unpaid servant (or slave) in lowly unranked position of non-class. Keeping Ruby low seemed to make Mrs. Biggsley (and even perhaps particularly her daughters) feel high. Ruby served more purpose than maid to Mrs. Biggsley, for the girl served as footstool which the woman could stand up upon in order to attempt to feel taller and of more worth herself. Deep within, Mrs. Biggsley must have felt herself a very small person, for she found a false need to attempt to feel bigger by squashing others into tininess in any way she could muster. This was a sort of blasphemy, even if only within nature (and beyond all Christian teachings or heavenly ways). One cannot grow taller by stepping down upon others. Such does not lift anyone.

Mr. Biggsley put his hand to many kinds of business and he (and the entire world around him) soon saw that he truly did possess a sort of 'the touch of King Midas', for everything he seemed to lay his hands upon did fairly promptly truly turn to gold round about him. If love of money is the thing, he surely felt the adoring warmth of it.

Because of his excessive busyness with his business, Mr. Biggsley was rarely at home, but his wife did not care, for she surely loved her husband's money far more than she had ever loved him. His money did warm her frigid heart. Coins were her happy delights. Gold was a blazing fire to her in a cold world.

Sometimes, if only when the entire family was without the house spending their money somewhere in the town (trying desperately to chip away at the mountains of Biggsley coin); Ruby could confide in Eliza and find consoling words.

"Will I die here, still an unloved orphan, Eliza?"

"What kind'o talk is that, my own beloved Ruby?"

"As a servant to the Biggsleys… is this my lot in life? Will I die in lowly servitude? Finish out my life as an unpaid servant? Are these the final grand plans God has had for me?"

"Nonsense!"

"But, how will I get out? Where could I go? What could I do?"

"I dare say some young man will…" Eliza began to get stars in her eyes, smiling with a warming heart for her dear Ruby.

"I cannot depend upon a Prince rescuing me from all this. I am stuck in a mire. I must think and do for myself. I can only depend upon myself." Ruby was depressingly serious.

"Well… I suppose…" Eliza's gaze drifted upwards as she began to attempt to contemplate on the matter.

"I have thought of things… don't think I haven't thought of a few ways to get away from here… but then… then I would have to leave you…"

"Awe… doona worry 'bout me… they do pay me, y'know… and I lay coin aside, y'see…"

"But… I would miss you dearly if I left here…"

"Oh… but, we'da have visits… or letters…"

"Yes, I suppose we would not truly be parted if I left here. I would not need go far. I could get work in town, perhaps. Then I could see you when you come to town. Yes, I should surely consider something… I am near old enough to garner something I would think… to set out on my own… if the right position would avail itself to me."

"Too true…"

"Thank you, my dear Eliza! You have given me hope… and courage to watch out for the chance to get away… to strike out on my own. One of these days, Eliza… one of these days…"

8

A New Horizon

I t was a delightfully bright sun-shining blue and cloud-dotted day when Eliza laid claim upon Ruby to go to town with her to pick up some supplies. Ordinarily, Eliza would certainly go on such a mission alone. It was always Mrs. Biggsley's command that Ruby remain home to work on her many chores. The housemistress did not wish Ruby free from constant labors, and besides, she and her daughters had grown so horridly fond of finding entertainment in tormenting Ruby in whatever way they could manufacture. With Mrs. Hanratty out of the house, this sport was straightforwardly accomplished without hindrance. Ruby was more easily toyed with. However, Eliza's spirit was stronger than usual that day, and thus she managed to convince her employer to allow Ruby to go to town with her.

Ruby was more than happy to get away (more from the Biggsley females and even the son than from her chores, all which would await her return to be certain) and a trip to town with her adored friend Eliza was like a joyful holiday from daily drudgery and persecution. The ride to town was bliss itself, with beautiful natural sights to see, delightful chattering company and fully felt, though temporary freedom from all the Biggsley household torments.

While Eliza was ordering some goods at the counter within the general store, her lovely young redheaded companion standing just slightly off to one side, Ruby's eyes glanced round the interior of the shop and soon found their curious way to following a tidy young woman's movements as she was putting an advertisement up on the board alongside other posted ads there. Ruby was tempted to saunter nearer to see more, for reasons unknown to even her. There was a sure silent almost instinctive nagging within her that drove her to advance , step by step, even as within herself she consciously resisted, considering such to be bold motions forward for no apparent reason. In a strange mood to begin to take chances out west (not unlike her 'Miss Mortimer-defying berry-picking and eating adventures' in her past out east), Ruby found herself reading over the shoulder of the crisp young woman.

The advertisement read something like this, 'Horizon House Private Boarding School for Girls is presently accepting applications for a new live-in maid, who must be qualified in general duties as expected, including kitchen work as a cook's assistant. A generous salary will be negotiated commensurate with previous experience. At least one solid affirmative reference preferred. Please contact the head schoolmistress of said school for an appointment or for more information regarding the position.'

Upon passing her before leaving the store, the pleasant-looking young woman smiled at Ruby as the redhead perused the freshly pinned up advertisement. Ruby's mind buzzed with this bright grand possibility. Was this her chance to escape the Biggsleys after all? Should she apply even this day? Could she contact the head schoolmistress before going back home to the Biggsleys' house? Could this all be achievable in the relatively short time that she had remaining in town today? A passionate sense to seize the moment filled her. Breathing heavily, her heart racing rapidly, Ruby anxiously awaited with mounting fervor, her first opportunity to speak with Eliza about this seemingly narrow prospect.

Eliza happened to glance back at Ruby and seeing the anticipative excitement written clearly upon her young friend's face, she paused her own focus to make her way over to Ruby, "What is it, my child?"

Saying nothing, Ruby pointed at the new advertisement, with one of her graceful fingers actually physically touching her apparent chance for salvation from the increasingly odious (at least on her account) Biggsleys.

"So the school be wantin' a new maid, then." Eliza smiled broadly.

Ruby near fainted with glee, though whispered in contained excitement, "Yes! Do you think it possible for me to make an application for the position this very day… before returning home?"

"Oh, yes!"

"What shall I do? I have never… what is first to be done?"

"Leave it to me, m'dear."

"But?"

"I knows the cook there. She'da have good sway with the mistress."

"You… and she… could help me gain that position as maid?"

"Yes, a'course. I'll finish here and then we'll go over."

"You think it a good place for me to escape to?"

"Oh, yes. I've heard plenty o'good things 'bout the place and the womenfolk who works there."

Ruby nodded. Outwardly quiet and apparently calm, she stood her ground anxiously with boldness, as if unconsciously fending off any other female who might vie for the position of maid at the private girl's school, before she had her own chance to go and claim it. In Ruby's view, Eliza could not finish up her business soon enough and when it came time to load up the wagon with all the goods, Ruby's limbs were in whirl during the process. A young man quickly found his way over to offer his help, and Ruby's enthusiasm in accepting his proposed assistance near caused the fellow to think she might be feeling as amorous towards him as he secretly felt towards her (for he had seen her in church many a week and had been attempting to catch her eye, waiting for her notice that he might smile his affections towards her). But, his hopes were dashed; his heart's desire seemed vain, as she generally tossed him aside after the briefest only necessary thanks. With Eliza's aid, Ruby was off to the school to beg to become the new maid and no young man (however handsome, rich or ambitious he may be) was of any notice to her.

At the school, Eliza Hanratty boldly strode into the kitchen through a familiar back door while Ruby most apprehensively waited in the wagon. Fidgeting and fretting with trepidation, Ruby wondered at the answer which could change her life forever; at least she surely felt this to be true, down deep in her bones. It was not long before Eliza waved Ruby into the kitchen and thus the redhead nervously climbed down from the wagon. Her legs felt an uneasy flimsiness as she forced them limb after limb forward to take her inside. Eliza introduced Ruby to the school cook, Miss Rhodes, all the while both older women were smiling warmly at the trepidatious young woman.

In her excited anxiousness and desperation, Ruby all but accosted Miss Rhodes with a forceful whisper of sorts, rapidly exclaiming her case, "Give me a chance… an opportunity to prove myself… I will make good as a maid and a cook's assistant… please allow me to come and stay on as… well, nearly anything…"

"Yes, yes… m'dear… I've heard all from Mrs. Hanratty here. I will look out for Miss Fenton directly… the head schoolmistress, you know."

"Please tell her that I will gladly work as your lowliest hardworking servant… I will work harder than anyone… for less pay than anyone… and I will be eternally grateful to you… for I will be better off than I am at present."

Miss Rhodes laughed at Ruby's pure enthusiasm, "I'm sure you can tell her yourself… but take care and do not sell yourself short, m'dear. There is no need to offer yourself up at a slave's wages. Indentured servitude is not the thing 'round here. Let me go find and speak with Miss Fenton and we'll soon see if she doesn't call you to meet with her instantly."

The school cook was briskly off and away to indefinite distant reaches of the large and handsome building somewhere, to seek out Miss Fenton in order to solicit an audience on Ruby's behalf. While Mrs. Hanratty and Ruby waited in the kitchen for further notice, hoping for a happy outcome, they spoke to each other in hushed tones and anxious whispers. With her arm about her young friend's shoulders, Mrs. Hanratty assured a suddenly fearful and now somewhat doubting Ruby that Miss Rhodes was a wonder of a woman and from her own lips it had been made clear that Miss Fenton was a treasure. Indeed, there were none but women of a happy spirit at the school and Ruby could do no better than to become part of Horizon House. Mrs. Hanratty was absolutely increasingly through-to-the-soul convinced that this was a godsend for Ruby to get her out of the Biggsley household forevermore, and did her utmost in warmest whispers to induce Ruby to believe in and take such a heaven-sent chance to start a new and far better life for herself.

Quite promptly, Miss Rhodes was escorting Ruby to see Miss Fenton, while Mrs. Hanratty was to wait in the kitchen. As they walked down a lengthy hallway, Miss Rhodes was as assuredly calm as Ruby was anxiously nervous, though Mrs. Hanratty felt a reasonable confidence that all would turn out very well. Miss Rhodes presented Ruby to Miss Fenton and then left the two alone.

Miss Fenton began, "Miss Rhodes has been telling me that her dear friend Mrs. Hanratty recommends you highly for our position of maid and cook's assistant."

In a general repetition of what she had previously pronounced to Miss Rhodes, at least in part, Ruby all but blurted near wildly, "I will gladly work as your lowliest hardworking servant for whatever pay you deem fair… and I will be eternally grateful to you for the chance… for any work I can do in your school for any pay, will surely cause me to be better off than I am at present."

Knowing only a little of the Biggsleys, Miss Fenton was still a good deal aghast that an adopted daughter should feel this way about having lived amongst such a wealthy and respected family that should have been as her very own. Was this a strange ingratitude of the redheaded girl or a true testament of the brief and candid hints that Miss Rhodes had intimated she had been told by Mrs. Hanratty? Miss Fenton tended to feel an inward sense that it was the latter, though reason or logic might dictate that she should think otherwise. Well, Miss Rhodes had given such a glowing account of the girl (based on a trusted and lengthy friendship with Mrs. Hanratty), that Miss Fenton decided on the spot (without taking the time or opportunity to allow for further applications from other girls or young ladies) to give Ruby a chance. A warmth in her generous heart told her that such was to be so. Besides, Miss Fenton took a sudden shine to the glowing freckled face, and her instincts pronounced to her that this lovely young lady with the brilliantly red hair was the one she should choose as new maid for her school.

"Well, my dear, you surely need not be anything like unto a lowly servant, for indeed, in my own consideration and belief, we have none such here. The position of maid that I need filled is of generally lighter and certainly shared duties, I would venture to claim. Our other maid is a cheery sort and I suspect that you two will get along famously. And you have met my kindly Miss Rhodes yourself, and will not fear to work as her assistant when needed?"

Almost too ecstatic to speak, though having swiftly found her ready tongue and mind regardless, Ruby thrilled, "Oh, yes, Miss Fenton! She… I mean… Miss Rhodes… seems a lovely woman… and I am sure I will get on with the other maid… and if I dare venture to express… I am certain that I will find you to be a genteel benefactress of a mistress."

Miss Fenton smiled, "I'm certain that you will. I aim to be genteel, to be sure."

In agreement with Miss Fenton, Mrs. Hanratty proposed a scheme to Miss Rhodes whereby Ruby could stay at the school and settle in right away that very day, promising to send all her few cherished things on to her there at the school as soon as might readily be accomplished. Ruby was happy to stay behind and more than relieved to know that she would not have to face Mrs. Biggsley to explain her leaving them and their household, and she certainly felt an eternal gratitude to Mrs. Hanratty for offering to explain it all away for her. Ruby could leave the unpleasant Biggsley family past behind her in an instant and set her sights that very moment on beginning to make her mark and place at Horizon House School even as she began to make her own way in the world.

"Thank you ever so much, Eliza!" Ruby exclaimed warmly.

"Yer very welcome, I'm sure."

"I'll never forget you and your many kindnesses to me."

"Well, you'll not b'able ta forget me since I'll be visitin' plenty often." Eliza lovingly teased.

"Yes, yes, please do visit as often as you can." Ruby was in earnest.

"And I'll see you in church, a'course."

"Yes, yes! We shall sit together in church every Sunday, just as usual."

"Sep, we won't be sittin' wi' the Biggsleys, that's fer darn sure."

"Oh, no! I never wish to sit with them again, and not even near them, if you don't mind."

"A'course, m'dear." Eliza Hanratty stretched forth for a grand embrace. Ruby complied with all gratefulness and adoration. Miss Rhodes smiled as a witness to the fond farewell that signified a new beginning for a very deserving young lady.

"Take care 'o my girl, Miss Rhodes." Mrs. Hanratty gently begged as she was out the door to be upon the wagon, off and away.

Miss Rhodes put an arm about Ruby's shoulders as the redhead waved and shed a few tears to see her beloved Eliza drive away, even as she did surely feel a great relief to be left behind to begin a new and brighter future of happiness for herself.

Mrs. Hanratty took a certain real pleasure in informing Mrs. Biggsley that Ruby had taken a position in town and would not be returning. Mrs. Biggsley was at first beside herself in displeasured shock and unbelieving dismay at the news, but what could she say or do about it? She would simply have to find another orphan to abuse and to use; else pay a dear sum (a generous pittance from her sizeable pocketbook) to find a maid, two or three who may be willing to take on all the work that Ruby had been used to do. Eliza Hanratty also took foremost care to gather up Ruby's things promptly, that nothing would go amiss due to the anger that any of the Biggsleys might feel towards Ruby for deserting her post without regard to any civility towards any of them. The Biggsleys had been brushed off by the orphan! 'How dare she?' they may likely tend to think, thought their cook. Eliza would deliver all personal possessions to Ruby, when she next went to town. All such things were safe with her in the meantime.

Miss Rhodes was delighted with Ruby right off. Being a long-time friend of Mrs. Hanratty, Miss Rhodes was generally of a similar frame of mind, character and temperament. She was the kind of woman naturally blessed and near divinely designed to find gratitude in all the pleasant attributes that Ruby possessed (through nature, from heaven and by personal practice). Miss Rhodes was all the more appreciative of Ruby's many positive qualities, since the last maid (whom Ruby was now replacing) had been supremely deficient in all that Ruby excelled in. A slothfully difficult female had been replaced by a diligent and pleasing young lady.

Ruby was radiantly joyous with unfolding pleasantries at Horizon House. The room she was given to call her own was more than she would have ever asked for in size and comforts. The food was ample and nutritious. The other maid in the school was as pleasing a female as Miss Rhodes. The teachers were each as gracious as Miss Fenton. Indeed, Miss Fenton promptly took pity on Ruby's shabby wardrobe and advanced her a generous sum (against her first month's salary) to get herself some new clothes right away. She felt treated with such fondness and respect that she could not be happier in this state of her new affairs. Ruby had not ever felt this fortunate in all her days of recollection. All at the school was perfection in Ruby's estimation.

In-between her sweeping, dusting and cleaning chores as well as her many little efforts to aid Miss Rhodes in the kitchen; to Ruby's enchantment, there was fully ample time for her to become acquainted with as many of the students in the school as she desired. Ruby was enchanted by so many charming earthly angels, and those girls of varying sizes did very promptly adopt Ruby as an older sister of sorts. Ruby brought back to life her past habits from the orphanage of mothering those smaller ones around her. She invented and read stories to her captive young female audiences. She drew pictures that fascinated them.

Such activities of elation brought to Ruby's mind her life so very far back and long ago at Humble House and her former friend Patsy. Ruby suddenly took hold of herself to finally write a long-overdue letter. She did not know if Patsy would still be working there at the orphanage, but she knew she should take the chance of beginning a correspondence with her old friend if she could. Ruby felt badly that she had never written a thing to her guardian ally in all this time. She knew that Patsy would have been wondering what had become of her and why she had not written. Ruby's life with the Biggsleys had been so demoralizing that she had not found time or heart ever to write to Patsy. The truthful reality was that Ruby did not wish for Patsy to know of how her life with the Biggsleys had turned out. She had rather let Patsy think that all had been a bed of roses instead of thorns. Rather than explain all her past with the Biggsleys to Patsy, Ruby set forth her happiness where she was now. As she spoke of the darling girls that she was now mothering, she was reminded to ask after a few favorite children she had known at the orphanage. Ruby did wish to know how life had turned out for many of them. She hoped that they had known better than she had herself. However, the Biggsleys were now in Ruby's past and she could look and think on her current happy situation. Ruby's present joy in time spent with the young girls made each workday light indeed.

So quick and overarching was Ruby's cheerful effect upon the young ladies of the school day upon day, that Miss Fenton swiftly took notice and began to formulate a happy plan for the young lady.

"Ruby, I have observed how wonderful you are with the girls."

"Oh, well… thank you, Miss Fenton." Ruby humbly replied.

"I have been taking notice. I hope you don't mind my spying on you, Ruby… but, I have seen that you are well-read, intelligent, talented and born to lead children… and surely cannot be destined to stay a maid, for I do believe that you should look to becoming a teacher here."

Ruby stared in a thrilled sort of disbelief at what she had just heard. Could this be so? Was Miss Fenton offering an upcoming teaching position to her? She could not seem to fathom that such a godsend could open up before her. Ruby had not been generally used to manna from heaven raining upon her.

Miss Fenton continued, "If you will agree, and I am certain that you will, we will look out for a girl to replace you as maid and once that is achieved, you could begin as a novice or sort of apprentice teacher, under my own personal guidance. Would you like to become a teacher here, Ruby?"

Ruby composed herself, "A teacher here? Me, a teacher at Horizon House?"

"Yes, Ruby. I would wish for you to be one of our teachers here."

"Yes! Of course I would!"

"Then that is precisely what we will do!"

"Oh, thank you! Thank you, Miss Fenton! And if I do not make a worthy teacher for your school… though I will try with all my might… if I cannot live up to your expectations, then please do relegate me back to being your maid, for I do not wish to go back… to go anywhere else."

"Oh, Ruby… I have seen enough to know that you will not be our school's maid once you have become our teacher. You were born to teach and guide children, and the girls of this school already adore you as if you had been their favored teacher."

"Thank you again and again, Miss Fenton! I will be eternally grateful to you!"

Miss Fenton offered the embrace that Ruby was earnestly wishing to bestow, and the older woman's joy at giving was nearly as great as the younger's elation upon receiving such a gift of an opportunity. That night Ruby could hardly catch a wink of sleep due to her excitement. She paused many a time to give little prayer upon prayers of thanks for her growing good fortune. Such blessings as she felt she did possess at present surely overshadowed past memories of injustices and sorrows endured by her.

A new maid was found without delay and Ruby was very soon being tutored in fine-tuning her teaching techniques. Miss Fenton worked as diligently as Ruby did in assuring them both that Ruby was a fine teacher for the youngest girls of Horizon House. The work was so very joyous to Ruby that she did not feel she was working at all. To be paid for such efforts seemed such a lucky thing indeed, and a teacher's salary was a good deal more than that of a maid. She nearly felt as if she were living a life that was every ounce as fortunate as her former days were not. Teaching the young girls of the school was as delightful as being a child again, though Ruby was warm day and night and well fed throughout. It was all as if an exultant dream.

To add to her current pleasures, Ruby was overjoyed to soon receive a happy letter from Patsy which also included an enclosed note from Scarlet, who had been very fortunate in her adoption. Ruby was thrilled to be able to begin a correspondence with both her two older and younger friends from the orphanage.

To Ruby, the gloomy smiling Biggsleys were all but forgotten to her, though, in an ironic twist (for in her recent past, Sundays had been her boon against the Biggsley tormentors), Sundays brought the family before her eyes, as she could not help but see them at church (in and out, coming or going). Sitting with and amongst Mrs. Hanratty, Miss Rhodes, Miss Fenton, other teachers, the maids and boarding students of Horizon House, Ruby did her best to ignore the icy (though still primly smiling) glances and even downright cruel stares of the Biggsleys females, in particular. Sometimes Mrs. Biggsley or her daughters would find their way over to smilingly firing sarcastic or caustic remarks at Ruby before or after a Sunday service, but these could not penetrate her soul nor bother her person in the least, for she knew that she had the last laugh and happiness now. The Biggsleys could not diminish Ruby's joy no matter how they might try to. Ruby chose to think not of Mrs. Biggsley and her girls, but rather to leave them to their own devices. Seeing the Biggsleys at church weekly or in passing in town occasionally, were the only events that marred Ruby's life and she would not spend a moment lamenting over such scars or fresh wounds due to the Biggsleys, for her life was now so very blessed.

There was much fond repartee amongst the teachers, cook and maids of Horizon House. Whether going to or from church, jaunts in town, mealtime or any other time that there was any reason to chatter back and forth, the women who worked at the school were all light and happiness. Ruby thought that perhaps this spirit of sisterhood emanated from the wonderfully kind and warm Miss Fenton (who was in charge of it all). What a difference leadership could make in a school, orphanage or home, Ruby thought. Miss Fenton endeared goodness at every turn that resulted in much happiness for all who were beholding to her benevolent rule; even as Miss Mortimer had engendered bitterness equaling unhappiness for all under her dominion. Mrs. Biggsley had provoked jealousy, distrust and very real confusion in her wake. Another musing of Ruby was that Miss Fenton knew how to choose kindly women to work with and for her. Of course, the result of Miss Fenton's actions and choices was a very harmonious place to live and work in. Not only did Ruby feel that she was among true friends, but, that she was a part of a type of family. All the young girls in the school benefited from this harmony. Indeed, disharmony was not permitted as a part of any program therein. Miss Fenton would not allow discord to take root.

Life at the school was so happy for Ruby that she began to think that she would never like or choose to leave. She believed that she could happily be a teacher at Horizon House forever. She was among friends who felt as if family and she felt great joy in imparting and sharing in much good amongst many young girls. As the months flew by, Ruby grew in confidence and faith. She began to truly shine. Indeed, all that Ruby could be (or could have been, given the nurturing love that was in so many ways denied her), began to take shape in all that she was now becoming. Her always cheerful nature (but sometimes subdued, due to suppression from without) from beneath sprouted forth like a prosperously burgeoning plant. Ruby found her true person springing forth. She was no longer the orphan that Miss Mortimer had mocked and that Mrs. Biggsley had procured for ill usage. Ruby stood taller, bolder, keener and stronger, so much so that she stood out as a young woman of poise, grace and self-assurance. The Biggsley females could hardly match the might of the Ruby that they no longer knew, though they did still occasionally and continually attempt to try to hold her down by whatever words or means they could muster, on Sundays and other days that they would see her in town.

Though the school was a treasure throughout, many of the girls of Horizon House did generally prefer Miss Steed above all other teachers there. Ruby was a true favorite among them. Her gentle meekness, lively humor, creative bursts of genius and spontaneous spirit did capture their hearts and imaginations. Ruby exhibited a true balance of retaining childlike qualities while still seizing maturity. Thankfully, the other teachers did not harbor any envious feelings for coming in second to her, for they too adored their own Miss Ruby Steed. Horizon House had never known so many giggles and joys.

Quite some time had elapsed and the joys at the school continued ever more. Ruby had most happily settled into her life as teacher. Though there were possibilities of beaux aplenty, Ruby paid the young men no mind, for she had set her sights to be akin to the cheery spinsters that she had come to know and love so well. At church or in town, when dashing young men would set their cap her way, Ruby would smile and send them on their way. She was gaining a sound reputation for being supremely unattainable, and this made her all the more desirable to the young men round about. Such was a grand contrast to the Biggsley girls and their many attempts to get the notice of any eligible bachelor. Mrs. Biggsley was bent on making profitable matches for her daughters, but all had been to no avail as yet. No matter how she toiled and connived, she could not find a single man to take a daughter off her hands. Young as they each still were, she wanted them married and wished them to attain rich matches.

At the end of a lengthy, though soul-satisfying day, Ruby was about to retire to her room when she was tapped on the shoulder from behind. She turned to greet her angelic benefactress.

Miss Fenton had news for her young protégé and thus she sought her out to favor her with a private audience, "Ruby, come to my room and sit with me awhile. I have refreshments and the fire is very welcoming. Come."

"Yes, of course."

Once in the room with the door closed, Miss Fenton served Ruby her plate and cup of delicacies and then began in quiet earnest, "I have received a request from a dear old trusted friend. She is like unto a sister to me, you see. She wishes me to recommend someone. This is the perfect situation for you, Ruby. I dearly wish for you to fully consider it."

"Situation?"

"Yes. This friend of mine is a fresh widow who is in dire need of a governess for her children. She has a lovely home. You would enjoy every comfort. She is very rich, Ruby. No expense would be denied you. This would be a very good step up for you. You would be amongst a higher set of people. Who knows what this could mean for you…"

"But, I…"

"Oh, I know you would not wish to leave us, and none of us want to part with you either… not for all the world, Ruby… but… sometimes a chance like this comes only once in a lifetime… and I wholeheartedly desire that you should take it."

"But…"

"What have you got to lose, Ruby? If you are not happy there, you can always return to us here. We would never turn you away. You will always have a place here, if you wish… but, this opportunity is something that… well… if I had ever had such a chance when I was younger, I would have taken it… I want you to take this chance, Ruby."

Ruby was all frightfulness and sudden melancholy. Leave Horizon House? Leave her cherished friends here? She was not ready to speak on the matter.

Miss Fenton could see what Ruby was thinking and feeling, for it was written so plainly on the young redhead's face. Mentor tried to assist apprentice, "Ruby, I know that you are happy with us and might wish to stay here all your life… but, life is a road that has twists and turns and sometimes a new path is set before you such that it begs for you to change course. You must have courage to seize the moment of opportunity, for it may never again present itself to you."

Ruby's mouth opened slightly, though no sound was yet uttered.

"Life is not always and perhaps rarely turns out to be what one hoped for, or even imagined, but sometimes destiny offers better things than one could have imagined possible. Who knows what this opportunity may offer to you, Ruby."

Ruby remained silently thinking.

Miss Fenton pursued her course, "Ruby. Simply consider it a trial. Go. Try being a governess for this family. At any time that you deem it needful, come back. I will keep your room as it is. We need not alter it or give it to anyone else until and unless you give me leave to do so. It will await your return until you tell me that you will not have need of it. I will keep your teaching position open here for you to come back to until you tell me otherwise. I deeply wish for you to take this chance. Do it for me, Ruby. I would not press and push you so, if I did not feel passionately from my heart that you should do this."

A tear cascaded down Ruby's cheek, and the second followed shortly thereafter, springing forth from the other eye. Miss Fenton disregarded her typically steady nature and pulled Ruby in for a sturdy embrace. Ruby began to sob at the thought of leaving her dearest counseling friend.

Miss Fenton attempted to lend courage, "Ruby, we will correspond. We will visit. You will not be so very far off. You will still see your friends here… and I will surely come to visit you there. I am such an old friend of Mrs. Eaton, the widow you will work for, that she will encourage my visits as much or more than you will."

Ruby began to calm and Miss Fenton furthered her encouragement in a light-hearted humorous tone, "Just think… you can avoid the Biggsleys altogether! We will not tell them where you have gone and you will be free of them at last! They will wonder about you all they want but we will not breathe a word of your new life. We will visit you often, and then when you visit us, you can do it all clandestine-like. What fun we will have hiding you from the Biggsleys! You will know all that they are about from us, but they will only imagine where you are and what you are doing. We can tell them you are among the wealthy and be done with it… such thoughts will drive those money-hungry Biggsley women mad with jealousy!"

Ruby laughed at these thoughts. She wiped her tears and smiled at Miss Fenton as their fond and comforting embrace subsided.

"There you go, Ruby! You will do it! For me, you will! And for you too, of course."

"I will try, since you wish me to… but, I would rather stay here in your school than go off to be governess to even the richest folk in the entire world."

"I know, Ruby… but… this could lead to even better things. I have seen the young men hereabouts and the way they look at you. There is not one among them worthy of you, in my estimation. You need to swim in a larger sea to allow an exceptional sort of man to find you out and catch you."

Ruby frowned, "But, I have no thoughts of marriage. *You* are happy without being married. Your students are your children. What more could you need?"

"Much more, Ruby… yes, I am happy with my lot in life, but… to own the truth, if I had ever been fortunate enough to be given a proper offer, I would have taken it. I would have accepted marriage, and gratefully so. Yes, a woman can be happy without a man… but… more happiness is possible with the right kind of man. Do not close all doors against yourself just yet, my dearest Ruby Steed."

9
Genteel Governess

It was with some tears that Ruby bade her dear friends many a farewell, as she set off away from the school. Fond embraces had been exchanged all around, as well as promises to correspond frequently and visit as often as may be possible. Ruby's heart was all aflutter all the way along as she ventured forth towards the Eaton household. Her mind abuzz with what this new situation might be like; she could scarce see what her eyes lit upon along the way. To be sure, she fought weeping too. She looked away and round about to rise and win against the discharge of water droplets in her eyes, though she saw little of any substance during the fractures of time between her tears. Amid her rolling curiosities about her future possibilities, she kept setting her mind on fond remembrances of Horizon House and hopes for upcoming visits with her friends there to come about very soon.

Once Ruby had agreed with Miss Fenton to forge ahead with the governess plan, more details had been communicated about the widow and her children. Mrs. Eaton and Miss Fenton had been especially close friends and neighbors in growing up. Recently having lost her husband to an untimely death, a still fairly young Mrs. Eaton needed a governess whom she could trust as implicitly as any family member, for, among other reasons, the new widow had some plans to travel abroad that would not include her lively young children. The few governesses that Mrs. Eaton had thus far tried had not been up to the task. They had not been of enough stamina and the children had hated them. Poor Mrs. Eaton was as much as at her wits end on the matter and thus she had contacted Miss Fenton, begging for a reference that she could truly count on. Mrs. Eaton could surely afford the best and she was willing to pay more than any going price to get the kind of young woman who could rise to and meet the challenge.

Miss Fenton had given Ruby a generous serving of encouraging speech before she set off on her new endeavor, instilling in her enough high hopes to take her a goodly length and height over any surmountable obstacles that could be expected amid such an assignment. All the way to the Eaton home, Ruby mixed those hopes with jittery fears. She could not help it. Though, when those wobbly fears were getting the best of her, she would pull back and remind herself that no matter what, she could always turn back. No, she would give this test her best effort and see what would be. She had Miss Fenton's sound promise that she was welcome to return to Horizon House at any time she needed, and she had given her own solid promise that she would not quit the Eaton children until and unless she knew that she could surely not succeed with them, as well as be happy in their home amongst them.

Upon reaching the Eaton house, Ruby was ushered in by a Mrs. MacLeod, the housekeeper, who then led her to the room that was to be her own as long as she should live there in that beautifully grand house. It was a lovely and spacious apartment that Mrs. MacLeod presented before the young redhead. Ruby was happy astonishment. The housekeeper explained that Ruby could freshen up and settle in a little before meeting the family. Though having been prepared to greet the Eaton family members first, Ruby was still relieved that she could take a little time to wash up and even change if she liked, before facing the moment when she would enter into the realms of this new family.

Once having readied herself, Ruby did not quite know what to do. Should she walk out into the hall and look about for the housekeeper? Did she dare run into Mrs. Eaton or any of the Eaton children without a proper introduction? Ruby felt uncharacteristically nervous to the extreme on this occasion. She strangely stood inside her private quarters at the door to the hallway for moments that seemed to drag on for hours. Her forehead beaded up with perspiration so much so that she took herself back to the washbasin to freshen her face once more. There was a knock at the door and in trepidation Ruby advanced back towards it. She opened the door and was relieved to see the friendly face of Mrs. MacLeod, who then led her down to a sitting room where she would await the family.

Mrs. MacLeod promptly offered Ruby some refreshments, which the new governess accepted most gratefully. Contentedly diverted by much needed sustenance, Ruby near forgot momentarily where she was and who she was about to meet. She had barely begun enjoying her small feast when a boisterous clamor was nearing the room where she sat nibbling and sipping. Mrs. MacLeod managed to halt the cluster of children all but about to spill head over heels into the room. She held them at the door with a stern command of looks and words, as well as with her bodily form.

"Whoa! Hold the line, dearies!" Mrs. MacLeod pronounced.

A burst of giggles and heaven only knows what else, burst out in a trumpeting of sound.

"I said, hold the line, you rascals! Wait until your mother is here as well. You are to wait to be introduced… all at once. You heard what your mother said, did you not?"

Ruby sat generally hidden around the corner, her eyes widening in a bit of fright to hear the goings on. She briefly wondered if she should continue consuming the array of cuisine still before her, but she was still hungry enough to quickly finish off the last of it before she knew her opportunity would be lost. And none too soon, for she heard another woman's voice calling to the children from a close distance, to hush and straighten up. Ruby wiped her mouth well with her napkin.

Mrs. Cynthia Eaton's voice grew closer and therefore a little louder, "What will she think of you, you earsplitting hooligans! We've gone through a half dozen governesses this past month or so and I am becoming a desperate woman indeed! What is a widowed mother of five raucous youngsters to do? I am beside myself in frustration! I stretched myself to the limit to find us a really good governess this time and you'd better not scare this one away or I'll not try so hard to hire someone nice next time! Do you want a beauty or a beast? Do not tempt me! I do not fear a differing direction where watchers of children are concerned, though, believe me, you should fear what your bad behaviors may lead to. I will hire a hard taskmaster if you truly wish it! Or… do you all wish to be sent away to boarding schools? Is that what you truly want? I am at my wit's end with each one of you, I tell you!"

Ruby wished to fade into the beautiful wallpaper behind her, if that were possible. She did not want to listen in on or intrude upon such an uncomfortable family moment in this way. She did wish that she could disappear to practically any place else to avoid the household familial discomforts appearing embarrassingly round the corner from her. She also instantly found herself wishing her way back to the school where life had been so peacefully easy for such a lengthy time. Ruby had virtually forgotten a life of challenge upon challenge and she did not relish the thought of facing such troubles now. Oh, but she feared that she should not have been convinced to venture beyond her just recent past life of perfection. Now she might have to taste some bitter fruit a lengthy while before finding her way back to the resplendent garden. Well, at least she did have an escape towards bliss, though she may have to go through a thicket of thorns before returning to paradise.

Between Mrs. MacLeod and Mrs. Eaton, the five seeming scalawags were shuffled into the room and lined up in front of Ruby. Ruby stood up from her chair, smiled and lightly bowed her head courteously.

Mrs. MacLeod took charge of the introductions, "Miss Ruby Steed, this is Mrs. Cynthia Eaton, and her children: Marcia, Camile, Albert, Arthur & little Jemma. This Miss Steed is to be your governess, children. Won't you say hello?"

In bellowing fashion, the children all chimed in at once with violent vigor, "Hello!"

Giggles and guffaws followed the unified greeting in a ruptured outburst, as convulsive wiggles and stares followed the laughter.

Mrs. Eaton attempted to aid her offspring instructively by her softer example, "Hello, Miss Steed."

Looking from face to face to face, Ruby complied, "Hello. I'm so very pleased to meet each of you. I hope that we will all get along famously."

Albert whispered too loudly to Arthur, "This one is really pretty."

The entire room overheard the complimentary remark. Jemma sniggered. Ruby smiled.

Camile whispered more quietly to Marcia, "Her hair is... awfully red."

Ruby smiled again, for she could not help overhearing that as well.

Mrs. Eaton wished to get on with things, "Mrs. MacLeod? Would you awfully mind taking the children off to the schoolroom for a while so that I can get a little better acquainted with Ruby on my own here?"

The housekeeper nodded and began herding the Eaton children, though inwardly she was increasingly tired of playing governess in-between governesses. She dearly hoped that *this* governess would work out and stay a goodly long while.

"Well, Ruby..." Mrs. Eaton began.

"Yes, Mrs. Eaton?"

"You don't mind if I call you Ruby do you? I can call you Miss Steed just as easily, but since I'm not generally a formal sort of person, I'd just as soon call you Ruby if you don't mind it."

"Of course, I truly do not mind at all. I am very used to being called Ruby."

"And please do call me Cynthia, if you'd like. I've asked Mrs. MacLeod and the other servants to do so, but she prefers to stay rather formal with me, as do they all. They all follow her, so what can I do? She takes charge and I prefer it as such, anyway. But, I was thinking, that since you are our governess now, and you will be very much a part of our family, I would as soon have everything less formal between us. You will be raising and teaching my children, after all. I don't consider you a servant, by any means. I suppose I will think on you quite as my own sister. I hope you will think on me as your sister… if not instantly, perhaps in time?"

"Yes, I am sure… to be sure, Mrs. E… Cynthia."

"You see? That was not so difficult! I am certain that we will like each other very much, Ruby. Give us time… just give us a little time… and we will all fit together perfectly. Well, well… why don't you go freshen up for our evening meal… and then it will be another day's end… though, tomorrow… you will begin your work as our governess." Cynthia Eaton smiled, patted Ruby's shoulder, and was off.

Mealtime was a mixture of chatter and chaos. Between Mrs. MacLeod and Mrs. Eaton, the five children still could not be brought to any pleasant level of decorum. Ruby did not attempt to aid as yet. She could see that she had her work cut out for her. She barely ate a thing, though she was not truly hungry for having feasted alone just earlier. Her mind was engaged on creative measures that she could instantly employ starting on the morrow, to bring this house of Eaton children into a sense of order and peace. That night she slept little as she thought much. She also prayed, for what else could a young woman in such a situation do? Ruby needed heavenly guidance for certain. A throng of invisible angels to silently aid with these children seemed in order and so Ruby prayed for heavenly beings to fly about them from tomorrow onward, though she did not know for certain if Heaven ever granted such wishes.

Ruby began her first work day as governess by trying to know the Eaton children better. She felt that she needed to first foster a sort of friendship with them, so she sat them all down together (at least she tried to have them all sit down together, for her success at this was sketchy and varied to say the least) in the schoolroom to ask each of them questions about themselves, and answer theirs about herself. Silliness permeated the room, but at least she kept them all in the room. It was a start. If she could not yet control their energies, she would insist on confining such activity to the one room and save the rest of the household the wild racket. It seemed to Ruby that it took an hour to accomplish a minute's worth of work towards any true acquaintance, but at least there was a sort of progress forward. She was gradually gaining a little knowledge about each of the Eaton children as they were about her.

It quickly became apparent that the Eaton children were in fact conspiring against Ruby. She could see what they were about. They would put creatures in places to frighten her with shock, and do all manner of unpleasant things in an effort to make her sorry that she had come amongst them. They wished for her to leave, just as all the other governesses had. Ruby was sorry to be there. She did lament having left her easy life at the school. She would have liked to leave this place instantly. Horizon House was a perfect dream even as the Eaton house was fast becoming a nightmare. Ruby could not but help begin to formulate plans for her escape back to her happy life prior to this situation; but, not as yet, for she would persist a while. She could wear them down, perhaps.

As young as Ruby still was, she was old and wise enough to understand that the Eaton children hated and scared off all prior governesses for want of attention from their mother. They had just lost their father, after all, and they likely craved love and attention from their only surviving parent. Perhaps they felt insecure and fearful that they might lose their mother as well. Ruby was given to understand from Mrs. MacLeod that Mrs. Eaton had recently taken a lengthy trip out east and planned another abroad to Europe very soon. This was why she wished to secure a dependable governess who was firmly settled as soon as may be. No sooner had Mr. Eaton been buried, than Mrs. Eaton had taken a trip. It was true that she had wished to escort her only sister back on her return trip home (for her sister had happened to be visiting when Mr. Eaton suddenly passed away from all the earth), and desired to reconnect with some of her other family there out east; but to leave her young children promptly after the death of their father seemed to make reason stare. Ruby could not fathom such a thing. Of course the Eaton children were behaving badly. As unreasonable as they seemed on the surface, Ruby could explain to herself the reasons why these young children would act in this unpleasant way.

Ruby believed that the children were feeling somewhat lost and abandoned in the least, and that they surely must harbor internal fears about losing their mother also. By going away so soon after the death of their father, their mother was as much as presenting dread and apprehension before her children. Had they not tended to worry that she might have an untimely death also? Should she not have channeled all her energies towards consoling her children and helping them to feel safe and assured that she would not also leave them through death? Leaving her children to travel (even though with her dear sister), seemed such a blow to her children. Had they not perhaps felt less loved by their mother, for she chose to travel with her sister rather than to stay home to console her children in a time of grieving?

Mrs. MacLeod further explained to Ruby that Mrs. Eaton made no secret that she was on the hunt for a new husband. Ruby tried to hide her shock and dismay from the housekeeper but she could not help thinking on the matter herself. Apparently, the children knew of this. They knew that their mother was anxious to round up a new father for them. This seemed a jot horrifying to Ruby. So sudden to forget a beloved husband and wish for a new one? She did not think that the children would feel too kindly regarding such an idea. It was all too soon, to be sure. A respectable year later would be one thing, but not this. Mrs. Eaton had barely worn black for a week and now she was draped in silks and feathers in all manner of bright colorations, hoping to attract a new mate. Such behavioral display was too much and too sudden, to be sure.

Mrs. Eaton had been much gone and very distracted since her fairly recent widowhood. Her mind seemed predominantly fixed upon finding the right man to marry. She had little thought for what her children may be suffering, especially due to her own negligence. From Ruby's vantage point, Mrs. Eaton was quite the faulty mother and this assumption strengthened Ruby's resolve to stay for the children. Ruby could suffer for their sakes. She wished to make things right for these poor, nearly orphaned children. Ruby knew what it was and how it felt to be an orphan. However, she could not understand how a mother could abandon her own children in such a way.

As Mrs. MacLeod brought Ruby a tray consisting of milk, biscuits, cheese, preserves and butter to her room one night, she harrumphed in forceful whispering, "Well... there she goes! Mrs. Eaton is to be promptly off and away to Europe in short order! It seems she thinks you are doing well enough with her children so she feels free to fly away! I surely hope that you will stay, Miss Steed. I truly don't wish to be left to herd those children again. The last time she took her trip, the governess ran off and I was left trying to keep the peace... and to find another governess."

Though she had been forewarned, still, Ruby was stunned that Mrs. Eaton would go off so far and long away so very soon, but this made her all the more determined to stay, "Don't you worry one jot, Mrs. MacLeod. I will be staying to help you hold down the fort. I have no intentions of abandoning either the children or you. I have climbed higher mountains than this one by far. I am made of stronger stuff, I assure you."

Not necessarily quite convinced as yet inwardly, Mrs. MacLeod outwardly held out hope, "Well, that is a comfort, for sure."

"She is *certain* to be leaving very soon, then?"

"Oh yes, Mrs. Eaton is going to Europe to try to find herself a prince to marry. She's got it in her head that she should marry a European prince... almost any country, mind you. Apparently, princes are very thick on the ground in Europe. Usually cash poor, sometimes land rich, but it's the pedigree she's after. She doesn't want for money, that's for dang sure... but she wants to become a royal by marrying one. Will I be prevailed upon to call her 'princess' or 'my queen' when she returns, I wonder?"

Ruby thought this an incredulously stupid plan, but said nothing of the sort. What was there to be said or done to stop the jolly widow from her course of action? It was clear she was setting sail to catch herself a foreign prince to make herself a princess. This was of import to her. What a silly woman she was quickly turning out to be. What would Miss Fenton think of or say to such behavior from her dear old friend? What would Mrs. Eaton's late husband think of such things? He would be turning in his grave, if he only knew. One would hope that he loved his children more than the mother seemed to. What a fate to happen to these poor children. No, they were rich to be sure: rich in material things, but poor in what was far more important to them. Well, Ruby would and could be as if a mother to these virtually motherless children. She would stand in the stead thereof and do the job that was not to be done otherwise.

Despite the efforts of the Eaton children to drive Ruby away, to cause her to think herself hated by them, to force her to despise them, to cause her to give up on doing anything with them; Ruby stayed. She persisted in patience, longsuffering, love unfeigned, virtuous efforts, valiant exertions and all such things of valor. Ruby counter-attacked with humor and warmth. She had known greater difficulties to be overcome as a child. As a young woman, she could stand this ground cheerfully. Ruby had determined to slog it out with these little warriors for what she feared might be a year or more.

To her great and joyous surprise, the Eaton children almost quite suddenly were worn down. Had they thrown up the white flag in defeat? It certainly seemed so. Ruby had won them over. Perhaps a few lessons learned from Miss Fenton had aided Ruby more than she imagined they might. It was not long before the Eaton children were living and learning with Ruby as peaceably as any of the children at the Horizon school.

"Ruby, why is the sky blue?" inquired Albert in earnest, as they all sat enjoying their luncheon which was spread out in picnic fashion on the Eaton family lawn outdoors.

"Well, I suppose I could tell you that the sky is blue because or even when it is no other color… and of course, we know that the sky sometimes displays other colors as well… or I could say that blue is God's favorite color and that is why he painted the heavens and blanketed the earth with shades of blue… or I could simply and truthfully state that I do not know for certain…"

Arthur thoughtfully added to the inquiry, "But, does anyone

know for true?"

"I've read some bits of theories it seems to me… maybe some men do know for certain… but I do not… at least I cannot recall… although I do begin to remember something about color waves or wavelengths all related to light going through prisms and rainbows coming out and how the sky lets blue through for us to see… and so I would wonder if the sky could quite possibly become any color if the elements and conditions allowed… but, do not listen to me, for I am no student of such science… we could perhaps find a book on such subjects to further enlighten us… or your mother could find a suitable tutor for such complexities… though I am certain that God does know all such mysteries."

Albert's mind drifted elsewhere, "Ruby, why did you not leave us when we were treating you so miserably?"

"Because I knew that you needed me to stay."

Marcia considered in question, "But, what if we had never behaved well for you, for the longest time, no matter how hard you tried to make us be good?"

Ruby smiled, "I knew that you all would behave well for me… eventually. You were not my first students, remember?"

Camile asked, "Do you miss the school?"

"Sometimes."

Marcia queried, "Do you miss the orphanage?"

"Not really… but I do sometimes miss a few friends I had there."

Camile inquired, "Do you miss your mother?"

"I cannot remember her."

Albert added inquiry, "Your father?"

"I do not recall him either."

Marcia hesitatingly asked, "Do you wish you could… remember your parents?"

Ruby became a little wistful, "Yes… I would like to at least have memories of my parents. I know nothing of them."

Feeling a depth of compassion for their governess, Camile posed, "Does that make you sad to forget your parents and miss your friends?"

"A little… but I do have you… each one of you… to call my own."

Arthur inquired, "Do you think your parents are in heaven?"

"I have no reason to doubt that they must be there."

Jemma added in question, "And you will see them there?"

"Well… if I am very good… and make it in to heaven… I surely think that I shall see my parents there someday."

Marcia put in emphatically, "You are very good already… more than good enough to get into heaven as soon as may be."

Ruby laughed, "Not too soon, I venture to hope!"

By the time Mrs. Eaton arrived home from Europe, prince-less and defeated in her dream of becoming a princess, she could not believe the transformation amongst her children. Such well-behaved angels they were now!

"Ruby! You have worked miracles with my little scoundrels. You truly are a worker of magic! If I had not known better, I would have thought these children to be somebody else's! How did you manage it?! And you are still here, after all!"

Ruby smiled, in spite of her secret hidden disrespect of the woman she worked for, "Of course I am still here."

"Well, well… I feared you would be long gone by the time I came home. I thought you would have given up on my brood and that Mrs. MacLeod would have been scrambling for one new governess after another."

Ruby thought, 'As she was required to do before because of your abandoning negligence.' Ruby bit her tongue to silence it. She thought of saying something in the vein of, 'Though I am only their governess, I wouldn't dare abandon your children… as you so easily have done…', but she thought the better of such a bold speech, though she wanted to shake her head at Mrs. Eaton for not thinking of it herself, and feeling the shame of the harsh reality and truth of the matter.

Though Ruby had said nothing, only smiling slightly, Mrs. Eaton mistook this quietness for a sort of shyness and continued, "Well…

it is very good to see you still here... still a part of my family... and since you seem to be the only living being who can set my children straight and keep them that way, I do hope you will stay with us for a goodly long time, if not forever."

Having successfully won the admiration or at least respect of the Eaton children, Ruby's next project was to help Mrs. Eaton to take more care for her very own children. For a time, with the mother having given up on catching a prince to marry right off, the children were treated to many happy moments with her. Mrs. Eaton was generally content in enjoying quiet days and evenings with her children and their governess. Ruby made her best effort to forgive the children's mother for being less motherly than she should be, and set her own sights on making many happy memories together. She stretched her spirit and creative powers to make certain that there was delight and calm day upon day and evening throughout evening. Ruby wished to bring Mrs. Eaton back to caring for her children as she should, and to thus help her children to feel more trust in and love from her.

One day when Ruby was out on her own due to a few hours off from her governess work, Mrs. Eaton was fairly accosted in her parlor by all her five children at once.

Marcia began, "Now, Mother... you must listen very intently... we all have something we must say to you..."

"Yes, my dears?" Mrs. Eaton replied, as her heart was thoroughly warmed upon seeing her five lovely children's wide-eyed faces all around her.

Marcia continued, "You know how very much we all love Ruby, though we tried to rid ourselves of her from the start?"

Mrs. Eaton nodded and smiled, "Yes, I saw or heard of the sad and sorry fates of every governess brought in to our household and I truly did not think that Ruby would manage to stay either... but... she has surely won you all over... and me as well... but I was an easier target for her, to be sure."

Marcia completed her thought, "Well... Christmas is coming round the corner and we wish for you to spoil our dear cherished

Ruby with many gifts. She has never been loved like we mean to love her. You must buy her all manner of pretty things."

Camile, Albert, Arthur & Jemma all nodded their affirmative thoughts to what their older sister had just said.

Mrs. Eaton could not agree more, "But of course I shall, my darlings! I will buy her jewelry and dresses… jewels and silks… all the things she has never been adorned with before in her life! We will fit her up like a queen!"

Jemma wiggled with delight, "Right now!"

Camile added excitedly, "Take us to the shops, Mamma!"

Albert sternly warned, "And you two girls don't tell our secret. It must be a very great secret!"

Shaking his head at everyone and showing forth a very severe face, Arthur reiterated, "Don't tell her the secret! That would spoil everything."

Mother calmed her children, "Yes, yes, my dears… we will shower our Ruby with gifts… and she will not suspect a thing until we place the many boxes before her on Christmas Day!"

Marcia begged, "May we go to the shops… if not this very moment… tomorrow, Mamma… please?"

Mrs. Eaton hesitated momentarily but then, "Well… yes… of course… I will take you out to choose gifts for Ruby tomorrow, then."

A fitting excuse was made to Ruby by Mrs. Eaton for herself and her children, when they left their dear governess to go out and shop for her the following day. Ruby was quite content to spend a little more time off of governing the children to write a few letters to Patsy and Scarlet back east, and to Miss Fenton, Miss Rhodes and Mrs. Hanratty in the nearer locale. Though she had come to thoroughly enjoy the Eaton children, Ruby still took personal delight in keeping up a goodly correspondence with her friends.

When Mrs. Eaton returned home with her children, the set of them were a happy bouquet, each and all loaded down with their secret parcels. Though the members of the family group tried to steal themselves and their parcels away to hidden places in order to escape Ruby's notice, she could not help but see the smiles and hear the giggles, and to elatedly wonder at the joy that had entered to fill the household. Ruby repented her past ill feelings towards her employer. It was true that Mrs. Eaton did exhibit her glaring flaws as a mother when Ruby first came amongst them, but was this merry evidence not proof enough to change her mind for the better regarding the matron of the home? Ruby felt such divine delight to witness (though mostly hearing from a distance in this instance) the happy family exchanges that this mother had created between herself and her children that day.

The days that followed were filled with similar blissful interactions amongst them all. Ruby now well knew that she had done right in leaving her happy situation at Horizon House, for this new horizon had proven successful after all. The Eaton family was at contented joyful peace.

A return letter from Miss Fenton was quite promptly forthcoming and her intention to visit very soon was a key message in the contents of such. The day Ruby's kindly mentor arrived brought delight to Ruby and her employer. Mrs. Eaton was only too happy to reacquaint herself with her childhood friend.

"Iris Fenton! Oh my dear, dear friend from so long ago! I should think that we might have seen one another long before this! You would have thought we were living on separate continents for the number of times we have seen each other in recent years! You have been too busy to visit me. I have been far too busy and away to insist on your visitation. But, finally, you have come to see me and here I am to avail myself of your angelic self! Come, come... sit down." Mrs. Eaton ushered Miss Fenton into her parlor, having had Mrs. MacLeod go fetch Ruby for the mutual visit of the ladies.

"It is so very good to see you too, Cynthia. I should chastise myself for staying away for such a length of time... but as always, as you alluded to, I have been so excessively busy."

"Well, well... you look no older... you still look so young. I fear the years have not been so kind to me."

"Stuff and nonsense. Of course you look just the same. You are as beautiful as you ever were."

Cynthia Eaton laughed, "Well… I am feeling somewhat old these days… I dare say that any man I might fancy as a second husband would think me a terribly old woman."

Iris Fenton counseled, as old friends are wont to do, "I highly doubt that, Cynthia, but… you need not be in any hurry to remarry."

"Yes, well… I suppose not… but who am I to speak of husbands to you when… well… oh, dear… forgive me, Iris." Cynthia felt keenly her misstep.

"No matter… not at all… I gave up on finding a husband long ago. In any event, I would rather have none than choose to settle badly… early or later."

Cynthia Eaton lowered her voice for a revelation, "Well… don't I know that only too well. Men are generally bad, I am too sorry to say."

"Oh, dear, no… I truly hope not. But, I simply never came across a good one who wished to offer to me… and thus… I have my happy life with all my little girls coming, growing and going."

Cynthia Eaton sighed at the thought of Iris's hectic life, "You have made something of yourself to be sure. Yes, you certainly do a worthy work in the world."

Iris Fenton smiled, "I did not dream of the life I have, for I dreamt of a husband and children… but… I have no regrets or complaints."

Just about the exact moment that Mrs. MacLeod showed up with the cart of refreshments, Ruby arrived as well, "Forgive me for having taken so long to come down from the schoolroom. I thought it a good idea to assign the children to a task that would keep them fairly occupied at length whilst we enjoyed a little visit without them first."

Smiling widely, Mrs. Eaton said, "Oh, yes… that is a good idea. Perhaps that will save our dear Mrs. MacLeod any trouble with my lively pups."

Mrs. MacLeod happily interjected as she was still serving the ladies, "Oh no... those little angels? They have been so very good since... well, they have been on their best behavior of late, and are a joy to behold."

Mrs. Eaton chortled and declared, "You mean they have gone from scalawags to angels since Ruby came to tame them! Do not fear to mention such, for it is too true and I will be the first to admit it and give Ruby her due."

Mrs. MacLeod admitted, "Ruby has indeed done wonders with them, Ma'am, I'm happy to grant you."

"Oh, grant me nothing! Let us speak truth in this house! I owe Ruby everything! I did not know what to do with my children and was running away from them in fright. Ruby came and now all is as it should have been before." Cynthia Eaton turned to Ruby with a graciously happy nod.

Ruby but blushed.

Mrs. MacLeod excused herself for a time.

Turning to Iris Fenton, Cynthia Eaton proclaimed, "It was pure divine inspiration that I finally felt compelled to write to you to beg for help... and you knew what to do... you were guided by God's hand as well... for you chose to send me Ruby... perhaps even a little against her wishes... and her good judgment once she arrived, I dare say... but, as you hear, it has all turned out providentially after all. We are as happy as can be, thanks to Ruby!"

Iris Fenton smiled broadly, patted Ruby's hand, and explained, "Ruby was the best I had to offer. I confess I more than hesitated to lose her, even to you... but, simply knew within myself that I must part with her for a more noble cause. I am only too delighted to hear that what I felt to be true, has turned out to be so."

Cynthia returned to her friend, "I thank you to the heavens for sending me Ruby, but please forgive me Iris, for you cannot have her back." She then turned to Ruby, "I hope you will never leave us for anyone, Ruby. I could not part with you. My children will always need you... and I dare say that I will eventually have grandchildren, so you will be with us always. So, even if you wished to marry, you would have to bring your husband here to live with us, because even then, I would not wish to lose you for all the world."

Ruby calmed her, "Rest easy, for I have no intentions of ever marrying."

Cynthia sighed, "Oh, dear, that hints greatly of unrequited love."

Ruby smiled, "Not at all, I assure you. I have simply known enough happy spinsters to be satisfied with such a life."

Cynthia speculated somewhat, "I suppose you have broken a few hearts?"

Ruby claimed in earnest, "Oh, I hardly think so. I haven't had the time or thought to so much as speak with young men."

Iris interjected, "Though many a man has followed her around with winsome eyes."

Cynthia agreed, "I do not doubt it. There is not such a beauty in all these parts. I am grateful that Ruby is content to hide away here like a nun, for if she went out much at all, she would have every single man in town clamoring for her hand. And then where would I be?"

Ruby blushed, smiled and shook her head.

Iris suddenly turned to Ruby, "Oh, I meant to tell you that Mrs. Biggsley asked after you… she wanted to know where she could send a letter to you… but I told her that you still remembered her and where she lived and that you could open correspondence with her at any time that you wished… though I did offer to pass on any message she might have."

Iris and Ruby exchanged knowing smiles as Ruby answered, "Thank you… but what could she wish to say to me?"

"Well, she had a piece of news as it turned out. It seems she's got both her daughters engaged to be married off!"

"Though they are still so very young?"

"She was in a hurry to find what she considered good matches in her estimation and I suppose she found two men rich enough for her tastes."

"Do the girls seem happy at their prospects?"

"I dare say that if money is all they care about, yes, but other than that, I heard that one fiancé is old and the other ugly. Neither sounds dashing or kindly in any respect, but…"

Ruby began to finish Iris's train of thought, "…but, those who have been taught to marry for only money…"

Iris finished, "… are satisfied as long as they get their coins."

Ruby wondered, "I would have thought that there might have been some rebellions towards preferences for young and handsome fellows."

"There was… but with only money to recommend themselves as well, their own prospects were so very thin… enough to cause them to bow to their mother's wishes."

Cynthia had been watching this piece of the conversation between Iris and Ruby and could not resist adding her own relative thoughts, "I had an offer from a European prince… but day upon day it became too clear that he was only after me for my money and properties… so I ran away home."

Iris smiled, "A narrow escape?"

Cynthia laughed, "Oh, dear me, yes!"

10
Mrs. Eaton's Brother

As the Christmas season approached swiftly into full swing, with Ruby's subtly gentle help and guidance, Mrs. Cynthia Eaton easily managed to be thoroughly attentive to her children in her varied duties of true import as their mother. Crowning the ample felicity throughout the Eaton family was the blissful, though semi-conscious and unspoken knowledge amongst all but Ruby, that another missing family member would be coming to add to the festive cheer during the days just before and throughout the Christmas holiday season.

Brandon Wallace, Mrs. Eaton's own brother, had finally returned home from his extended travels out east. Though he did not live in the Eaton home, his own house was not afar off and it was quite usual for him to spend a good deal of time with his sister's family (being that he had no other family of his own, as yet). Before he had had to go east on business, he had visited more than usual in his attempts to console his sister's family as they suffered in grieving over the death of Mr. Eaton.

The day of Brandon's arrival, Ruby happened to miss the grand reunion, for she was out visiting with the neighborhood's pastor and his wife, as she had agreed to help them in planning for and implementation of an upcoming church Christmas social. The Eaton family could not help singing Ruby's praises to Brandon in her absence.

Marcia proclaimed as she danced in twirls, "Wait 'til you see her, Uncle Brandon! She is *so* beautiful! You will not believe your eyes at her beauty!"

Camile agreed, cuddling her doll in an excited swinging motion, "Oh, yes, she is very, very beautiful!"

Jemma added, looking up as she hugged her uncle's leg, "And very *nice* too."

Albert and Arthur's heads were nodding vigorously upon hearing about Ruby being very nice (since they were still boys young enough to tend to think beauty an irrelevant notion).

"So you have yourselves a treasure, then?" Brandon asked his sister.

"Oh, yes, assuredly… but don't you get *any* ideas about her for yourself, my brother, for I will not part with her, even to you in marriage!"

Brandon ignored Cynthia's comment as best he could.

Marcia stopped dancing and asked of her mother, "Will she be home for dinner?"

"Yes, yes… of course she will."

Marcia thrilled, "Then you will meet her very soon, Uncle Brandon!"

Camile dreamed, "Maybe you will fall in love with her… I think?"

The boys giggled as did Jemma.

By the time Ruby arrived home that evening, Brandon was fairly a forgotten settled fixture in the house and might have had to introduce himself to Ruby had not Mrs. MacLeod remembered to do the honors, after helping Ruby out of her coat and other such things once she was inside the front doors.

Ruby and Brandon were both reserved with each other, though plenty gregarious with the other members of the family. The family was so lively that nobody besides Mrs. MacLeod noticed Brandon observing Ruby quite regularly from whatever vantage point he happened to have.

When the evening was wound down enough for Mrs. Eaton to begin sending her children off to bed, (like unto many a mother) she chose to utilize bribery of the richest kind, "Now children…

take yourselves off to bed like perfect angels and I will promise to finish up all my Christmas shopping tomorrow! Otherwise, I do not know when I will have time to buy some of those things that you have been begging for of late. Give your uncle goodnight hugs and be off with you!"

Each day prior to Christmas Eve, Brandon came to the Eaton home. Each day into each evening, he quietly observed Ruby. Each day the Eaton children chattered about the coming glorious day.

Albert suggested in begging fashion, "Mother... Mother... why must we wait until Christmas morning to open our gifts? I know of many children round about who open their gifts on Christmas Eve. Why cannot we also?"

Mrs. Eaton answered emphatically firm, though smiling, "No... no... it has long been our own tradition to wait until Christmas morning. I can tell you that I have experienced gift-opening on Christmas Eve and though it suits many, I say this: then there is nothing to go to bed for... nothing to keep you excitedly awake waiting for... nothing to rise early for... no... in our home, we will wait until that very special morning."

Albert persisted with Arthur's begging assistance, "Please?!"

Marcia aided with an offer to possibly pacify with compromise, "Perhaps just only one gift on Christmas Eve? Could you give us each something that we could play with before we go to bed... or to cuddle as we drift off to sleep?"

Brandon joined in, "It sounds a capital idea to me, dear sister."

Mrs. Eaton agreed. And so it was on Christmas Eve. After a dinner of goose and all the expected trimmings, the Eaton children were each delighted to unwrap a toy that they could play with, to distract them, if only a little, as they anxiously awaited the grand day of many gifts on the morrow.

Bright and early on Christmas morning, Brandon arrived as if Father Christmas himself, laden with packages of gifts for everyone: each wrapped neatly and beautifully. And though he had come as early as could be, the Eaton children had all been up for hours, biting at their bits like horses about to race, excessively restless in their wait to commence the magnificent day. Mrs. MacLeod helped the cook do her happy duty in preparing the giant bird (a duck of prodigious proportions) and other such bounteous fare for all to enjoy a little later on. Ruby had been assisting Cynthia Eaton in anything she desired, to make everything perfect for that festive day of joyful celebrations.

Camile shouted gleefully, "This will be the happiest Christmas ever!"

Jemma put in, excitedly, "Oh, I can't wait, I can't wait!"

Arthur chimed in, "Me too!"

Albert begged, "When do we open our gifts, Mamma?"

Marcia added, smiling joyfully, "I can't wait for Ruby to open *her* gifts!"

Ruby raised an eyebrow in wonder, though she felt supremely humbled and her heart was thoroughly warmed in the knowledge that Marcia should think of her governess's happiness before her own.

The day unfolded into the most blissful in Ruby's life. Not only did she delight at witnessing the thrills of the children upon receiving her own gifts to them (as well as enjoying all the giving and receiving joy that abounded all around), but Ruby was overcome with a depth of slightly unexpected happiness due to having been treated as a true member of the family (for she was especially doted upon). Among the many choice gifts that Ruby received from Cynthia Eaton and her children, was one perfectly wonderful cameo broach, which had been especially chosen by Marcia, Camile and Jemma. The Eaton girls also chose to gift their beloved governess with a beautiful crimson-red dress. Ruby had never been lavished with any such a bounteous treasure in all her living days. She was truly overwhelmed by the Eaton family generosity towards her.

Though not saying anything regarding, Brandon could not help but take full notice throughout the day of the loving admiration and high esteem that his sister's family held for their own beloved Ruby.

That evening as the children were scattered round playing blissfully with their new toys, Brandon could not contain his opinion and thus he leaned over to Ruby with a quiet revelation, "I am truly impressed… no, I must say that I am fully amazed… with what you have done for my nieces and nephews. Your guidance of them has been most remarkable. They are changed creatures, I dare say. From hooligans to angels in a matter of months! How did you do it, I ask you?"

Ruby's answer was humility itself, "Oh, thank you, but it was nothing."

"I do not wish to accuse you of any dishonesty on the point, but I happen to know too well that nobody else could do a thing with them. I lost count of the governesses that came and went… and my sister and I were generally at our wits' end as well. Truly, you have done a wonder with them. Surely, you must employ some sort of magic wand in the schoolroom."

"Oh, no… there was no magic… but only such as love, patience, example and prayers, sir."

"I have to give you great credit, to be sure."

"Thank you, though I do not wish to accept too much credit where it may not truly be due me. All the children wanted for was a little persistence on my part. In no time, they were easily compliant, for they were angels easily enough."

"Angels in disguise by far, I would say. Only you among many could seem to find their hidden worth. You are certainly too modest, but I will allow you *that* for your comfort's sake… and simply thank you from my heart for the service that you have rendered my sister and her children."

"You are very welcome… and I thank you for your generously kind compliment, Mr. Wallace."

Cynthia Eaton had overheard Ruby's last words and could not but interject, "Oh, please… I beg you call my brother Brandon. We *all* do and you are a part of our family now, Ruby. You simply must comply with this ardent wish of mine."

Ruby only nodded a smile in obedience.

Brandon was soon romping with his nieces and nephews, playing ruffian to their bounding childhood energies. Ruby sat back, observing with enjoyment the brisk and hearty play. She thought in those raucous moments that a man was certainly good for wearing children out through wrestling and other rough play. It was clear that the Eaton children delighted in their uncle's shenanigans, and also that he took great pleasure in tossing his sister's children about.

Ruby could not help but admit to herself that Brandon was a reasonably handsome man, and that his pleasant manner and boyish charm shone through in his interactions with the Eaton children. With herself he was quite reserved, as he seemed to generally be, but with the children his liveliness was unleashed. This unguarded prankish amiability did indeed magnify his attractions. If Ruby had not for quite some time determined that she should like to remain a governess or a teacher forever in this life (and therefore remain a happy spinster), any thoughts of allowing herself any feelings of attraction towards Brandon, she would have nevertheless checked for propriety and ethics sake. What would people think of a governess upstart throwing herself at the brother of her employer? Ruby was certain that such attentions or behavior should simply not be broached. It would be tantamount to scandal.

If Ruby had not placed severe blinders on herself so completely, she might have begun to notice how very often Brandon did come over to visit the Eaton family, and how regularly he would begin conversations with her. Ruby had not known his habits prior to her arrival it was true, though, Cynthia Eaton and her children did seem to remark on Brandon's frequent visits. Mr. Brandon Wallace was spending some of his days and many of his evenings at the Eaton household, so much so that he began to seem always around. Ruby and Brandon had become very familiar with each other within the Eaton family sphere.

It was usual that Brandon would not attempt to come visiting when aware that his sister was not to be at home (for propriety sake regarding the governess, according to his thoughts), but on one such occasion, he had come calling not knowing that Cynthia was to be out for the day. Ruby had set the children upon some task or other prior and thus they were busily engaged in preoccupations when their uncle had arrived unexpectedly. Mrs. MacLeod brought him in to where Ruby was quietly reading on her own, whilst the children were so excessively occupied at a little distance and a little beyond a corner.

Brandon inquired, a little uncomfortably (at suddenly feeling left somewhat alone with Ruby), "And where is my sister?"

Ruby smiled reassuringly, after sensing Brandon's discomfort, "She wished a day out at the shops on her own."

"Oh, I am so sorry to have disturbed you... I assumed I would see my sister here... I suppose I should behave better and try a habit of making appointments instead of always dropping by as I do."

Pursuing a completely relaxed demeanor in order to set him at his allowable ease, Ruby countered, "But you are her brother. Surely appointments are never necessary for you? You are a true part of her family."

Brandon relaxed a great deal, "I suppose you are quite right. Thank you for acquitting me of my supposed folly."

"I am only too happy to aid you in what is right."

Ruby and her employer's brother engaged in appropriately varied conversation before they each relaxed to such a degree that they began to speak on more personal subjects.

Brandon suddenly lowered his voice enough to guarantee it's concealment from servants or the children, "Ruby, I say again that you have given my sister and her children a priceless gift. You cannot know how lost she and they seemed after... and I'll even dare to admit, even before her husband's death."

Ruby did not know how to respond except to offer a gracious nod.

"Perhaps you should be aware... perhaps I should tell you... Ruby, has my sister spoken of her marriage with her late husband?"

"No... I cannot say that she has."

"Have the servants revealed anything?"

"No... is there something that you wish to say to me that is of import?"

"Yes... well, I feel that you can be trusted... that you are a part of the family... that maybe you should know... well, that my sister was secretly and... I fear to say... horribly unhappy in her marriage. To be painfully frank, when that indiscreetly womanizing scoundrel of a husband died, it was generally a relief to her to be free of him and his ways. He was a torture to her, I must say. I tell you this to help you understand why she has not been... might seem to be less than... the best of mothers... sometimes. Many might wonder why she ran off to Europe in search of a prince to marry. That silliness on her part was hard upon the heels of her becoming a fresh widow and suddenly finding herself free to spend money as she chose. She thought she could seek out a man who would love, instead of to be cruel to her. I suspect she wished to be far away from anyone who knew her husband and how he had mistreated her. She was as if a little girl wishing for her prince to save her from the unpleasant life she had come to know. I grant you that she was wrong to run off and leave her children in that way... and to leave them so much to their governesses, but, I only tell you to apprise you of a larger picture of my sister. She had not been the best of mothers to her children in a goodly long time. I would venture to say that when a husband is not good to his wife, it is very difficult for her to be as good a mother as she might have otherwise been. I make no excuses, but only an explanation. You need not reply to this disclosure. I hope I have not overstepped my bounds in revealing such intimate details to you."

Ruby was thoroughly contemplative, "Not at all... your disclosure has been most instructive and I thank you."

Looking round the corner, Arthur was suddenly aware that their uncle had come. Boisterous joy ensued. The Eaton children accosted their uncle with energetic delight.

Before Brandon had a thought to return to his own home that evening, Cynthia Eaton arrived weighted down with parcels. The children were promptly all over the packages, attempting to ascertain which might contain something for each of themselves. While their mother confessed to them that she had brought home a few things for their distraction, they were only a little disappointed to discover that most of the contents were new possessions, personally for their mother.

When it was duly past time for Brandon's departure, he turned to Ruby, "Thank you for our pleasant conversation, Miss Steed."

As Ruby smiled, about to respond in kind, Cynthia Eaton boldly interrupted, "Brandon! I've told you time and again to call our Ruby by her given Christian name. Please do not persist in saying Miss Steed! It pains me to hear such formality in this household of mine amid my family members. I simply will not allow it!"

Brandon tried again, "Until we meet again, Ruby."

His sister was satisfied, "There… now does that not feel better?"

Farewells were soon entirely accomplished, Brandon was gone home and the children were eventually sent to their beds.

Cynthia coaxed Ruby to accompany her for warm cups of milky drinks and pleasant evening conversation by the fire in the parlor. The ladies settled in nicely, enjoying the calm of the final quiet moments of the evening together. The fire crackled in a lively manner, lending generous flickering light to the room and outshining the numerous candles that were burning their brightest in their own attempts to brighten one of the loveliest rooms in the generously decorated house.

Cynthia began her side of their conversation in earnest by telling Ruby about her adventures out prowling the shops that day and then, out of nowhere, she could not resist a far more serious subject nearer to her heart and foremost in her mind, "You must wonder why my dearest brother Brandon is not married, my dear Ruby. A young man as handsome, kind and rich as he is, and not married, must set a quick mind like yours to wondering, I would wager. Well, as you have not asked but must surely be curious, I will tell you: his heart was injured some years past. He fell in love with an alluring girl, from what we long had thought were good family, who turned out to have a heart of stone. She jilted my dear brother… almost at the altar; I tell you. She ran off after somebody else. I don't like to recall the particulars, but Brandon was in shock and his heart was fairly broken for a while. I know he got fully over her fairly quickly, but where young ladies are concerned he has been gun-shy ever since. You know, since his broken engagement with that girl, I haven't seen him talk so much to one young woman as he has with you of late. He is truly quite attentive to you, my dear. It's all got me to suddenly thinking. Now, don't you dare to break his heart... and indeed, I wouldn't wish to lose you to marrying him either, for he would take you away from me... so please do endeavor not to entice him, and resist any charms he might throw at you. Please stay governess to my children and grandchildren forever."

Ruby was taken aback a good deal but pulled herself together enough to reassure her employer, "Oh, no... you need not worry on that count...for I have no intentions of marrying at *all*... I have had no immediate or future hopes or thoughts regarding marriage in the least... indeed, I have fancied myself the happy spinster of sorts... but, if your brother ever did have any inclinations my way, it would surely not be due to any machinations on my part... and if he ever hinted in that direction, I would hint the other way... though if he outright accosted me with a proposal, I would gently let him down... I am certain that we could remain goodly friends, for it would be my greatest desire to do so for all your sakes."

Cynthia Eaton was well satisfied with such an answer.

The following days continued much as the former had. Brandon was over amongst the family a great deal, and there was great delight amid the Eaton household. The weather was still unwelcoming out of doors and thus everyone happily stayed cooped up indoors, where there were always fires blazing in abundance and plenty of warming foods. Brandon's business affairs were held at bay with ease by his own design, as he was only too contended to spend a great deal of his waking hours amongst his family.

Cynthia Eaton did still notice her brother's attentiveness to Ruby, and though Ruby also took note of such warmly kind attentions from her employer's brother, she did her utmost to create a guarded though friendly wall to stand firmly between them. Brandon did not quite know what to make of this beautiful young woman. He thought that he detected hints of her heart warming towards him, though he surely sensed a marked cool professionalism in demeanor emanating his way from her. Though it was not truly his way of behaving, Brandon could not help but reach beyond his generally cool natural reserve to pursue Ruby's friendship to some noticeable extent. The Eaton children were not wholly unaware of the goings on between their uncle and their governess. They reveled in what they saw (at least the attractions on their uncle's side). They encouraged more. They cherished the thought of Ruby truly becoming a full member of their family through marriage to their uncle. Indeed, they did sometimes whisper their secret suspicions and hopes to each other.

One day, Albert embarrassed the pair when he took one of each of their hands, clasped them together, and proclaimed, "I thee wed!"

At that surprise gesture and proclamation, all the children giggled in blissful happiness at the prospect. Ruby's face was more crimson than Brandon's, but both were thankful that at that moment Cynthia was not in the room. Ruby believed that this tiny event, however entertaining for the children, would not please her employer and unbeknownst to Ruby, Brandon knew such as well; for, he had been privately scolded on more than one occasion by his sister, not to dare to take her prized governess away from her to his own home through a marriage to Ruby.

Brandon did increasingly treasure his growing friendship with the governess of the Eaton home, and he felt certain that she also welcomed the warm acquaintance with him. He wondered if perhaps she did not fancy him for a husband, for she might have loftier hopes. She was so very beautiful after all (it was an obvious fact to him), and he had been in front of his own looking glass enough to know that his own face was surely not equal to the finely delicate and uniquely perfect structure of hers. Brandon had too many times at church seen how other eligible bachelors had looked at the fair Ruby, and he felt his ire rising at any thought of their attempts at attentions towards her. Thankfully, Brandon thought, that Ruby was never out much beyond sitting with him and his sister's family in their pew at church. She was so seldom out alone where she could be prey to young men. Brandon knew the power of this fact and, wrongly or rightly, he cherished it with a certain jealousy.

All young manly eyes could see and surmise that Brandon Wallace had prior claim to the Eaton governess. Few men, if any, would dare to cross such a line to usurp Brandon's own rightful and unwritten (though subconsciously claimed) territory. Any young man who wished to pay any attentions or addresses Ruby's way would have to cross the line that Brandon Wallace firmly stood upon. In a small way, Cynthia Eaton knew this unspoken societal truth and was grateful for it (for this kept her own governess safe from any marriage), and in a clear way, Brandon did as well. He felt somewhat guilty within that in this way he was thwarting any attempts of any man towards marriage to Ruby (for her prospects were severely limited: indeed, in reality, they were but nothing), but, he could not help but take full advantage of the social phenomenon. Brandon was deeply drawn to Ruby and he could not bring himself to step out of the way for any other man.

Ruby was generally oblivious to the many young men who stared at her throughout the church services each Sunday. Likely one of the few who was insensible of her own attractions, Ruby did not see what so many others saw in her. In fact, even the pastor was aware that church attendance was up markedly amongst eligible young men (as well as the Eaton family) since Ruby had come to town and begun regularly attending his Sunday sermons. He did not mind in the least degree. Ruby was a welcome addition to his congregation in more ways (and persons) than herself.

One day when Ruby was planning a little trek on her own to the shops in town, Brandon had happened by (just as she was about to leave) and upon hearing of her day's outlined itinerary, found himself suddenly bold enough to offer to accompany her on her outing. Ruby feared to acquiesce to his charming offer, though she could not seem to resist nor did she wish to offend by declining. Whether or not Brandon was fully conscious that he was defending his territory from other eligible males in town, he at least was following his instinctive impulse to take advantage of the opportunity to spend a good portion of a day mostly alone with Ruby. She likewise attempted to follow her own impulsive instincts by suggesting that Marcia or Camile might wish to come along as well (as a chaperone complete). The two older girls were keen enough as to romantic dreams (and to the secret tender hopes of their uncle, as they believed), that they orchestrated a sudden urgent grand puppet theater: a dramatic event that all the Eaton children *must* stay home to attend and to perform in.

Ruby was on her own (alone with Mr. Wallace) for a good part of the day, and not only could Brandon Wallace protect his Ruby treasure from any advance of other men, he could advance his own agenda if he so chose. Even Cynthia Eaton could not be prevailed upon to assist Ruby in slipping out from Brandon's grasp, since she had just spent several days in a row tiring her purse out at the shops and did not seem alarmed at the thought of her brother taking her precious governess on an afternoon outing. She felt safe and assured that Ruby would be kept as her very own possession, neither to be scooped up for marriage by any strange gentleman nor to be talked into matrimony by he who had been her intimate visitor in the house for so very long. Brandon was Cynthia's brother and she tended to regard Ruby as also her brother's sister. Their governess was as a sister to them both, in Cynthia's estimation.

Though Ruby had as much as attempted to escape Brandon's company; she could not deny within herself that it had turned into a more than lovely day with him in attendance. Ruby could not suppress her enjoyment. Brandon was in top form. His common tendency to hide his truest self was thrown to the wind. He chose to let his inner spontaneous self show forth. Brandon was in a rare mood to enjoy the moment and he did not hold back. Indeed, he was uncharacteristically forward. Helping Ruby in and out of the carriage he drove for her, that she might go in and out of the shops, Brandon exhibited uncommonly chivalrous gestures on behalf of the fair damsel. Ruby could not refuse to give in to his gallantry. It was all too much enjoyable flattery and delight.

When it was high time for Ruby to return home for the evening meal, Brandon insisted that she allow him to indulge her with the best meal that could be bought in town.

Ruby protested, "Oh, no…. I could not. I must go home."

"Why? You are not needed at home tonight."

"But your sister…"

"My sister does not necessarily expect you to return home, as yet."

"But what will she think?"

Brandon offered explanation, "She will think that you or we are late… but she will not mind it. She can sup with her children without you there."

"But she will…"

"Perhaps she will assume I am buying you a meal."

"Are you certain? I…"

Brandon insisted, "She knows that you are safe with me. She will not worry over you."

"Though I…"

"Do not worry your pretty head. If my sister feels any distress, she will deal with me first, and then I will set her straight. Let me handle my sister if need be."

"But I cannot allow you to buy me…"

Brandon heartily interrupted his fair companion, "Buy you a meal?! That is nothing! How can you think it of any consequence at all? Besides, I am famished and cannot wait so very long before eating. Please do me this favor and allow me to eat before I faint! You must accompany me! I know it is the province or fashion of ladies to faint… though not deemed customarily belonging to men… and indeed not widely considered admirable in a man… and so of course you would not wish to cause me to embarrass myself by fainting."

"But I…"

"You must… you will allow me to feed you one small meal that *I* may eat. Where is the harm… the crime… the sin? There is none."

"Well, I …"

Brandon smiled, "I wager your dear pastor would heartily approve. Indeed, only the other day did he ask me why no young man was courting you. He could not imagine why none were. He thought *that* particular deficiency of circumstance a crime and a sin, indeed he did."

Ruby could not help but laugh, though a little nervously at the thought of being talked about in that way (especially by the pastor... with Brandon).

Brandon continued in that vein, "Well, I dare say he as much as told me that perhaps I should get on with such attentions. I would say that he nearly... commanded me... to court you!"

Ruby could not believe this, "No! He would never! He must have been joking... no, I think it is *you* who are joking!"

"No, I am in earnest. You cannot believe that the pastor would speak so to me, but it is so... there it is. Well, he did not specifically command or tell me to court you, but he did wonder aloud to me in private that I was not paying my addresses to you in that way. He said it seemed a natural thing, given that we are such good friends... and in close connection because of my sister... and both young and... well... each very marriageable. He claimed that I, actually meaning we, might be ignoring a true commandment, so to speak."

Ruby surely did not know what to say to such a bold speech from her employer's brother. She sat dumbfounded in Mr. Brandon Wallace's carriage. She looked him plainly in the eye and then looked away. Her look of innocent shock amused Brandon to no end. He threw his head back in laughter and then, "I have shocked you greatly, have I? Well, I'll not press the matter. Not tonight, anyway. I'll let you ponder the pleasing idea a little for a while, I think. Let us forget for now the pastor's advice to me regarding you, and we shall enjoy a wonderful meal. I am light-headed for want of food."

From that moment, through their delicious meal, and on the ride home, not another word was spoken about courting and marriage by either Brandon or, of course, by Ruby. Only polite quiet conversation passed between the pair. Brandon was indeed thinking of marriage to Ruby. Ruby was truly pondering the matter, as he had suggested she should. She could not help it. She felt that she must face some facts. The pastor's counsel aside, Ruby knew that she had been feeling various kinds of fluttering in her heart and stomach regarding Brandon for quite some time. Despite her near promises to her employer, and all her attempts to remain the happy spinster she imagined herself to be forevermore; she believed that she was and had been falling in love with Brandon. How could she help it? He was handsome and charming. He was hardworking and successful. He was kind and delightful. He was attentive and bright. He was good and so very jolly. He was wonderful with the children and also to his sister. Ruby had no doubt that he would make some woman a gentle, loving husband. Why should she *not* be that woman? He would protect and provide well for a wife and children. Why should she not be that wife? Why should she not have his children? He deserved a good wife and children. He seemed to be choosing her to become his wife and the mother of his future children. Why should she not comply? She felt assured that he would dote on her all the more after marrying, and she would feel free to finally dote upon him. Such a union could make them both very happy.

Ruby could not sleep that night for pondering the matter over in her mind and mulling it about in her heart. She got out of bed numerous times to pray over the idea, even though she had previously sent supplications heavenward at length on the subject before retiring into her bed. Ruby was a confusing combination of excitement and wondering. Brandon loved her! Well, he had not quite exactly professed as much, but he surely hinted strongly towards that fact. She did believe that she truly loved him. He had all but asked her to marry him! Well, he had suggested that he was attempting to court and then marry her. She could not but smile at the idea, though she had not let herself think on any such contemplation before this night. Oh, but she could not make such a decision wrongly. A choice for marriage was such an all-important question of which answer must be correct. Had not Cynthia Eaton suffered the bitter consequences of a selfish unfeeling husband? Had she not been miserable? Her greatest luck in matrimony seemed to be the death of her rich husband. Of course she had her children. They were worth far more than gold. Though, a woman dare not contemplate children if she is not given a worthy offer of a husband. What goodly woman would marry simply to secure children for herself? Indeed, what kind of woman marries simply to obtain gold? No, a question of marriage must first and only be asked with regard to the man who offers it. Is he worthy? That is the material point. In the beginning, the question of marriage is all about the man and how he will husband his wife.

Her thoughts returned to Brandon: he was truly a worthy man. However, were the feelings that Ruby had been harboring truly love? Was this love such as the truest? Did she feel a love that would lead to the greatest happiness in matrimony? Was this fluttering feeling more than infatuation? Ruby desired to ask herself if she truly loved Brandon. Did she love him more than she could ever love any other man? Could Brandon cause her to never want towards thinking of any other man? Was Brandon the happy ending of all quests in love for her? She wished to find the honest answer within. She sought an answer from above. She believed that she seemed to see no other than him. Was this proof of love? Was it proof of true love? And this worthy man Brandon: did he love Ruby more than any other woman? He had loved before. Did he love more now? Would his love for Ruby be the end of seeking? Would he remain constant to Ruby all the days of their lives? Oh, but Ruby's mind was swimming with these questions and she feared that she might not be able to trust the answers she would give them. Her mind may be clouded since her heart was so full. How could she see clearly through such a fog of passionate feelings?

As the night wore on, desiring at least *some* sleep that night, Ruby finally took hold of and reminded herself that Brandon was only just hinting towards beginning to court her. Why should she struggle over a question of marriage at this point in time? Could she not simply enjoy his courting efforts for a while and decide the matter later? Brandon had said that she should ponder the idea a while, did he not? Yes, she could gradually ponder as he commenced his courting efforts. She could relax and observe a while. She need not decide on marriage to Brandon tonight. She had time.

The next number of days was as if a dream. Brandon was

over much and Ruby enjoyed his subtle though especially pleasing attentions her way. Cynthia Eaton scarce noticed a thing amiss and neither did the Eaton children, though they had been known to hope for a marital union of their uncle to their governess from fantastical time to time. All seemed as it always was: as things had grown to be expected. Ruby was a part of the Eaton family as Brandon long had been. Jolly days and evenings lazily rolled by, as Ruby and Brandon each secretly and independently contemplated a future life together.

Just on a day that Ruby might have expected Brandon to come and finagle a way to get her out of the house and alone with him in a supposedly needed trip to the shops, he did not come. Ruby found herself looking out for her fine Mr. Wallace. She could not but feel disappointed that he was away.

Instead of the expected from Mr. Brandon Wallace, unexpectedly, Cynthia had news of a disconcerting nature, "Oh, dear… Ruby, I must speak with you. Come to my parlor where we can speak privately."

Ruby was predictably alarmed and followed her employer into the favored room where they each promptly sat down. Cynthia continued, "She is come *home*!"

"*Who* is come?"

"Oh, my! What will she do? What will Brandon do? What will happen next, I wonder?!"

Ruby did not know what to ask and so sat still, quiet and ready to hear whatever Cynthia wished to tell her.

Cynthia continued her whirlwind of speech, "She was off to schooling and travels and such. Well, at first she was off after another fellow… but that all ended badly… though I know not the particulars. We all came to think that she would find some European to marry… you know… someone very rich. What else would she have wanted, but someone richer than he whom she had already won? He was rich enough and everything more. More in the way of money could have been her only object… or perhaps someone a bit more dashing… or even something of the dangerous. Some young ladies seem to hunger after that sort of thing… that type of fellow... you know."

Ruby continued to sit, quietly and still.

Cynthia seethed, "Oh, but I despise her. I hoped that once in Europe, she would stay there endlessly. With her having been gone so very long, she was mostly long forgotten... though, when remembered, I had truly hoped we would never see her again... well, if only married securely to another man. Oh, what can I do to save him from her clutches?!"

Ruby began to sense a wrenching feeling bubbling up within her. She contained the appearance of such, determined not to show a hint of it outwardly.

Ruby's employer continued, "I've already had word that she saw him in town early this morning! Oh, what dread! I thought he was over her, but... she... she is so *excessively* conniving... that little hussy! Has she begun her deception and second snare of him so soon?! "

Ruby was becoming certain of whom Cynthia was speaking and of whom might be ensnared once more.

"I am certain that she has come to break Brandon's heart again... or maybe to marry him after all!"

Ruby sat calmly as her heart was breaking, wrenching her soul along with it.

Cynthia fumed, "Oh, but I detest even the sound of her name! Rochelle! Is that not the very sound of evil manipulations?!"

Ruby thought not, but did comprehend why her employer might believe such a thing. Ruby reached out to stroke and soothe Cynthia's hand nearby, trying to offer some kind of meager comfort, even as her own mind and heart could not find any comfort for her.

11
Wild Abandon

As the snow began to clear, Cynthia Eaton started to feel a real impatience that she could not quite contain nor explain to even her own mind: she felt compelled to seek out society beyond her home and family. As invitations to balls and dinners came her way, she sought out that other company, leaving her children more and more to their governess. In Mrs. Eaton's mind and heart she tended to believe that her children were better off spending their evenings with Ruby anyway, for the dear redhead would tuck the children into their beds with delightful stories that would enrich their dream-worlds like few other persons ever could. Ruby did do her utmost to take care of every need of the Eaton children, particularly with their mother absent so very much, though with Mrs. Eaton generally home early in the days; the children did not tend to feel abandoned to any degree, when their mother was out partaking in nighttime social affairs. Mrs. Eaton could dine, wine and otherwise, whilst her children slept.

Brandon had been away from the Eaton household, on business as he said, but both Cynthia and Ruby feared that something relative to Rochelle may have had more to do with his absence than anything. Cynthia worried aloud to Ruby that Brandon might be spending some of his hours captured by Rochelle and thereby would become transfixed by her evil charms towards marriage once more, even as Ruby's heart began building a fortress against her former attractions towards Mr. Brandon Wallace. It was entirely possible that Brandon was avoiding Rochelle, but Ruby wondered if he might be avoiding her as well. It was true that Brandon had indeed been going away on business, on short trips to here or there. It was also true that Brandon and Ruby's associations with each other had taken a very different tone than before Rochelle's return to the territory. Ruby could not help but feel uncomfortable, wondering whether Brandon's heart had turned away from her and back to his former love, and Brandon had no doubt that Ruby had heard rumors regarding Rochelle in reference to himself, which discomfited him as well. This co-knowledge had created a wedge of general silence between the two and neither knew quite what to say to the other to ease their communications. This general discomfort between Ruby and Brandon was not especially noticed by Cynthia Eaton or her children. Life did seem to be going along quite as usual, though Cynthia was somewhat nervously awaiting the outcome of Rochelle's expected manipulations on Brandon.

The next Sunday that Brandon was in town to go to church with the Eaton family, Ruby's discomfort was thrown into a thorough tizzy when Rochelle buzzed around Brandon like a bee. Such was the first sighting of the Miss Rochelle Behr for Ruby, and 'twas a painful display to her indeed. Congregational eyes were agog with the way Miss Behr threw herself at Mr. Wallace. All who had not known from before were soon apprised by their friends at church that this Rochelle Behr was indeed the hussy who had left Brandon Wallace nearly at the altar, and now she had returned after a lengthy absence of travelling, to quite obviously attempt to finally get married to her former Mr. Wallace after all. Most did not approve. Some enjoyed the entertainment. All wondered what the end result would be. To anyone who knew the still young man very well at all, Brandon was visibly distressed by Rochelle's overly pressing attentions. Cynthia Eaton worried. Ruby felt compelled to quietly ease away from Mr. Brandon Wallace, the more she saw Miss Rochelle Behr so explicitly near him.

Ruby did not see or hear any hint of Mr. Wallace all that next week and then that following Sunday, he was noticeably absent from church, as his business affairs had taken him away for a greater stretch of time once more. The entire congregation looked for Mr. Brandon Wallace, but he did not appear, to a general disappointment; for most folks wished to see the saga continue for amusement or interest sake. Since Miss Rochelle Behr could not further her agenda to secure Brandon for herself once more, she took the opportunity to ensure that the fair redheaded beauty would not pose an obstacle to reuniting herself to her former beau. Miss Behr accosted Miss Steed outside the church the first practical moment after the services were ended.

Rochelle Behr began, "Well, and so you are the Eaton *governess*, I am told."

Ruby said nothing but, "Yes."

"You have apparently made yourself quite indispensible to Mrs. Eaton, I understand."

Ruby said and showed nothing.

Rochelle leaned in close to whisper, "Of course you know that Brandon and I were engaged to be married before I had to go away for some travels and education? It is now only a matter of time before we are betrothed again, I am certain that you and all surmise... and you do surmise correctly... you can all count on that. I don't know why he thinks himself unengaged to me anyhow. I was his fiancé before I went away and I think myself his fiancé still. 'Twould be terribly ungallant of him to back out, do you not think?"

Ruby simply raised an eyebrow, fixated on a passing cloud, inwardly wishing to be away, elsewhere, anywhere.

"I don't wish to distress you, but some say that you were trying to catch Brandon Wallace for yourself. Is this true? Did you wish to marry him? I can't imagine so... you would not attempt to climb above your station to marry the likes of him, would you? *You*, a lowly governess, have not set your sights so high, have you?"

Ruby looked away, wishing Rochelle away.

"Did you think you and he... quite the thing?"

Ruby intensely desired not to converse with the young lady, "Not at all, I assure you."

"I thought not."

Ruby looked at some children running by.

Rochelle smiled slyly, "Well, well… the content governess… the settled spinster, I presume… yes, well, that sets my mind at rest. I would not wish to fight with you over him. He might be a little hesitant to begin with me once more… but he will be mine again, I can attest to that. Indeed, I see him as mine still."

Ruby only nodded and looked away.

"I suppose you think me bold, Miss Steed?"

Ruby forced herself to briefly look Rochelle in the eyes, "No more than some, Miss Behr."

"Well, Miss Steed, I believe in speaking plainly and I believe in speaking my mind."

Ruby pained at hearing Miss Behr say her name again, "Yes, of course."

"May I call you Ruby, Miss Steed?"

Ruby pained all the more, "You may, if you like."

"Oh, good… for I would like to think myself your friend."

Ruby could not imagine why Rochelle should wish to be her friend, other than in some unknown way to further her own designs to recapture Brandon. Ruby could not believe that Rochelle could feel any confidence or justify any right in claiming a friendship. Ruby only nodded.

Miss Behr continued, "You are a part of the Eaton family, and in a way, so am I. Brandon and I will wed soon enough, I will become Mrs. Wallace, a sister to Cynthia Eaton, aunt to the Eaton children…. and then you and I will be fast friends. We will see each other oft. Indeed, perhaps you will care for and be governess to Brandon and my children. You shall quite likely be employed by me."

Ruby did not wish to think upon such a horror, but smiled slightly, trying desperately to hide her pain, "I cannot imagine that Mrs. Eaton could spare me, even for *your* children."

"But Brandon and my children could be brought over to you. There. Cynthia would not say no to her brother on that count."

Ruby tired of this Miss Behr and her tortures, "I could not say what Mrs. Eaton's wishes would be in such a case. I wonder why you speak to me of that which I would have little or no control over."

"Oh, I merely suggest the future of our friendship. Of course you are Cynthia's governess, but I do know that she adores her brother and if he desired that she share her governess with us, she would do it."

"Unless he would not ask such a thing of his sister."

"Well, Brandon would ask anything of his sister if I told him to do so, for he adores me fully as much as he did before, and once we are married, well… you can imagine how his adoration will grow all the more."

Ruby thought this last statement boldest of all, but did not raise an eyebrow, nor did she show forth her inward flinching. She attempted to appear severely bored, and did then sincerely look longingly over at the Eaton carriage and horses that stood waiting a little beyond them. She craved flight from Miss Behr. Ruby's wishes were granted as one of her hands was forcefully grasped by Marcia, and her arm was tugged towards her blessed escape.

Ruby apologized in the midst of her happy rapid departure, "Excuse, me, Miss Behr. I must away…"

Miss Rochelle Behr stood left alone for a moment before seeking to find her father for a return home to their abode of opulence.

In the coming weeks, Ruby did all in her power to avoid Miss Behr at church, finding creative ways to shield herself with Cynthia Eaton (who was herself avoiding Miss Rochelle Behr) or the wonderful Eaton children. Miss Behr was all frustration as she fiercely desired to make certain that Ruby would pose no barrier to her designs on Brandon Wallace. Easily sensing Cynthia's disapproval of her, Rochelle was not inclined to attempt to work her machinations on Brandon's sister; and as long as Ruby stood by Cynthia's side, or nearby with the Eaton children, Miss Rochelle Behr was at a loss to exercise her manipulations on Ruby. With Brandon Wallace gone off on business elsewhere so oft and extendedly, Rochelle Behr was frustrated aggravation itself. Since Miss Behr dared not show herself at the Eaton home, Ruby was safe from the manipulator, as long as she did not go to town on her own. Ruby was content to stay home, safe from the Miss Behr.

As Ruby played governess as well and blissfully as any ever could, Mrs. Eaton contented herself in continuing to take advantage of attending to her own social hungers. Every party, dinner or ball she was invited to, she would not but attend. Usually strolling or stumbling in quite late, if she did find Ruby up by the fireside, she would wish to share all her entertainments and pleasures with her doting governess.

One such night, Cynthia arrived home in time to visit with her governess, "Oh, Ruby… my dear… I am so glad that you are not off in your room… for I have news…"

Ruby helped Cynthia onto her favorite comfortable chaise in the parlor, for Ruby could see by the way that her employer walked, that she would be far better off sitting as soon as may be.

Cynthia exhaled with a sort of swoon, leaning fairly forward towards her fair governess in a forced whisper, "Well… do not breathe a word to anyone at present… but… you know that young dashing fellow… that I told you about before? Well, he danced me into the garden tonight… and fairly proposed to me at once! What do you say to that? Well, I said yes, of course!"

Ruby smiled and nodded, for she did not wish to dampen Cynthia's giddiness at being engaged again, but it was the third time that month already. Ruby knew that it was the wine that got her employer into such fixes, and she might well regret herself in the morning and be obliged to end another betrothal before the day was through. Mrs. Eaton was in a fair way to be considered throughout the territory as a very silly woman. Ruby wished she could aid Cynthia in these matters somehow, but what could a governess do from home to protect her employer from embarrassing herself when she was gone out?

Still very much a little worse off for the too much wine that she had consumed earlier, she leaned forcefully back on her chaise and all but bellowed, "Oh, but he is a passionate fool for me! You would not believe the things that he says to me! Desperately in love with me he is! I feel like I am a young woman again. That is what a young man can do... for an older woman like me... you know. Oh, Ruby! I am in love again!"

Ruby smiled. She groaned inwardly. Cynthia Eaton in love again? Heaven forbid! Would it be four or more times by the end of the month?

"Oh... I know what people are saying... what they always say... that this one is after my money too... but, I say he is different... I know he truly loves me..."

Ruby smiled once more. She did not for a moment believe that this beau was different than the previous brief fiancés that Cynthia Eaton had accepted and then fairly promptly dropped. A string of young men had all proven to be far more interested in Mrs. Eaton's riches than her other worthy attractions. This new young man would likely turn out to be the same. Oh, but Ruby wished she could impose more sense upon her employer. All the hints in the world did not seem to faze Cynthia Eaton in the least. She seemed headlong determined to marry the wrong sort of fellow, and was in a fast way towards a bad marriage. Her first marriage had been a torturous prison to her, and Ruby could not fathom why she seemed to attempt to doom herself to an even worse state of matrimony. She did not want for money, property, or even children. She did not truly need a man. Why did she so crave love? And how would the wrong sort of fellow satisfy her in that realm over the long term anyway? She was certainly better off without love, in such cases as these.

Mrs. Eaton ecstatically tilted her head, "You should have seen us dancing... he was a prince... and I was his princess! He made me the belle of the ball! I can't believe he would choose me... of all the young ladies... well... you know... he says... he can't believe I am not as young as all the rest of them. Oh... and... Rochelle Behr was there too... why must she come to these parties too? Well, she kept staring at us... I fancy she was envious... but then... what do you know? There was Miss Behr with an older fellow! I wager she's given up on my brother... at least for now. Well, he's made himself so scarce... that she's had to look elsewhere. I think maybe she fears she'll end up a spinster... so... now she's got her clutches on this rich old gent. Well, I hope she marries… and soon… for then Brandon can finally come home to us… instead of making business excuses to get away from her."

Ruby did not let her hopes rise on Brandon's account at all. Mrs. Eaton was only talking, fueled by wine. It could mean nothing, after all.

As had become a necessary usual nighttime habit, Ruby helped her tipsy employer to her bedchamber.

Few days had passed before, Brandon had suddenly returned. He did not appear to allow Miss Rochelle Behr a moment's access to him before he made straightway to the Eaton household. His sister reveled in his return. The children delighted to finally see their uncle once more. Ruby stayed aloof. Cynthia was all joy and let her brother know it, forcing him to stay the day and feeding him all manner of dainties while they visited happily. She did not bother to announce her numerous engagements to him, for she had broken off another one: all had happened in his absence and she could hope that he might not hear of all or any of them any time soon, if ever.

Nearly deciding to cancel her plans to go off to a dinner party, Brandon encouraged his sister to go and not stay on his account, for he promised to remain until her return, and then they could visit much more. Ruby's heart fluttered in a kind of nervousness or even fear, as she contemplated a good part of the evening alone in Mr. Brandon Wallace's company. Miss Steed steeled herself. She could spend a good hour or more putting the children to bed while Brandon read by the fire or some such thing, and then she could retire early, thereby leaving only the required modicum of polite slight conversation with Brandon in-between. Yes, she would be quite safe. Thus she so determined to orchestrate.

However, once Cynthia had gone out to her dinner engagement, and Ruby tried to excuse herself from the brother's presence, Brandon had the audacity to inject himself into the bedtime story activities. Ruby could see no way out. It was her role and her duty to make certain that all five of the Eaton children were safely and soundly settled into their beds before she could relax with a warm cup of something by the fire, or take herself to her own apartment for the night. Brandon knew this. He took full advantage of it. He thoroughly enjoyed watching and listening as Ruby told her stories to the Eaton children. He took great delight in seeing them marvel at their governess's fictional creations. Knowing that it was obviously owing to his intruding on the nightly custom; he also could not but warm to Ruby's nervousness that night. He liked to think that he could cause Ruby to feel undone. She still was affected by his presence. This was a good sign, he thought.

Once the Eaton children were secured into their beds for the night, Ruby attempted composure as she begged a cup of something warm from Mrs. MacLeod, and Brandon did the same. Ruby tried to seat herself alone, in a way, by the fire, but Brandon would have none of it. Ruby had moved her chair in a position that announced desired solitude, but Brandon ignored her physical plea and pulled his chair very close to hers. Once Mrs. MacLeod had brought them their drinks, the two sat quietly, sipping, watching the flames dance. Ruby dared not glance over and up at Brandon, even as he generally stole extended staring gazes at her instead of the fire. Ruby sat, silently planning her escape from the man that she felt so drawn to. She could not risk her own heart, whilst knowing that his heart might still belong to that odious Miss Rochelle Behr.

Soon, the silence was broken by Mrs. Eaton's brother, "Well... what do you say about my sister?"

Ruby was taken aback and looked over, with a strange and curious cast to her face. She did not answer, for she dared not imagine what to say.

"I hate to say it, Ruby, but... it is all over town and beyond that my sister is behaving in a terribly silly way."

Ruby's eyes widened. Her tongue stayed still. Her heart jumped for having heard her name on his lips.

"I can't count the number of times she has been betrothed of late... and I won't bother you to remember either."

The concern on Ruby's face showed.

"Yes... you feel it too... I worry for her, Ruby. I fear she will marry some young buck and be miserable. We both know it is her money they are after."

Ruby's heart leapt again. Oh, but must he say her name again? She still said nothing.

Brandon did not seem to notice Ruby's silence, "This wild abandon must cease. There must be something you and I can do together to save her from those men who would deprive her of all her coin, and worse: all her happiness. We must save her from herself, Ruby."

Ruby sighed. Her heart ached for him. Why could he not speak to her without speaking her name? Somehow, hearing her name in his voice pained her. Seeing her name on his lips was a type of torture. She looked away. Into the fire drove her penetrating gaze.

"I have distressed you? Forgive me for stating my concerns so plainly, Ruby. I suppose I have no right to ask for your assistance. She is my own sister, after all. I feel it is simply that you may hold more sway over my sister than I do or can. I thought that maybe you could be instrumental in helping me stop her from…"

At this, Ruby could join in, forgetting her own heart, and feeling for Cynthia's welfare, "No… you are right… you and I… together… perhaps we can work to help her see…"

"Yes! We can surely come up with something! At least we can work towards… well… for now, you can hint here and there… and I can offer a more direct approach on the subject… and perhaps we can offer her diversions at home as well… together…"

"Yes, of course. I will do my utmost to help divert her from the path of conniving young men."

"Yes! Exactly! They are conniving to be sure. I generally think of some young women as conniving, but it is too true… there are conniving young men as well."

Ruby could not help but think of Miss Rochelle Behr. She sat suddenly silent once more. Her heart sighed.

Brandon continued, "I suppose I have been remiss in protecting my sister. I have had my own concerns. I have been away on business too much and Cynthia has come too close to another bad marriage…

indeed, a far worse one, I am painfully certain."

Ruby looked into Brandon's serious face. Oh, how could such a good man as this have been fooled by such as Miss Behr? Ruby hoped that he could see clearly now. She offered, "I suppose I have been remiss as well. There must have been something I could have said or done... to help her see more clearly... but I have feared to... to disappoint her... in her gleeful moments."

"Yes, well... I will have no fear on that count. I will have to be diligent in showing her the follies and vices of her future fiancés as she gathers them up one by one."

"I shall try to help... where I can..."

"I will search out their pasts if need be! And if needs must, I will stop them at the altar in the church!"

Ruby could not help but smile. This freed Brandon to do the same. Their conversation took a far lighter tone and they enjoyed each other's company as they had so often done in times past. A comfortable spirit existed between the two of them for the time being and they cheerily talked of many things. Miss Rochelle Behr was nowhere near either of their thoughts. Brandon's gaze was firmly affixed to Ruby's countenance. He could not look away. He did not wish to. Ruby looked from the beautiful fire to Brandon's visage, back and forth, throughout their conversing. She might have liked to fairly stare into his eyes, but she surely did not have the courage to do so, and thus, her sight took refuge in the fire between times. She did not play coy, she simply was. Nevertheless, this demure demeanor in Ruby was all the more an attraction to Brandon.

Cynthia Eaton was finally home again. She was not so affected by wine as in too many nights prior. She joined her brother and governess in the parlor for pleasant conversation. Soon, Ruby left brother and sister to their own private conversing as the governess redhead took herself to her room and then to bed.

Ruby could not sleep that night as soon as she may have expected or hoped to do. She began to recall those things of marriage that Brandon had spoken to her not so very long ago. It all seemed so very faded in the past as if a dream and yet here and now, all was flooding back to her. Had his former tender feelings towards her faded? Did she still love him as she had begun to so recently? Ruby thought on the idea that love is a tender plant that must be continually nourished in order that it not begin to wither towards dying. Love must be fed to flourish. She knew that her fond feelings for Brandon had been bridled and then had diminished somewhat because of Brandon's recent neglectful absence and particularly due to Rochelle's appearance and dogged annoyance. But what was she to think now? Brandon's behavior towards her near the end of that evening approached as tender towards her as it had ever been. Though, Ruby determined that she could not possibly free her heart again towards Brandon until all was settled in obvious separation between him and Rochelle. As long as Rochelle considered herself engaged to be married to Brandon, or at least until he made it perfectly clear to all that there was no such betrothal or ever would be again, Ruby must stand afar off from him.

12
Second Skimmings

The following Sunday, just outside the church and prior to the meeting (while Brandon was doing his utmost to steer clear of Rochelle who was too successfully hounding him), Cynthia Eaton was determined to introduce Ruby to one of her own former fiancés.

"Ruby… here… there is someone I wish you to meet. This is Mr. Dodge."

Ruby politely nodded. Her thoughts could not help but question why her employer would want her to know a man she had quickly engaged herself to and then more swiftly broken with.

Mrs. Eaton clearly delighted in attempting to bring the two young people together in acquaintance. Ruby was thankful that the church service was about to begin and excused herself to round up the children to go inside the meetinghouse. Once seated, Cynthia sat whispering to Ruby of all the redeeming qualities of Mr. Dodge. Ruby wondered why Cynthia Eaton would think so very highly of a man that she had so publicly spurned, and further, why she could possibly wish that Ruby should like him. Throughout the meeting, Ruby felt the eyes of Mr. Dodge gazing at her, and the few times she looked over to verify this phenomenon, he was smiling openly. Ruby was mortified.

Mrs. Eaton whispered to Ruby even as the pastor preached, "Mr. Dodge is truly quite enamored with you. He is blatantly staring at you. Is this not thrilling? Such a handsome young man… and he is besotted with you. Are you not pleased?"

Ruby did not wish to answer in whispers in the midst of the sermon and yet her employer expected it. Ruby whispered as quietly and briefly as she could muster, nearly begging, "Let us speak of this after the meeting."

"Oh, yes… of course. We will enjoy your conquest afterwards."

Though Cynthia Eaton did not fall into the temptation of continued whispering to Ruby about Mr. Dodge, she did continue to look over at him, enjoying as he enjoyed staring at Ruby. The redhead shrunk from the display, doing her utmost to ignore it all, forcing her mind on the sermon and only looking at the pastor or the Eaton children. When the meeting ended, both Ruby and Brandon busied themselves with attending to his sister's children, for Mr. Wallace was avoiding Miss Behr as energetically as Miss Steed was avoiding Mr. Dodge. Mrs. Eaton tried to aid Mr. Dodge in his quest towards Ruby. In the midst of all this aiding, avoidance and pursuance, Miss Behr and Mr. Dodge bumped into each other and so then suddenly began enjoying a new acquaintance one with the other. Mrs. Cynthia Eaton's hopes were thwarted. She was all disappointment. Brandon and Ruby's annoyances were curtailed.

This was only the beginning of some continued annoyances for Ruby, particularly. Cynthia Eaton was not anywhere near done passing off her old beaux onto Ruby. It seemed a sudden sport or hobby for the governess's employer. Ruby could not think what end result Mrs. Eaton might desire, but, nevertheless, one after another, Cynthia Eaton subjected Ruby (at church or in town) to being introduced to this past fiancé or another (or at least to be told gushingly at length about each fellow).

Ruby tired of these silly exercises, but what was a governess to do with an employer who insisted on such habitual diversions? Ruby was beholding to Cynthia. As beloved a governess as she might be, she was still second class to a degree. Ruby could not truly insult nor refuse Cynthia Eaton on any count. Ruby believed that she must suffer her employer's strange whims. As each former beau was tossed Ruby's way by Mrs. Eaton, governess was compelled to be gracious towards employer, even as she tried to politely repel each fellow with firmness. As the employed, Ruby was required by etiquette and propriety always to defer to her employer's oddities in order to keep her own position safely held in the household. Her livelihood depended upon it. Not considered equal in class to the woman of the house, the governess therein deemed it quite necessary to offer obeisance to the woman who was far above her. No matter how benevolently Mrs. Cynthia Eaton might behave towards her, Ruby knew her place. Her current life was held in her employer's hands. As governess, Ruby was not truly a part of the family, no matter how often her employer claimed it to be so.

Thus and so it was that Cynthia Eaton continued to attempt to pass off her second-handed beaux upon Ruby, and Ruby's ability to halt such attempts was truly limited because of her second class status of sorts as the governess. Ruby began to become weary, feeling like second skimmings, indeed. As happy as Ruby tended to be in the Eaton home and particularly with the children therein; from time to time, Ruby yearned for Horizon House, where the women who worked there were generally on a more equal footing. There was not such a distinction of rank between Miss Fenton, the other teachers and maids there.

One day, after Cynthia had been telling Ruby of another old beau and how they must be introduced, Ruby thought up a tactic that might begin to save her from such unwanted attentions, "Dear, dear Cynthia. You have me pondering on a very serious matter. Do you wish me off and married, and out of your house?"

Cynthia Eaton was all shock, "Ruby! Whatever do you mean?!"

"Well, you have been introducing me to young man upon young man for quite some time now, and it seems that you wish me married off and away from you and your children."

"Oh, no! Well, now that you mention it, I can see how it would seem that way... silly me... I suppose I have been working against myself... if you do end up marrying one of these fellows I've been throwing at you, I will only have myself to blame for losing you!"

"You see! You need not introduce me to another fellow at all. You can be done with this pastime. Put your energies to better use,

I beg you."

"Well, you know, this all puts me to mind… I think that I have been tossing men at you for two reasons… one, I seem to have run out of new men for myself to consider and so out of habit I was throwing you in the way of young men, since I was temporarily out of the way… and, two, I admit that in my heart of hearts I would love to see you married… you know… eventually. I do not wish to lose you, of course… but, my selfishness aside, you are a treasure and a rare beauty, and as such, you were born to marry well."

Ruby thought on the kinds of men that her employer had been pushing at her. These were all Cynthia's cast-offs. Though not quick to ascertain their deficiencies at the onset, Mrs. Eaton had subsequently discovered that each of them was left with merits horribly wanting. It did seem strange to Ruby that Cynthia would think that any of these men could have anything remotely to do with marrying well.

Ruby risked, though chose her words most carefully, "It is very generous of you to think me born to marry well… and please do forgive me for being so presumptuously bold by questioning you thusly… but, as you have told me of the follies and vices of each of these men… for you have rejected each of them for marriage yourself, and for good reasons too… would you do me any justice by offering any of them to me as a potential husband?"

Cynthia Eaton pondered in earnest for the briefest moment and then plain and honestly answered with a laugh, "Right you are then! I am corrected! I have been a silly friend indeed!"

Ruby sighed, feeling great relief, though containing her feelings to the faintest degree, "Thank you… you are very good."

Cynthia sighed as well, "Still, I do believe that eventually I will lose you as governess to my children… you will marry one of these days, I am certain… but… we will be friends still."

"Dear Cynthia, I have no current intentions of marrying… I am content to be governess to your children."

"Oh, but what a waste that would turn out to be… if such as you did never marry… someday soon, Ruby, you must marry… and have children of your own."

Ruby smiled, "If God places just the right man before me, and lets it be known unto me that I should marry that man, then, I do believe that of course I must comply with such a heavenly plan… and I'm fairly certain that I would be happy to do so."

Cynthia smiled, thought on the subject at hand a short while and then, "Perhaps someday not far off, you… and I… shall each find the proper husbands, after all."

"Perhaps."

Then without much thought at all, Cynthia suddenly proclaimed with a most casual smile and attitude, "What if Brandon were placed before you by heaven?"

Attempting to ignore her flushing cheeks away, Ruby did her utmost to return in an equally easy fashion, "What would you think I should do?"

"I would think you should comply. I would hope so. Indeed, yes… then you would become my sister even as you would also become an even better friend…"

Ruby wondered how to reply and not knowing for certain with any confidence, remained silent, only smiling faintly.

Cynthia continued, "But… *that* is highly unlikely to happen. I am only dreaming. I fear he will wed that perniciously horrid Rochelle Behr after all. What will I do then?"

That settled by her employer, Ruby only smiled warmly and tried offering comfort, "Whatever will be… you will manage."

"Yes, yes… I suppose I will."

It was only the following evening that Cynthia Eaton took Ruby aside, "What a scolding I had from my brother today! Sit. Let me tell you. I thought he had brought me to town to treat me to something delicious and what do you think? He planned it all to express his displeasure with me! Yes, you may be well surprised that a younger brother would take it upon himself to tell his older sister what was what in his mind against her… but there it was. He told me that he could contain his disappointments in me no longer. He told me of scandalous rumors being bandied around about me… you know… due to my many engagements… my numerous beaux… and he was speaking very protectively about you, my dear… he cautioned me against further exposing you to ridicule as well… you know… by always introducing you to the young men that I myself have already discarded as unworthy for marriage as far as I was concerned."

Cynthia looked at Ruby imploringly. Ruby stared back in return, not knowing what on earth she might say to all that, as yet.

Cynthia further implored, "Well? What do you say to that?"

Ruby attempted, "I do not know quite what to say…"

Cynthia aided, "Well… after I began to recover from the shock of Brandon scolding me about making a fool of myself so publicly by getting myself engaged to so horribly many young men of late… you know… for I am his older sister and he is not inclined to scold me as a rule… indeed, I cannot recall his ever truly scolding me before… Anyhow, I could not but notice that his concerns were similar to yours… you know… about me throwing my cast-offs at you. You have been kind on that count but he was most emphatically unpleasant on the point. My brother is surely looking out for you, my dear. I do think that he holds a soft spot in his heart for you. I do."

Ruby wished to turn the focus of the conversation away from herself: herself and Brandon, "I am certain that Brandon wishes the very best for you and he sees that each and every one of those young men was so very unworthy of you."

"Yes, of course, but… you must see so much more than that. He knows them so unworthy of *you* as well."

Ruby continued to take her opportunities to help Cynthia, "I suspect that your brother desires that you will make every effort to be discriminating in your choice of suitors and… to behave more discreetly, perhaps? I am sure that he wishes that you do what you are able to prevent more rumors from being bandied about."

"Oh, yes, of course… but… he was thinking of you… in a *most* protective way. I could not but notice his kind thoughts for you. His mind was assuredly fixated upon your welfare. Ruby… perhaps Rochelle Behr is fading away in his thoughts and you will replace her in his mind some day."

Ruby did not wish to speak of these things to her employer and so desperately tried her utmost to sway the conversation away from Brandon, "I suppose I cannot imagine what your brother thinks of me... or of Miss Behr, at this juncture... but... may I say that it is wise counsel for you to discriminate in the realm of considering potential husbands... and the more you are at home in the evenings, the more your children do benefit by having their mother around."

"Oh, Ruby, you are exasperating the way you divert away from speaking with me about my brother, particularly in reference to yourself. If I did not imagine otherwise, I would wonder if you secretly detested him!"

Ruby could not allow that, "Oh, no... I think very highly of him... of course. I am simply setting my energies upon being your governess."

"Now, what is the fun in that?! I wish to speculate about how much my brother admires you... and how much he may be thinking of you... Let us not be simpletons! You are a rare beauty, as I have proclaimed before... and I see how many young men stare at you at church and in town... why would not my own brother notice you in this light as well? He is a man, after all. He is not blind, to be sure. Indeed, he has impeccable taste, generally... and it is a wonder that he would not prefer you over that overbearing Rochelle... who throws herself at my brother at every turn, I need not tell you. Yes, her father is rich... but Brandon is in no need of money, for he has plenty of his own."

Ruby attempted diversion, in a way of a subtle lesson for Mrs. Eaton, "I must agree with you on one clear point: it is fairly mortifying the way Rochelle does throw herself at your brother. I wonder at any woman putting herself in the way of a man in that fashion. It seems a foolish way to look out for a husband... and makes a fool of her in the process."

One of Cynthia's eyebrows was raised, "If I did not know better, I would detect a hint of scolding in my own direction."

Feeling sharply that she had overstepped her bounds, Ruby looked down humbly, "Oh, no... not at all... not at all, Cynthia.

Please forgive me if I gave such an impression."

Recovery was attained on both sides and Cynthia happily announced, "I have news! Iris Fenton is coming for a visit!"

Suddenly relaxed once more, Ruby was truly pleased, "Oh, that is wonderful news, indeed!"

"This is the second time she has come this year! This must be due to you, Ruby. She waits years between visits for only me, but for you…"

"Oh, no… do not say such things! Let us think of it this way: she has two reasons to visit instead of one."

"Oh, all right. I will acquiesce to your thoughts of which are kinder to me than I am to myself."

Cynthia took part in no outside engagements. Fully focused on her friend's impending arrival, she ordered up particularly especial foods and had the entire house cleaned: a lengthy treatment of every imaginable thing, whether it needed it or not. Cynthia Eaton had long admired Iris Fenton, and always wished to make a very good impression upon her when she came to call.

Iris Fenton was in a fair way to faint from hunger and thirst by the time she arrived at Cynthia Eaton's door.

In her entryway just near the front door, Cynthia near knocked Mrs. MacLeod over in her attempt to swiftly greet her guest, "Iris! You look a fright! Was your journey even tolerable in the least? You must be famished and dying of thirst by now! Come… come… let us sit in my parlor. Mrs. MacLeod will fetch us refreshments. Go, Mrs. MacLeod, go! Can you not see the woman is about to faint with starvation?! And have Ruby brought as well… you know… when she can safely break away from my lively children."

Cynthia settled down in mood as her guest and she sat down on upholstered silken chairs. She found calm, "There. Rest easy… food and drink will be here shortly… and so will your beautiful little redheaded protégé. What brings you to town… besides Ruby and me, I mean."

"Oh, nothing really… all things were at hand at the school and I felt the need to think of myself… to take a rest. And what better place and with what better company could I find than to come visit you and Ruby?"

Iris did not speak of her knowledge from Ruby's letter of worry regarding Cynthia. Iris had been summoned in secret by Ruby. Ruby had thought and suggested that perhaps Iris could come to aid in helping Cynthia see that chasing after young men who were chasing after her money, was not the proper or correct way to go about finding and marrying the right man. Iris was certainly up to the task. Cynthia revered her as a wise counselor indeed, and both women knew it. Iris full well knew that she could have easily directed their conversation towards a destination wherein she could swiftly offer wise hints about propriety for her friend, but she preferred to wait for more natural opportunities in order to remain completely subtle in her approach. She knew that she had ample time to bring about the true purpose of her visit.

Ironically, it was Cynthia who brought up the subject of marriage, or machinations towards it, "Well, Iris, do you remember that little hussy Rochelle who dropped Brandon and broke his heart some years ago? She has returned and is on the hunt once more. I fear he may be in a fair way to succumb to her wiles once more."

Iris felt concern, "Oh, no... he could not be so trusting of her as before?"

"Well, perhaps not... he has been holding her at bay, it seems... but I did run into her in town t'other day and she spoke to me as if a betrothal is definitely on again between her and my brother... and she also said something quite insulting and untrue about Ruby."

"Oh?"

Cynthia raised her eyebrows, "Yes, she said something to the effect that the lowly governess thinks she can vault herself up to Brandon's station... that Ruby is after Brandon for marriage... for his money!"

Iris leaned forward, lowering her voice, "Oh, no. You know that Ruby would never marry for money. She is entirely too much like me for such as that. If she liked Brandon, it would be purely for his merits, I assure you. This hints greatly of jealously and bitterness,

I suspect. Rochelle must be afraid that Brandon prefers Ruby over herself, and she is attempting to thwart Ruby's interests through you. I surmise that she means to have you stop Ruby from catching Brandon."

Cynthia lowered her voice as well, "Well... I have not seen anything to worry me on that count anyway. Brandon and Ruby are as brother and sister, and that is all."

"Are you certain, then?"

"Oh, yes, quite... well, I would certainly say so on Ruby's side. As for my brother... well, one can never be certain... he does take prodigious care and concern for our Ruby... it is possible that he thinks of her... but she does not seem to think of him at all."

Iris fairly whispered, "And if you are wrong, what then? Would Ruby wishing to marry Brandon worry you?"

Cynthia followed suit and whispered as well, "Well... I suppose Rochelle made a correct point... you know... about the stations of folks and such. Ruby is only a governess of unknown family and, well, Brandon is... well, quite rich, you know."

Still in a whisper, Iris willingly showed her insulted feelings, "Cynthia! You shock me! I thought we left the class or cast systems back in England and Europe. We live in a new world here, particularly on the western frontier, my dear. Did not you and I have fairly humble beginnings? Your marrying rich did not raise you above me in class... surely you do not think *that*, my friend."

Cynthia repented, "Well, no... of course not... please, do forgive me."

"Let us not forget what a treasure Ruby is. What woman of any station or money could compete with such a pillar of virtue and sweetness? Rochelle Behr has a rich father. Do you esteem her higher than Ruby because of her father's money? No, indeed!"

Cynthia's eyes widened, "Indeed not! I despise that gold-hunting hussy!"

"And you clarify a material point: Rochelle aspires to money, though she truly needs none, while Ruby with none does not."

"Ruby is an angel."

"There you are. You see clearly now. Character counts for worth... money for nothing."

"Well, money *does* come in quite handy."

"It surely does!"

Both ladies laughed at that, and just then, Ruby had arrived at the parlor door. Mrs. MacLeod was not far behind with the overdue refreshments. The three women enjoyed light and delightful conversation, as the Eaton children quietly busied themselves upstairs with projects that Ruby had set them upon.

Iris commented, "Ruby, one would think that there are no children in the house. What have you done? Tied them up and gagged them? What is keeping them so very quiet?"

Ruby smiled, "I only gave my students particular tasks to perform and they are so very focused on their work that they make little sound. They are wonderful angels."

Iris looked at Cynthia, "A treasure, I tell you. You have robbed me of my finest former treasure. I cannot believe that I ever allowed Ruby to leave me to come and work for you! She works wonders like no other."

Ruby was humbled and a little embarrassed at the accolade.

Cynthia could not refute such a compliment for her governess, and quite contrarily, felt compelled to add, "To be sure! She came and turned my little heathens into saints!"

Iris boldly stated, "Do not forget the treasure you have in my Ruby, Cynthia! And if you do not treasure her as I do, send her back to me! I still and likely shall have no other teacher quite as wonderful as she!"

Cynthia enjoyed fighting over and for her redhead, "No! You may not have her. Ruby, never leave me, no matter how much Iris may beg for your return! I will pay you ten times over what she could ever afford to pay you!"

Iris laughed, "Cynthia! You shame me by tossing all your money about! Though, I cannot blame you in the least for wishing to spare no expense in keeping Ruby from me and to yourself. Ruby, do not refuse more money on my account! Let us make certain that you take all the money she is now offering you not to return back to me! I will help hold her to that bargain or take you back this instant!"

Quite suddenly, from the door, Brandon's voice was heard, "I am very sorry, Miss Fenton, but you cannot take her back. Ruby is truly ours now. My sister could not do without Ruby and her children would be lost once more. Ruby belongs here with us. If need be, I also will pay dearly to keep her here... for my sister's family."

Iris looked over and detected more in Brandon's eyes than a defense of his sister's right to her governess. Ruby's mentor was quite convinced in that one instant that Brandon could not do without Ruby, in and of himself. More than a little thrill chilled up Iris Fenton's spine. She glanced from Ruby to Brandon and then back and forth somewhat (though discreetly), while the conversation carried on in the room, taking twists and turns as most conversations tend towards doing. Iris determined that she would clandestinely do what she could for Ruby and Brandon, while she was there to secretly help her friend Cynthia. It was a mission about marriages. She, who had never married, nor ever come truly close to it, seemed surely to be needed to make certain that her friends would each marry well.

Soon, Brandon was taking Ruby away and up to see the children on some pretext or other. Ruby excused herself to return back to her students, with their uncle.

Iris Fenton took the bull by the horns, seizing the opportunity she saw before her, "So you think your brother thinks only of Ruby as his sister then?"

Cynthia was comfortable, "Oh, yes. Indeed, yes. I've never seen a hint otherwise... well... not really... nothing obvious, to be sure."

"Then you are not looking, my friend. I saw sparks in Brandon's eyes just now. His mind was long ago emptied of that Rochelle and it appears filled with Ruby, I am certain of it."

"No... it could not be... surely not... I have seen nothing to... well, very little to give any alarm on that count..."

"As I say, you have not been looking... perhaps you are too close to see. Perhaps it all has been coming on gradually and thus you have not seen it growing. From my vantage point, comparing before until now, it seems so obvious to me. I do think Brandon besotted with Ruby."

"If Brandon were besotted with Ruby, surely he would have begun attempting to court her by now?"

"Perhaps he has been held back... by obstacles. They could both be holding back for any number of reasons. No, I am convinced that Brandon sees only Ruby."

Cynthia was half amazement, "I suppose, but what of Ruby? Do you think that she...?"

"Oh, yes... well, perhaps she is holding back far more than he is, but... I do think I see a certain something in her eyes for your brother."

"Oh, dear... what will I do if she leaves me to marry Brandon? I do not wish to lose her."

"You will gain a sister... a treasure of a sister... and a dear and faithful friend. Do not be selfish in wanting to keep Ruby as your governess... especially when she could be so much more to you... think... cousins would begin appearing for your children! What greater happiness could there be than to increase your familial happiness?"

Cynthia pondered silently, nodding slowly.

Iris continued, "Brandon deserves wedded bliss... and so does Ruby. Oh, they do seem made for each other to me. Do not hold them apart when they may very well be destined to join together."

Cynthia still sat musing the matter over.

Iris dealt a drop of levity, "You do not wish Brandon to marry Rochelle, do you? Save him, my friend! Save him from that hussy, or any other for that matter, by helping him win your governess in matrimony!"

They both laughed aloud. They continued quietly talking the new idea over. Cynthia became more and more amiable to such thoughts. The two ladies hatched a plan. Iris would take Ruby out for a drive to the shops to garner gifts for a few ladies back at the school, and Cynthia would attempt to talk sense into her brother.

While Ruby and Iris were out and alone together, Iris Fenton spoke very plainly to Ruby regarding her suspicions about Brandon's heart. Ruby exposed very little of her own heart to her mentor, but she did listen intently to all that Iris had to say to her.

"I encourage you to follow that possibility a while to see if it might be a true dream for you. Do not think yourself the poor and lowly governess, Ruby, for you have many rich virtues and beauty to offer any man, no matter how rich in worldly goods and gold he may be. Marriage is the ideal state in life for a woman... or a man for that matter, Ruby. If you can find a worthy man who will honor you as he should, marriage is a heavenly state on earth. It is true that I myself am a spinster, but this was a secondary choice, not my own first desire... but was born out of a lack of a better choice for me. I would have married, if such a man as Brandon had loved and offered to me."

After Ruby expressed her concerns about Brandon possibly still being taken by Rochelle Behr, Iris Fenton continued to tell Ruby of Brandon when he was young: how he was such a dear boy, and she truly believed him to be very dear still.

Iris continued to explain, "When Brandon was young and somewhat gullible; he was manipulated by Miss Behr into falling for her. He was dashed and embarrassed when she ran off to chase someone else, but realized fairly quickly that he was most fortunate to have escaped her clutches. He never loved her deeply. It was only a youthful infatuation. I do not think that Brandon will be so unwise as to fall again for her now, no matter what machinations she conjures up to catch him. Indeed, I do think I see that his mind is already quite fully occupied with you instead... and I do believe that his heart is fully yours as well."

13
Distractions

Abrilliant blue sky set off the lovely little church that wonderful Sunday. Mrs. Cynthia Eaton, her brother Brandon Wallace and her governess Ruby did joyfully well shepherding the Eaton children into the building. Delightfully uplifting hymns were sung and the pastor delivered a rousingly inspiring speech. The happy little building was filled to the brim that day. It seemed as if a special occasion somehow. The sun brushed magnificently brilliant paintings into the simply stained glass arched windows surrounding the entire congregation.

Something about the pastor's words dug deeply into Cynthia Eaton's soul and she seemed to receive a certain epiphany about herself. Quite there on the spot, as she sat in the pew with her blessed family around her, she inwardly repented of her most recent sins, both of commission and omission. She determined to think on men for herself in marriage much less and to put her thoughts upon her children far more. Many of her friend Iris's words of personal counsel during her recent visit (for the two old friends had taken some time away by themselves) had sunk profoundly back into Cynthia's mind. She had been a most slothful mother and a terribly silly woman. She had made a public fool of herself of late among undeserving men. Such did seem a little apropos, since she felt a most undeserving woman. She had such angelic children and a doting brother. Her governess Ruby was practically a saint. Indeed, though her life had been filled with some past sorrows due to the negligence, ignorance, selfishness and general unkindness of her late husband, God had removed that man from the world and had given her another chance at a far happier life. She had seemed bent on her own destruction and had done no favors for her children in the process. It seemed as if her first worthy work as a lucky widow was to happen upon the good fortune of asking a dear friend a favor. Thus was sent to her an angel in earthly disguise to care for her children, until she found sense enough to begin to do it herself. She determined to begin to truly mother her children, as the best mothers ever had done.

Once out in the sunshine, Cynthia easily took note of how her brother pined over Ruby from afar, while braver men (in the societal sense) incessantly approached and spoke subtly of their attentions towards her. All manner of men seemed abuzz around Ruby while Brandon stood back and watched. Brandon had always been generally reserved and had not ever realized his own worth. Such excessive modest and humility was why the likes of Rochelle Behr could have ever caught him, and perhaps a part of why he allowed the hussy to harass him still. And such related timidity was why Brandon was barely moving in Ruby's direction. Even with a strict talking to from his own older sister, urging him to go after Ruby while he still had the chance, Brandon held back. He stood back. He feared to tread where other men were beating down a trodden path towards the beautiful redhead.

While Brandon stared at Ruby being accosted by swarms of men, Cynthia stared at her brother, wondering what could be done to help him. Cynthia Eaton could begin to see that Rochelle was as if a giant wedge holding Brandon and Ruby apart, for Brandon could not find the emboldened rudeness to shake off the hussy and Ruby appeared wary of allowing her heart to weaken towards Brandon much because Miss Rochelle Behr was so often near him. Brandon saw the men swarming around Ruby while Ruby saw the hussy buzzing around Brandon. Unexpectedly, Cynthia believed she was given the inspiration that she knew may be needed. There was something she could do for her brother and Ruby after all! She would host balls and parties! She could throw all eligible men at Ruby, at once in her own house! Brandon would surely feel jealousy as Ruby received generous attentions from all those men. Cynthia could force Brandon to risk himself to save Ruby for himself and from all those men! Add to that, Cynthia could send minions of men after Rochelle to keep her quite busy and away from Brandon, as well. Cynthia Eaton had never been one to manipulate, as many women are wont to do, but for such a goodly cause, she knew that it would not be difficult to swiftly learn to exercise such typical feminine machinations.

Cynthia Eaton knew that she may indeed be required to plant many seeds into Brandon's mind. She might be forced to give him many suggestions and numerous speeches to encourage him on. She felt certain that her brother was fearful of being rejected by Ruby. He did not have the confidence to ask for the fair redhead's hand in marriage. He could not believe that such a specimen of perfection could ever love him enough to marry him. Brandon was too reluctant to pursue her on his own accord and Cynthia believed that she needed to help him along. Pitting some beaux against him, perhaps a desperately in love Brandon could be roused enough to finally try for Ruby's matrimonial hand. His sister had no doubt she could force him to pull it off, and as soon as may be.

Arrangements for the first dinner party were planned and ordered by the lady of the house: the food, the decorations and the gowns for Ruby and herself. Invitations were sent out. Since inviting Rochelle could not be avoided (because of her father, who was an acquaintance and neighbor), Cynthia Eaton planted a seed of desire with the boldest young man she could think of, pulling him aside in town one day, and telling him that Rochelle had been mentioning how much she was drawn to him. Cynthia knew the fellow well enough that this would be enough to keep the hussy occupied for that one night at least.

As Cynthia's party planning worked its way into full momentum, Ruby and Brandon began to worry. Was the merry widow going to become the silly woman once more? Soon Cynthia could not help but notice her brother and governess quietly worrying over her from slightly afar, and smiled within to realize that an added benefit of her efforts to bring Brandon and Ruby together had inadvertently brought them mistakenly together all the more on her own behalf. She was giddy within herself. What a boon! What a blessing this was! Seeing her brother and governess friend worry over her in this way caused her to implement her exertions all the more ostentatiously. She exaggerated her activity and thus Brandon and Ruby consulted one with the other all the more. As Cynthia openly talked of preparations to host dinner parties and balls, Ruby and Brandon worried together over the hostess.

While the first dinner party drew nearer, Ruby wondered and asked her employer what her duties might entail.

Cynthia enjoyed responding giddily, "I've grown so very fond of you, Ruby… you simply must attend all my dinner parties and balls. Once we have the children in bed… with Brandon's help of course… for I wish him to attend all my parties as well… and you know as well as I do that my dear younger brother cannot refuse me… we will enjoy late night social functions until I tire of them as much as you both are certain to do."

Of course when Ruby and Brandon spoke of this matter together, later on, they were each pleased to note that they would both be able to chaperone Cynthia and keep her from too much harm in the way of gold-hunting young men or any other man who would be wrong for her in marriage. And so, the dinner parties and balls began to take place, unfolding evening after evening, with Cynthia, Brandon and Ruby each determined to work their plans throughout and to fruition.

Cynthia's self-designed plan seemed only too easy to set about, for eligible men were so very willing to line up to try for the beautiful governess. On the western frontier, of course, there were many men vying for the attentions of the relatively rare numbers of ladies to be found in such general wilds. Ruby was the belle of each ball. Cynthia made certain of it. All was orchestrated to showcase the lovely redhead. Usually, Rochelle was breezily out of the way for the most part, for her father's money was enough of an attraction to the kinds of men who were after that sort of mercenary thing in a wife. All Cynthia need do was to point the materialistically inclined fellows towards the rich man's daughter. Watching Ruby being watched, approached and all but courted by many a man, Brandon stood back, complying with feeling severely jealous as per his sister's wishes to finally propel him in a culminating fashion towards his destiny in marriage to Ruby.

First there was a Mr. Riley. He was certainly handsome and young enough, and even came with a small fortune, but there was something wanting, even if Ruby had been interested in anyone besides Brandon Wallace. It was a wonder that Cynthia Eaton had never considered Mr. Riley for herself in the past, but, she had generally considered from amongst only those young men who were actively considering her (and pursuing her money). She had not been conniving enough to find subtle ways to go after the right sorts of men, young or older. She had simply chosen from those who placed themselves in front of her. Well, she had certainly given up on such things for now, for her focus was on helping Ruby *appear* to be considering such men for herself. All that aside, Mr. Riley was rather a boring chap. He could not carry on an interesting conversation to save his life. This unremarkable characteristic did not bother Rochelle, however, for when she saw Mr. Riley's interest in Ruby, even before she realized that Ruby had no interest in the Riley fellow, the hussy was throwing herself in front of the supposed sudden suitor, simply to prove that she was more desirable than the redhead. As Mr. Riley aimed at Ruby, Rochelle was busy trying to captivate Mr. Riley, while Ruby was energetically attempting to ignore him, as Brandon was feeling protective envy for the dearest angelic governess, while at least Mrs. Eaton looked on. All this playing before Cynthia's eyes was like pure gold and royal dainties at once.

Next, there was a Mr. Besser. He might have quite possibly been acceptable to the pastor at first glance, for he was full of scriptural quotes and sermons, but to most young ladies with their minds firmly intact inside their heads, this fellow was beyond boring. He was truly irritating. There was a sacrosanct self-righteousness about the man. He seemed to think that any woman that he should choose to tip his hat towards should fall at his feet in thanksgiving for such a blessing.

Not only was Mr. Besser an irritant of human nature, but he was rather unpleasant to look at as well. And to converse with the man for any length of time would convince any person with any level of intellect and quality of discernment of character, that he was terribly hypocritical, for he obviously preached one thing and did another. Ruby actually hinted openly at horror in being attended to by the fellow, and while Rochelle looked on in happy amusement, Brandon felt true pity for his dear, darling friend, and thus he invented excuses to take Ruby up to check on the children and other such things, so that she would be spared such unwanted attentions. None of this escaped Cynthia's sight, and while she felt true guilt for seeing Ruby tortured in this way by the Besser fellow, the result was too happy to continue in any remorse. Such ends did surely justify such means.

Then, there was a Mr. Derringer. Well, he was a rough sort who caused Ruby's eyes to widen with shock almost every time he spoke to her. She jolted back like a startled pony at his every attempt to attract her. To some women, he was of course ruggedly handsome and alluring in an untamed sense, but to Ruby, even his large and aromatically strong cigars were enough to repel her. She avoided him at all costs while he nearly chased her around the rooms. What an animalistic boar he was turning out to be. The man was so overtly wild western that even Cynthia Eaton wondered at how she might have him removed from the party that evening. She did not know the social consequences, but soon determined never to invite the man to her house again. Society be dashed if such a man must be a part of it! Seeing poor Ruby running about as if prey, being hunted by a rabid beast; Brandon felt true concern for his redhead, rather than feeling any jealousy towards the swine of a pursuer. In fact, it was Mr. Brandon Wallace who took matters into his own hands and surreptitiously encouraged Mr. Derringer to take his leave early that night, all that the fair damsel would be spared such relentless pursuance.

Subsequently, the illustrious Mr. Jardin minced in and onto the dance floor with a town beauty, before noticing the rare redheaded magnificence. He thought Ruby almost as beautiful as himself. Mr.

Jardin enjoyed dazzling everyone by speaking in foreign languages: first in French, of course, and then in Italian, German and even in Dutch! He did not care whether anyone could understand a syllable he said, and in fact, he generally preferred that everyone listened to the lilting and musical qualities of his voice and speech rather than anything he might have to say. If anyone in the company knew anything of these foreign languages at all, they would have found utter confusion in the rambling nonsense of disjointed words and phrases only strung together to impress the naïve listeners with such uncommon sounds. Though Mr. Jardin had resided in America for many years, he was surely still quite thoroughly European in his views, habits and accent; and always dressed so finely and with such frills that one might mistake him for one of the ladies in the party. Most, if not all of the women, would prefer to talk of fashionable ball gowns and such *with* him, than to let him speak regarding anything of love and marriage towards them. Ruby easily left Jardin to other ladies, to talk of finery that she was not cognizant of nor cared one jot about.

Mr. Colt could speak of nothing but his cows. Oh, but you would think that the world was made up of nothing but cows and all that they produced. Indeed, some of Mr. Colt's musings were only fit for a barnyard! Mr. Dallas did nothing but lament over his lost love, left way down in the south; so much so, that all around him encouraged him to go back to claim her for his own. Mr. Kansas was all business. He bragged about his investments in a way that even annoyed the men around him. These three supposed courters posed no threat nor caused any jealousy in Brandon regarding Ruby, but Brandon Wallace did feel the general need to rescue his maiden thrice more. As he took Ruby away from these men, Cynthia sighed and smiled blissfully. All was working according to her plans. Soon, Brandon would rouse himself enough to finally ask Ruby, and then Cynthia Eaton need only host one final singular party, or set of parties, centering 'round the marriage of her brother to her governess.

Now, there was the amiable, rich and handsome Mr. Wesson. It was true that he was a little old for the tastes of one still as young as

Ruby, at least for a serious consideration towards marriage. Indeed, one would have thought that Cynthia should consider him for herself, instead of allowing him to offer himself as a little pawn in her game of love and matchmaking. Well, Ruby enjoyed Mr. Wesson's company well enough as did he enjoy conversing with her, Brandon's jealousy was roused enough, Rochelle was kept away from Brandon to a greater degree, Cynthia was pleased with this continued success, and all were exhausted from the exercise. But nothing truly came of any of it. Cynthia was becoming frustration itself after all! The poor woman had spent so much in the way of money and energies, and all for what?! Ruby knew that many men quite liked her, though she should likely have known this before, only from having gone to church many times and to town a few. Brandon's jealousy had been raised here and there, but again, this had already been accomplished by happenstance and circumstance at church each Sunday and occasionally in town. Rochelle had been diverted and distracted by other men. Many a neighbor and friend had feasted and made quite merry so very many times at the grand Eaton home. But all for what?! There had been no proposal. Brandon and Ruby were not yet engaged. What confusion!

The Sunday following Cynthia's having grown tired of throwing dinner parties and balls to no true avail, she spied her brother standing off and alone, pining for his Ruby, who was attempting *not* to be surrounded by a few young men who were trying to garner her notice. Cynthia thought she sensed Brandon's pulling back from Ruby, as if he dared not venture in to vie for her, or perhaps simply that he did not wish to win a woman who was so easily adored by other men. Cynthia did not know what her brother was about and she determined that moment to take him aside to find out what the matter might be. A few short hours later on that day, when Ruby was quite busy entertaining the children, Cynthia found an excuse to take Brandon off and away for a discussion. Well, the dear sister had said barely anything at all before Brandon was scolding her for her interferences.

"I know what you are attempting to do, sister."

"What? What is that?"

"You have orchestrated endless feasts and dances in an effort to make me jealous by showing me how well Ruby is admired by other men."

Cynthia chose to remain silent on the point.

Brandon continued, "It was a worthless exercise... or should I say a very costly one? You did not need to expend all that outlay and effort to show me that Ruby could have as many suitors as may be, my poor, silly, dear sister. I see every week at church. I see whenever Ruby is in town. I hear. Jealousy brings me no closer to admiring, desiring or attaining your fair governess."

Cynthia was most vexingly flabbergasted, "Then what will, my boy?!"

"That is not your concern. If I will win Ruby, I will do it in my own time and in my own way. Whether or not I wish to is not your affair."

"I know, of course, but..."

"Cease and desist from playing matchmaker for me. I do not wish you to do so. I do not need you to try for me."

"But... I..."

"I think it not right for you to attempt to interfere in my affair of the heart. I do not wish to discuss it further. If Ruby is right for me... all will play out properly in the right time."

"But, Brandon... my younger brother..."

"Yes, you are my older sister... but you must learn patience. Be still."

Cynthia acquiesced to her brother's wishes, determined to exercise all due diligence towards greater patience (at least where Ruby, Brandon and a marriage was concerned) and also determined to turn her attentions back to her children who had certainly felt the want of a (much distracted) mother of late.

Fate aided Cynthia in turning her attentions towards her children, for, one after another, in cascading fashion upwards as to their ages; Jemma, Arthur, Albert, Camile and then Marcia all became ill. The three youngest were hit the hardest. Fevers filled the house. All else in the Eaton home also became ill, though none were quite so taken as the youngest children were. The family doctor was called and he swiftly came to the aid of all. Brandon was ordered to remain in the household throughout the nights until he was entirely well. Reassured that it was only something that should be recovered from in fairly short order, for a certain fever had been wreaking its havoc throughout the town, all settled into resting, and aiding nature in taking its due course in the matter.

Between the women of the house, the children were attended to most generously. Brandon even aided Ruby in telling stories to distract the children from their discomforts. Cynthia rose to the occasion and became the most doting mother, bringing whatever nourishments that were deemed helpful. All was easing towards normalcy.

By the time most all were beginning to feel far better and even nearing to their usual robust health, Ruby had taken a turn for the worse and the doctor had come back to worry over her. She had run herself ragged caring for everyone else, he said. She had succumbed to something more serious. It was her lungs. There was a foggy something that had settled in deep down, disrupted her breathing and would not seem to shift. The doctor talked a great deal with Ruby over her past consumptive kinds of troubles (particularly in her childhood, and the horrid cold conditions of the orphanage), and chose to lay down the law in the house such that Ruby would be watched over with great care. She was to have absolutely no duties to concern herself over. Indeed, she was to remain in her quarters, sleeping or at least resting as much as she possibly could do. As Mrs. MacLeod generally came and went from Ruby's room, Brandon was lingering around one corner or another, ready to ask how the governess was doing, for he had not left now that he was well. His brow was so horribly furrowed in his obvious concern for Ruby that Mrs. MacLeod began to smile at her own speculations about how this most eligible bachelor might be inclined towards the lovely, (though lowly with sickness) redheaded maiden.

When Ruby finally felt well enough that the doctor allowed

her to come out to sit amongst the rest of the household, Cynthia, Brandon and the children treated her like a queen. She was forced to sit at the head of the table, and summarily doted on with word, deed and delicious foods.

That first evening as they all sat together with the house's best china for dinner, Marcia lamented, "Ruby! We were so very worried for you!"

Camile added, "Yes, we were all saying our prayers for you!"

Arthur chimed in, "We thought you were gonna die!"

Brandon scolded, "Arthur!"

Arthur retorted, "Well, we did!"

Jemma smiled, "I knowed you wouldn't die, Ruby."

Marcia corrected, "Knew... you knew she wouldn't die."

Jemma frowned at her older sister, "I know. I said that."

Marcia began, "No... you said... oh, never mind."

Albert added, "The doctor was very worried. I think he thought you might die."

With lowered voice, Camile turned to her brothers, one after another, "Albert... Arthur... stop talking about Ruby dying!"

Ruby simply smiled at the loving attention.

Albert continued, "Well, we were all so sick... well, I was so sick... at first I thought *I* might die."

Arthur agreed, "I was so sick I thought *I* would die too."

Marcia settled things, "Well, we're *all* better now."

Camile tried to help, "Even Ruby."

Arthur amazed, "*Nobody* died."

Marcia frustrated, "Yes. Talk no more of *anyone* dying, I beg you."

Cynthia changed the subject, "Please pass me some of that wonderful bread, Brandon."

Brandon aided, "Would you like some butter or preserves with that?"

"Oh, yes, thank you, my dear brother. I shall take both!"

Brandon turned to Ruby, "What would you like? Is there anything more I could give you?"

14

Wedding

The pastor had requested a private audience with Ruby. Cynthia had offered the service of her carriage, but Brandon had intervened with an excuse to go to town himself and so had taken Ruby to her appointment, with plans to fetch her afterwards. Ruby was certain that she and the pastor would be discussing something to do with an upcoming event which was scheduled to raise money for charitable purposes, and so she was quite in a wee shock to hear the message he had for her. The pastor said that he was representing a goodly fellow, in a most important mission of communication. A Mr. Huntingford, a member of the congregation whom Ruby had seen here and there, had recently been to see the pastor to ask for his aid in regards to his hopes to begin courting Miss Ruby Steed. Mr. Huntingford had decided that in absence of a father (since Ruby did not have one of her own), that he should ask Ruby's pastor (for such a man is a sort of father of his flock) for such fatherly permission seemed within propriety and protocol to the fellow. The pastor had decided that prior to outright giving permission to the young man, perhaps he should speak with Miss Steed first, to see which way the winds blew with her, relative to her general or specific attractions or hopes. And so, the pastor was asking. The pastor more specifically wished to know if there might be any possibility that she might like to be courted by Mr. Huntingford.

Having fairly entirely recovered from the little shock amid all the lengthy explanation on the pastor's part, Ruby proceeded to attempt to offer her most gracious thanks and then gentlest apologies in declining any courting or offer from Mr. Huntingford. She certainly did not wish him to continue considering or begin working towards any offer of marriage to her, knowing full well that she would reject his attempts entirely. Ruby tried to explain that she currently had no interest in being courted, for she was quite content in the Eaton household and with that family. After advising Ruby regarding her general divine duty to hope and avail herself towards a worthy match in matrimony, and her repeated or more specific disinclination relative to Mr. Huntingford, the pastor said that he would endeavor to let the fellow down gently on her behalf.

As Ruby waited for Brandon to retrieve her, all the while that she was attempting her utmost efforts not to think on the recent near offer to herself, her mind was sharply reminded of (and then her attentions were firmly turned towards) another goodly and worthy, though older fellow in the congregation. Mr. Winchester Massey! She began pondering most seriously to herself. Would not Mr. Massey make an exceptional husband? Would he not be an excellent fit for Mrs. Eaton?! Ruby had seen him staring at her employer from afar. Surely he must be in love with her! Thus, before parting, she took the opportunity to seek out and ask the pastor about this man, and was given a glowing report (much to her smiling satisfaction). Having seen Brandon driving up, as Ruby and the pastor parted, unbeknownst to her, the pastor wondered within if she had her eyes and heart set on marrying the older, richer, Mr. Massey. He would have to give the man some hints about Ruby later on, to be sure. Perhaps since he could do no good for Mr. Huntingford, he could lend the favor over to Mr. Massey. It was a pastor's duty to try to bring happiness to all those within his flock, was it not? It was requisite that he preside over them like a father, to be certain. He was required to be as if a divine patriarch on earth. If he could not help the one man towards happiness with Ruby, maybe he could help the other. Surely, it could not hurt to try.

Even as Brandon helped Ruby into his carriage, she was bursting with gleeful news, "Brandon! Why did we not think of it before?"

"Think of what, Ruby?"

"Mr. Winchester Massey, of course!"

"Mr. Winchester Massey?"

"Yes! Of course! It is a revelation! I do believe that I have been given a revelation! As if from heaven above! The idea is divinity itself!"

"Mr. Winchester Massey?"

"Yes!"

"Ruby, please do tell me what you are trying to tell me!"

Ruby laughed and, "Yes! Of course! Well, let me just get to the point."

Brandon was a slight bit flabbergasted, "Please, yes, do get to the point."

"Well... the point is this: the pastor reminded me of something... that Mr. Winchester Massey is always staring at your sister."

"The pastor noticed this precise fact?"

"No... he only reminded of... well...when he... well..."

"Ruby! What?!"

"I am certain that he is in love with her."

"You are certain... because..."

"I have seen him staring."

"You saw him looking at her?"

"Yes. Well, it is the way that he stares at her. Why have I not seen before... I mean... why did I not notice... or realize... before... it has been so obvious, now that I have been reminded... now that I think on it. Mr. Massey is certainly in love with your sister. And the pastor gave me a most wonderful report on the man. He is rich, he is good, he is a widower, he has no children... which adds to his loneliness, of course... and he *loves* your sister!"

"Did the pastor say so?"

"Yes! Well, he did not *say* that Mr. Massey loves your sister... but he did say everything else I mentioned."

Brandon showed an ounce of concern, "That seems a fairly material point to be missing."

"Oh! That is beside the point! I have seen it for myself... before! I have just not *seen* it before."

"You have seen it… but you have not seen it?"

"Yes! I finally see it."

Brandon laughed, "Oh, Ruby, you think and speak precisely like a female."

Ruby looked at him severely and then, "Well, I am a female. I suppose that fits like a favorite old shoe."

"Yes, I suppose it does."

"So… what will we do to bring them together?"

"Oh, dear… more female thinking."

"Is matchmaking only thought of by females, then?"

"I really do not know for certain… but such things do seem the domain of women."

Ruby smiled, "Well, if it is my domain, I can take it all on myself… but… a little assistance from you would be most helpful."

"Are you really quite certain that Mr. Massey is in love with my sister?"

"Really quite certain."

"I suppose we could attempt something."

"We must!"

Brandon wished to be helpful, both for his sister's sake and even just simply to please Ruby, "What do you suggest?"

"Well, we both have tired of seeing your sister distract herself with far too many young men: all of whom we do believe primarily were after her for her money."

"Yes, her efforts have all been placed in the wrong directions."

"Let us each now come to a right understanding of the correct and fitting sort of man for your sister… he should likely be of similar age, disposition, wealth and society."

"Of course."

"Well, from what the pastor told me, Mr. Massey surely fits this perfect mold… and from what I have seen myself, he has admired your sister at church for quite some time. He is a shy fellow who likely cannot seem to bring himself to dare approach your sister, never mind court her. Thus, we must help him along."

"I suppose."

"What do you know of him?"

"I know that he has been a worthy man of business in these parts for many years. He is well respected among his peers. He is not given to drink, or to women or…"

"Well… it is obvious that he is not given to women. He barely speaks to them. It is a wonder that he ever was once married in the first place! We will surely have our work cut out for us."

"What work do you think we can do?"

"I can surely plant seeds of excitement in your sister's ear… it will be easy enough… you know, when we are at church, I can point him out and speak in complimentary terms about him… you know… whisperings to your sister to get her thinking about the man."

"Saying may be easier than doing… but you speak as if you have done some such thing before?"

"Oh, no… but, it should be easy… as easy as child's play. I am certain that it will work. He and your sister are both ripe for love."

"You speak as if you were born to match-make."

"Well, I am a woman."

"I suppose so."

"You suppose… that I am a woman?"

"Oh, no… only that you and… well, women in general… are very likely born to matchmaking."

"Yes… well… likely too true… quite right… so, I will work my matchmaking magic upon your sister and you will have to work on Mr. Massey."

"Work on… how? What would I do or say?"

"Oh, be friendly-like to him… work at knowing him better… perhaps there may be pertinent things that you could learn about him… from him… or from others… and, anyway…. once you know him well, you could… well, begin to hint or speak tom him of your sister…"

"Oh… you seem to make it all sound so very easy…"

"It will be… it should be… you are a man of business… you can speak to other men of business… well, consider it your business to begin to work upon this man for marriage to your sister."

"I may need your assistance… your counsel… I may need to speak with you often as to what should be said or done."

"Of course… we will be partners in this business venture. We will work our marital magic together."

Brandon smiled at that phrase from Ruby relative to himself. He enjoyed thinking of the need to coordinate and speak with Ruby so very much on his sister's behalf, though the thought did occur to him that he was acting the part of an outrageous hypocrite (if he should truly interfere in his sister's affair of the heart, since he forbade her to do so for him). But of course, he could not say such to Ruby, and any concern or hesitation he might express would be put down by her. He knew that he could not pose any argument against her plan. He assuaged his guilt by inwardly telling himself that since he would truly be leaving most everything to Ruby anyway, and he would only be helping in some small ways here or there, he did not truly need to feel that he was the guilty hypocrite. Besides, he thought, Ruby and he could save his sister from herself and a foolish match, by helping her towards a worthy match with this Mr. Massey, or any such goodly fellow.

The following Sunday, since Brandon was unable to attend church, having been called away on some pressing business matters, Ruby felt the full weight of beginning her loosely planned scheme to get Cynthia married off to Mr. Massey. She would have to do everything herself this week. Time was of the essence she sincerely felt, and she must strike while the iron was hot: or, more precisely, she must take advantage of every Sunday, since church was the only place that she could count on Cynthia and Mr. Massey seeing each other. Since there were no daily opportunities to place their figurative hands in each other's, she must make great strides each Sunday. The two weren't getting any younger, after all! And it was entirely possible that some *other* woman might suddenly see the gem that Mr. Massey surely was and a shy fellow like that might be caught by the wrong sort of woman in a flash! Add to that, there were still many of Cynthia's old beaux milling about and she might be fooled to the altar by one of them any day, after all! Ruby must save the pair of them. She had worthy work to do. Yes, it was the Sabbath day, but, it was the Lord's work in a very real sense. Surely, heaven would smile upon her worthy efforts of divinity at church in this way.

Ruby began everything well enough, by discreetly pointing out and quietly mentioning the man to her employer, "Do you know Mr. Massey at all?"

Cynthia's reply was rather bland, "Not really."

Ruby felt an ounce of desperation, "Well, I have heard that he is a very lovely man. He is a lonely widow... and very rich."

Cynthia seemed only mildly interested, "Really?"

Ruby was determined, "Yes... any woman would be very lucky to catch him in matrimony."

"Well, I have rarely spoken to him. He seems a little... standoffish, I think."

"Oh, no... he is only very shy. Shyness is such a wonderful quality, don't you think? A reserved man is to be desired in so very many ways."

"I suppose. I have never thought much about it."

Ruby invented something, hoping she was not truly telling a falsehood, especially in church, "Oh, yes... I have heard that a quiet man can make a most wonderful husband to most any woman... and a reserved man like Mr. Massey is not inclined to wander from a wife in any respect. I understand that he was a very devoted, kindly husband to his wife... you know... before she passed on beyond all the earth."

Cynthia's interest was suddenly peaked a little, "You seem to know a great deal about this Mr. Massey, Ruby."

"Oh, yes. The pastor was telling me all about him... that he is a very worthy... a goodly fellow."

Cynthia counseled, "He seems a mite old for you, though, Ruby."

Ruby was flabbergasted, "Oh, yes... of course... oh, no... I was not thinking of him for me."

"Oh, good..."

Ruby dared not venture further with her employer just yet. She decided to take another line. As soon as she was able, she forced herself forward to speak with Mr. Massey. She hoped that she could begin to build a bridge whereon the two potential lovebirds could walk towards each other.

"Hello… Mr. Massey. I am Ruby Steed."

He was all embarrassment and could barely speak in return, "Oh, yes… I know."

"I thought that since we have been fellow parishioners for quite some time, that perhaps I should finally introduce myself to you."

Mr. Massey looked around, obviously avoiding meeting eyes with Ruby, "Oh, yes… well… all right."

Ruby continued in her attempt to try a conversation with the fellow, but it was of no use. He seemed thoroughly uncomfortable and always seeking an escape from her. Soon, he was off and away and Ruby was left standing there alone, wondering what she might have said to offend the man. Or was he simply dreadfully unsocial? She threw out all thoughts regarding Mr. Massey and Cynthia for now. The hope seemed somewhat impossible for the time being.

Later at home, Cynthia took Ruby aside to converse, with all intentions of wise counsel, "Ruby. It is all over the congregation."

"What is?"

"That you are after Mr. Massey."

Ruby was all shock, "What?!"

"Yes… well… I would not have believed it, save for the fact that you seemed to talk of nothing but the man today… and then there you were introducing yourself to him. I was quite taken aback by your bold forward behavior. It simply was not like you to do such a thing. They say you are after his money."

Ruby was speechless.

"Yes, I also heard that he was mortified to have such a young beauty throwing herself at him. He is an honorable man… a kindly widower. He does not wish to give anyone the wrong idea about himself. I do not think that you should trouble him any further. Even if you are enthralled by him, Ruby, he does not wish for your attentions towards him. I doubt he would ever marry you, no matter how much you might wish for such an event. Even the pastor told me you were after poor Mr. Massey… and Mr. Massey was frightened near out of his wits when the pastor told him that you were asking about him."

Ruby was only shaking her head wildly, wondering if she should expose the entire truth to Cynthia. She decided to dare, for what else could she offer as explanation, "Oh, dear… Cynthia… you all have it entirely wrong. I do not think of Mr. Massey for myself. I was only trying for you… for your sake… and for his. I have seen him stare at you, Sunday after Sunday. I asked the pastor about him… for you. I was convinced that Mr. Massey was in love with *you* and I thought that I would play matchmaker for you… you know… to help bring you both together. Oh, what a mess I have made of things. What a fool I have appeared! I am so mortifyingly embarrassed!"

"Mr. Massey? In love with *me*? Do you really think so?"

Quite recovered from her own mortification due to her employer's instantaneously surprising response, Ruby smiled, "Oh, yes. I would wager all my savings on it. The way he watches you… he *must* be in love."

"But he *never* speaks to me."

"More proof of love… particularly from a *shy* man."

"Yes, I suppose so."

"I think the man so very in love that he is terrified to speak to you."

Cynthia smiled warmly, "Silly man… and I do mean silly in a fond and endearing sense."

"Well, he is horribly reserved."

Cynthia gushed, "Beautifully reserved, I think."

"Yes, I suppose so."

Cynthia was ecstatic, "Oh, to think that he could be in love with me… and all the while I have wasted my time with stupid young gold-mining fellows!"

"Well, perhaps you should bring yourself to talk to him. My talking to him only frightened him away… but I do think that your speaking with him may have the opposite effect."

"Perhaps… next Sunday… perhaps I shall approach and speak with him."

Ruby offered, smilingly, "Well, I will watch from afar and attempt to decipher the meaning of his reaction to you. I doubt he will seek escape from you as he did from me."

The following Sunday was a grand success. Ruby laid low, hoping all might be forgotten from the week before. Mrs. Cynthia Eaton easily made her way over to Mr. Winchester Massey to begin conversing with him. More correctly, Cynthia took the opportunity to invent an excuse to speak with the pastor just as he was talking to Mr. Massey. This resulted in introductions between the two near strangers. Mr. Massey was more than amiable. Indeed, he was fairly overt in his friendliness towards the lovely Mrs. Eaton, though it seemed clear to Ruby even from afar that Mr. Massey was exerting himself to the utmost degree in order to carry on as long a conversation with Mrs. Eaton as he could justify within propriety. He must *truly* be in love with her! The entire conversation went so swimmingly well, that by the end of it, Mr. Massey had luckily garnered an invitation to dinner that evening at the Eaton home. Perhaps more the truth of the matter was that widow had garnered an *acceptance* to dinner from the widower. At any rate, the pair of them were as delighted as doves, and neither could wait to see each other over table, no matter what might be served up to eat.

When Brandon arrived to visit a little with the Eaton family later on in that evening (for he had finally arrived home from his business travels), he was quite shocked to see his sister and Mr. Massey sitting together in the parlor, as if longtime lovebirds. Pleasantries were exchanged before Brandon took himself up to find Ruby sending the children to bed.

Once alone in the hallway with Ruby, Brandon began in hushed tones, "What has happened?! How did you manage it? They look positively mad in love! They nearly seem betrothed already! Ruby! You are a matchmaking *genius*, I think!"

"Oh, no! I nearly bungled the entire affair. What a catastrophe it all was *last* Sunday!"

"Explain! Ruby, you must explain *all* to me."

Ruby whispered forcefully, "Well, my efforts last Sunday only resulted in everyone, including your sister and Mr. Massey, thinking that *I* was after him and his money!"

"No!"

"Yes!"

"How did you salvage things?"

"Well, your sister pulled me aside to counsel me… she was most concerned… and I was forced to tell her the entire truth…"

Brandon inquired, "You did not mention my part in our plans… I hope."

"Oh, no… only that I was attempting to match-make the pair of them together because I thought him worthy of her and in love with her… and she quite took to the idea… instantly, really."

"Truly?"

Ruby fairly beamed, "Oh, yes. And today, she took matters into her own hands, and as you can see… he is truly in her hands completely."

"I cannot believe it!"

"Yes… she walked up at church and got herself introduced to him by the pastor… Mr. Massey was enamored… she invited him to dinner… he accepted… he came… and they have been pining over each other ever since. Like magic, the thing seems done. They will be married before we know it."

Brandon was happy shock, "Oh, my heavens."

"Yes… it does seem something of the heavens."

"This is too much! Why did you not push my sister in his direction sooner?"

"Well, better later than never."

"To be sure."

The pair of them whispered delightedly in the hallway for quite some time, all the while the other pair of them sparked together in the parlor. Brandon and Ruby chose to leave Cynthia and her new beau alone and quietly retired to the kitchen where Brandon could find much-needed nourishment. Mrs. Macleod thrilled with the two about Mrs. Eaton's happy developments as she served up leftover this and that.

Much later that night, after both Mr. Massey and Brandon Wallace had gone home, Cynthia pulled Ruby in to her room for a private conversation, "Oh Ruby! I am so very grateful to you for telling me about Mr. Massey! What a gentleman! What a wonderful man he is!"

"And he seems to be yours... if you desire him."

"Oh, yes. He has adored me from afar, he claims... and for a very long time, actually. I do... I do find myself very drawn towards him."

"That is truly quite wonderful."

Cynthia was all happiness, "Oh, yes, yes... and I would not be surprised if he made me an offer very soon. He so much as hinted towards that this very night! Is that not wonderful?!"

"Wonderful and exciting... he does seem to be such a lovely man."

"Oh, yes... I am certain that he is everything that I could ever wish in a man... in a husband... I am really quite thrilled at the prospect of marriage with him... oh, but do not tell a soul. Let us wait to be sure that I did not misunderstand his intentions."

Ruby could not but smile, "The man looked thoroughly in love to me... and there would be nothing to hold him back from offering his hand to you?"

"Oh, no... I cannot foresee anything in our way at all. I suspect it is only a matter of time before he does ask me."

"And you will say yes, of course."

Cynthia thrilled, "Of course... and, I cannot wait!"

Ruby warmly offered, "I hope he does not keep you waiting, then."

"Oh, Ruby... I have not ever told you before... but... my first husband... you know... my dead husband... well, he was *never* much of a husband. He treated me quite badly, to own the truth... and he shamed me quite publicly with his... well... habits with... other women. Over the years, his behavior grew worse and worse. He did not even attempt discretion and all in town knew that I was spurned by he who should have loved and been true to me. Life was mortification and misery with that man."

"Oh, I am so very sorry…"

"And he did not treat me very well in my own house, either. I was often humiliated in front of the servants because of how he spoke to me… and I was always so very sad. I had lost heart in everything… even in my children… and… well… I suppose when I was finally free of his tyranny and injustices, I went wild… I spent his money madly almost to spite him… I became so very silly… with other men… as you have seen. This Mr. Massey… well, I know very little of him… but I do know that he was gentle with and true to his wife while she lived… and he knows a good deal of how I was mistreated in my past marriage… and so, you know… he understands why I abandoned caution and good sense for a while. He thinks very highly of me… he does not hold my recent silly past against me… like others might… Oh, Ruby, he is so excessively kind and good. I will be so very happy with him if he… well, I do hope he requests my hand in marriage, for I would love to be married to him."

"Well, I will hope and pray for a speedy path to the altar for both of you."

Before the neighborhood had a chance to begin to be abuzz with the possible beginnings between Mrs. Eaton and Mr. Massey, Cynthia wore a most beautiful new ring, and their engagement was announced and spread round about. Everyone, the pastor included, thoroughly approved the match. Mr. Massey was an honorable man near Mrs. Eaton's age and wealth, and all saw a marriage between them as most respectable and full of happy prospects.

One day as Ruby assisted Cynthia in her wedding plans, for there would be a dinner and ball for the occasion, bride-to-be told her governess, "Oh, Ruby… I do hope that you will be as blessed as I feel right now. You surely deserve such happiness in marriage."

"Though, for now… I am content to stay governess to your children."

"And I am very blessed to have you, my dear."

"Thank you. I feel blessed to be a part of your family."

"I only wish… if Brandon would… if you two… you could…"

Ruby did not wish to speak of such things and so, most energetically, "Let us talk of flowers. We must settle on how many and which colors… and which kinds of flowers, of course. Cynthia, you must focus on your favorite flowers and colors. You must make a final decision almost this very moment!"

Cynthia was successfully diverted and Ruby did her utmost to keep her employer's mind on the task at hand.

Within a very short space of time, the grand wedding, dinner and ball took place at the Eaton home. A good portion of the higher elements of society folk in town attended. With Ruby's coaxing to please only but herself as the bride, Cynthia had chosen to generally only invite those she deemed to be her truest of friends, though, for appearances sake, there were a few persons who were allowed on the list, though they did not measure up to the best of friends and character.

The wedding was a lovely event, neither Mr. nor the new Mrs. Massey outshining the other in smiles, exuberance or obvious joy. Because Brandon, Ruby, Mrs. MacLeod and others took care of so very many details for Cynthia (to leave her free to rest as much as may be in her flutter of excitement), she was able to arrive at the altar fairly fresh and looking a good deal younger than her years would ever confess to. Mr. Winchester Massey thought himself the luckiest man on earth. As Mrs. Cynthia Eaton became Mrs. Cynthia Massey, a mantle of the happiest of wives settled upon her in spirit. Though she believed that she would love this man contentedly deeply and blissfully so, she did not know it for certain at that moment; but she would know married life as she had never known before, for it would be comparable as night to day for her. She had been blessed greatly in this man that she had chosen to accept. He would assuredly make her a very happy woman all the future days of their lives together.

The dinner was a delicious spread of varying fare, all chosen and prepared to include favorite dishes of the bride and her groom.

Perhaps there were too many courses. Perhaps the selections were too varied or strangely paired together for some tastes, but, no matter. To please all others was of no account. The tastes of both Mr. and Mrs. Winchester and Cynthia Massey were satisfied greatly and thus the couple of honor was prodigiously pleased. All was as good as need be, for the dinner was for the new couple, after all.

The Eaton children (who would relatively soon become just as known as the Massey children, as they had ever been known of before) were each on their best of behaviors, having been primed by mother, uncle, governess and more: to conduct themselves perfectly. To add incentive to all of them, they had been summarily, thoroughly and for some duration instructed that if they behaved themselves well and properly throughout the wedding at the church and the dinner at home, they would be allowed to stay up for the dance afterwards that entire evening, rather than being swiftly put to their beds for the rest of the night. It may or may not have been considered a rare thing by the attendees to see children dancing about during such a ball, but the newly-wed Massey's and the children of the bride did not care one whit what anyone might think of such a thing. During the ball, Ruby was prevailed upon by each of the two Eaton boys many times over, to dance with them and she gladly complied. The three Eaton girls commandeered their uncle Brandon for dancing too many times to count as well. More oft times than not, Ruby, Brandon and all the Eaton children filled the center of the ballroom floor. Thusly, most energetically preoccupied, in their heart of hearts, Ruby and Brandon each were glad not to feel compelled to dance with anyone else that they truly might not wish to be thusly connected to; though each surely did think of dancing together, for they as if danced together amid the children as it was.

Rochelle and some others were noticeably absent that evening, for Cynthia hoped to later successfully pretend through hints that a few invitations must have gone amiss somehow, and thus Brandon and Ruby were both spared much discomfort of that pressing kind.

Throughout the latter part of the evening of dancing, there had been one man who stood off and aside, watching Ruby intently. Few took notice of him as he quietly noticed the fair redhead from his generally hidden corner. When Ruby took herself outside into the garden for the cool breeze and a breath of fresh air on her own, the silently brooding sort who had been watching her every move, followed her out to where she stood admiring the stars and the moon. The night air sunk deeply within her, in the midst of every taken lengthy breath and thus she did not hear the stranger advancing quietly behind her.

As the man leaned uncomfortably close and spoke to her, after her initial understandable start of fright and subsequent quick composure, Ruby could smell an excessive amount of liquor emanating from his breath. She instinctively backed away even as she tried to behave and speak politely in spite of what she felt was rude impropriety on the fellow's part. When the large man backed the lovely governess into a secluded corner, she wondered if she might be compelled at some imminent moment to take drastic, forceful and violent measures to defend herself from whatever stupid fancy or malevolent intent the man might have in mind to attempt towards or against her, out there in the darkness.

Inside, the new Mrs. Massey had just waved Brandon over to her, "Why have you not danced with our dear Ruby all this evening? I know that you and she have been fairly occupied with my children, but, I would have thought that you would have found a way to dance with each other at least a few times... but I have not seen it... though I have watched for the occasion. You have highly disappointed me, my brother. What are you about? Our ball is to be over very soon, and you must dance with our beautiful and deserving governess at *least* once. I saw her going out towards the garden in the back. Please do retrieve her for a dance before it is too late this night. Go on, dear brother, go get your Ruby... dance with my governess!"

Brandon obediently complied with a happy excuse to beg Ruby to swing about on the ballroom floor with him. In a matter of a few swift and lengthy steps, he was out of doors and looking for his favored partner. Before he could see her, he heard a feminine peeping noise of suppressed desperation. His eyes followed the distressing sound to where Ruby was most energetically attempting to push a brute of a man away from her even as he harassed her in a most unpleasant manner. Brandon did not think twice before acting at once. In what may have been no more than an instant, he was suddenly at Ruby's side and was forcibly tossing the rogue off to one side after punching him squarely in the jaw.

Brandon could not tell precisely when he had called out the words but in the midst of the tussle he had loudly demanded, "Unhand her, sir!"

The villain was off and gone away out of the garden, one hand comforting his freshly bruised face.

Brandon was all concern for his fair redhead, "Ruby?! Are you all right?"

"Yes... yes... thank you, Brandon. I am safe. There was no true harm done."

"Well... it is a good thing I came when I did, or there may have truly been some harm done to you. Who invited that blackguard to the party in the first place? I don't even know his name. I do not think that I have ever seen him before. Have you? I don't believe that my sister had him invited."

"I cannot recall ever seeing him before. I suppose he came... with somebody."

"Well, he is gone now. Well... I... well... are you certain that you are quite well?"

"Truly. Quite well. Thank you."

"Well... my sister sent me to... that is to say... she told me you had gone out here... I came... to fetch you... to dance with me before this evening of dancing is over. Cynthia tells me that the ball is near done and that if I wish to dance with you, I must do so very soon. I do truly wish to dance with the most beautiful woman at the party, and therefore, I had better get you on to the dance floor with me before it is too late this night."

Ruby blushed.

"Will you? Will you dance with me, Ruby?"

Ruby smiled, "Yes... yes, Brandon... of course I will."

Brandon put out his arm for Ruby to lay hers upon that he might lead her into the ball for at least a few turns around the room.

As Ruby reached to put her arm in Brandon's, she heard a shot ring out. Brandon felt it. The shock of the unexpectedly sudden event threw them both to the ground. Gun in hand, the brutish blackguard who had been thwarted by Brandon in his attempt to accost Ruby, bellowed out something of spoken revenge from the garden gate in his drunken stupor of rage, and then was off and gone forevermore.

Brandon tried to get himself up but one arm failed him. He felt quite ashamed of himself for his weakness until Ruby proclaimed that he was bleeding from that particular upper arm. Brandon was not surprised to realize that he had been shot, for the wound stung tremendously. He did his utmost to suppress his wincing for the pain. Even as she cried out towards the house for help and tore at the skirt of her beautiful dress in order to swiftly wrap any available cloth around Brandon's profusely bleeding arm, she could see that her dear Brandon was suffering in pain though still trying to be brave in outward appearance.

In very short order, the new Mrs. Massey was at her brother's side in fitful concern. Mr. Massey and at least one other man helped Brandon inside, where his wound could be attended to by the doctor who most fortunately happened to be one guest of the wedding party. Ruby followed closely, feeling immense fear and trepidation for her very dear fellow. Indeed, Ruby, Cynthia and the Eaton children, all anxious worry, waited with baited breath for the doctor's pronounced diagnosis of Brandon's wound.

15

Proposal

As the good doctor wished for an operating room near the kitchen to ease the difficulty and facilitate the safety of removing a bullet, the patient was taken into such a convenient room in all haste. Every person who still remained at the ball had gathered round at one of the doorways of this particular sitting room as the physician examined the wound. The victim of the shooting was somewhat prostrate on a lounge, exercising full courage in near silence as the doctor prodded and poked at the bloody bit of opened flesh on his arm. Few could see much at all, for the crowd blocked a perfect view to all but the front spectators, but cascades of whispering revealed all or most of what was transpiring and any imagined, supposed, assumed, speculated, anticipated or predictable seriousness of the tragedy. Most ladies took themselves off to sit for maintained composure or to generally faint for the sight of blood (or at least any hint of seeing or hearing of such horrors).

The Eaton children had been assured by Ruby that Brandon would surely be well, as she ushered them up to settle down to bed for the night. The briefest consultation between Cynthia and Ruby had resulted in the belief that it was best to send the children to their beds, being that it was so very late in the evening and far past their usual bedtimes, as well as the glaring fact that they were far too young and impressionable to witness, to any degree, a bloody operation on their own uncle's arm. It could do no good to allow the children to worry off to the side, whether such concern may be fully justified or not. By the time the Eaton children were settled in for the night and their inwardly anxious governess was able to bring herself back down the stairs to focus her full attention on poor Brandon once more, the physician was ready to give his educated conclusion to all listening ears. Ruby was all anxious worry, thinking Brandon's injury somehow her fault, for it was obtained because of his defense of herself. As the good doctor began to speak, she was especially attentive to what he might say.

Only a flesh wound, practically just a graze, the bullet would not be found in Brandon's arm, for it was somewhere out in the garden. A collective sigh of relief was heard and felt all around. Some of the youngest men in the company fought in flight to be first to find the lump of metal out of doors, but upon hearing that detail, Mrs. Massey swiftly instructed her own new husband (in a hushed commanding request) to do her the favor of retrieving the bullet as a souvenir of the horrendous event for either Brandon (should he so desire to have and keep it) or perhaps for her own boys who would think it a true treasure to share between the two of them.

On the morrow, all had calmed down enough for Brandon and Ruby to encourage with insistence that Mr. and Mrs. Massey should take their wedding journey as planned. Mrs. MacLeod also assured Cynthia that Brandon would be well looked after in her absence. The doctor had cleaned, sewed and bandaged up the wound on her brother's arm and thus Brandon was well set to rest in his sister's home until he was quite fully recovered. Between Ruby, Mrs. MacLeod and all Cynthia's dear children, Brandon would be well taken care of while Mrs. Cynthia Massey could enjoy a wedding journey with her new husband. Mr. Massey had taken great pains and spared no expense to plan a most wonderful trip for himself and his new lovely wife, and so he was very pleased to be able to drive his bride away in his most luxurious carriage that next day. Ruby and the children smilingly waved from the front doorway. Brandon, who was resting in obedience to the orders of the physician as well as his sister and Ruby, had said his own goodbyes prior to the grand family send-off.

While Mrs. MacLeod spearheaded the cleaning up of the

household (for there was a great confusion of clutter due to the party the night before, as well as the tragic injury and surrounding kafuffle regarding), Ruby took charge of making certain that Brandon was entirely comfortable and very well fed. Marcia, Camile, Albert, Arthur and Jemma took great delight in scurrying from the kitchen to Brandon's room with all manner of delicious foodstuffs, as well as taking turns reading or telling him stories. Each of the children also took their turns in trying to take charge of all things. Brandon and Ruby oft looked at each other in enchanted amusement as his nieces and nephews, each one of her students, energetically served and entertained.

Within a day or two, just when all thought that the wounded victim was well on his way towards speedily healing, Brandon's injury took a turn for the worse, for the bullet wound and surrounding arm became inflamingly tender and sore. In point of fact, Brandon suddenly felt so noticeably ill that even he, acting as brave as could be, thought it prudent to request an urgent visit from the doctor. Shortly after the dear doctor arrived, he pronounced a serious infection having set in and voiced his dire concern for the patient, who was now beginning to suffer under a sort of infectious fever relative to the inflamed injury. New greater measures for the invalid were commanded from the medical man. Poultices of every variety were suggested (and some adopted), blood-letting was offered (though declined), medicines were ordered (and a few doses actually taken) and the strictest bed-rest and attention was required (and duly complied with). Brandon, Ruby, Mrs. MacLeod and each of the children agreed to do their part. The physician would come and go as he could.

Rather than a near instantaneous turn-around towards rapid healing and health as hoped, Brandon fairly quickly became somewhat delirious under his fever. The adults in the house agreed that the children should not see their uncle in this distressingly unnatural way, and so were to be kept generally apart and out of the invalid's room. Though Ruby knew full well it her personal required duty to put the majority of her attentions and time towards the children, she instead begged Mrs. MacLeod to keep the children occupied that she might predominantly care for Brandon herself.

Barely admitted to herself inwardly, Ruby was wrenched with worry for her dearest Brandon. She could not deny her feelings from within: she did love him and in a most doting way. The more she cared for his every need, even though he was oft barely aware of her presence beside him or generally within his room, the more her love for him grew all the deeper. Whether he was more conscious or confused, seeing Brandon lying prostrate on a bed, suffering, feverish, wounded (for her sake) and possibly near death (for the physician had warned that they must be prepared for anything), tugged powerfully at Ruby's heart. She was coming to feel that she wished he would swiftly gain health and then speak of marriage to her once more (and in an ever more meaningful way than before), that she might speak or at least hint to him of her truest feelings towards him and then joyfully agree to spending the rest of their earthly days together as man and wife.

At night, in one of his feverish fits, Brandon forcibly grasped Ruby's hand and begged in a raspy whisper, "Ruby! Do not leave me! Stay by my side always… I am in very great need of you… you are… you are everything to me."

Governess attendant consoled delirious patient, "Of course, dear Brandon… of course… I am here."

"If I die… you will not forget me?"

"You will not die. Brandon… you *must* live."

"But… you would not forget me… if…"

"I could not… ever forget you… but… you will *live*…"

"If I live… would you… will you… consent to… to be my own?"

Ruby was startled. Did he mean what she thought? Was he in his right mind to be asking such a thing? She could not find a way to answer him just then.

Brandon continued, speaking desperately from his feverish state, "Ruby? Ruby… are you there beside me?"

"Yes, of course, Brandon."

All agitation, he held her hand far more firmly, in a very tight grip as he spoke again, "Ruby? Please say that you will be my wife. Tell me you will marry me… and I will live… for *you*… I will live…"

Ruby was speechless.

Brandon near cried out, "Ruby… I cannot live without you… you must marry me… if you will not, perhaps I shall die… I cannot think of any but you… you must agree to marry me… that I might live."

Ruby wondered at the power of the fever to cause Brandon to say such things. Could the words truly originate from his conscious mind? Should she answer from her heart? Would he remember all such speech later on when his health and mind returned to a normal state? Could she only say yes to calm a feverish invalid, regardless of the future reality?

As Ruby wondered, Brandon was far from calm, "Ruby? I beg you answer me! Will you marry me?"

Ruby finally gave in, choosing not to worry as yet whether or not the offer was a valid one, "Yes, Brandon. I would happily marry you if you wished it."

"I do… I *do* wish it… I wish that you will be my wife… when I am recovered."

"Recover then… get *well*, Brandon."

"I can if you love me… for I do truly love you, my Ruby."

Ruby dared not profess her love to him, for she could not under such circumstances. She only gently squeezed, patted and stroked his hand. He was thoroughly comforted. Brandon dropped off to sleep. The fever did not disturb him as it previously had. His slumber was deep and lengthy.

Brandon's fever broke a few hours later amid his active dreaming in the late darkness of night. When he finally awoke the following day, his mind was fresh with his dreams. Dare he attempt in his current consciousness amid daylight to ask Ruby aloud of what he had dreamed of and hoped for in the night? Could she possibly answer him affirmatively as she had done within his feverish dreaming?

The physician had come early to check on his key patient and was delighted to find Brandon out of danger. Ruby had entered the room shortly after the doctor had nearly finished with Brandon, and was all the more relieved and happy to hear the good news. The joyous report was then fully tempered by the physician with warnings to both patient and nursing caregiver to continue all required doctoring care with due diligence that there be no relapse into dangerous territories of infection. Soon the physician was off and gone to administer to others in his personal care, with a promise to check back again within days (unless notified that he was needed earlier).

Ruby and Brandon were alone in the room. Mrs. MacLeod was at that moment herding the children to their breakfast. Ruby still stood where she had entered, holding Brandon's breakfast of choices on a tray. While preparing in the kitchen, she had not known whether or not Brandon would be ready for anything beyond fluids or perhaps some dry toast as well, but she had garnered every possibility for the invalid regardless of what he may wish to try. Ruby's feet were as if planted on the spot. She could not move forward towards her patient. His hunger was mounting. He wondered when he might sample from the tray. Both tried to push thoughts and questions from their minds, regarding words spoken between them the night before.

Brandon braved first, "Well… dear Ruby… what have you there for me this fine morning?"

Ruby smiled and stepped forward as she spoke, "Every good thing possible…. I did not know if you would only wish even water or tea… but… I gathered every likely morsel I could find for you to choose from."

"It seems that you anticipated my recovery. I am truly famished and think I just may consume everything that you have kindly brought for me."

"I do dare you to try, sir. It would please me greatly to see you so thoroughly fit for all these foods. I confess I am delighted that you are feeling so much better."

"And I have you to thank for my recovery."

"Oh... no... I..."

"You cared for me so diligently... what a fine nurse you do make."

"Oh, no... I am certain that..."

"Do not dismiss my compliment. It was duly earned."

Ruby only smiled.

Brandon proceeded to eat fairly heartily, though he did not persist in finishing every crumb that the fair Ruby had brought to him. It would have been too much for most any person just recovering from such an illness, and he was not such a fool not to admit to the fact, to himself or to Ruby. She said nothing hinting of chastisement or any reminder of her earlier daring challenge of consuming all on the tray, but only of her agreement to the wise prudence in eating no more than the body begs for in healthy need.

Ruby had been sitting nearby; offering pleasant conversation as Brandon had been eating and drinking. Her thoughts were most predominantly settled upon making her patient more comfortable in every way. She continually forced her mind away from her hopeful thoughts for a continuance of the former night's conversation. Did he remember, she wondered? Could he possibly have forgotten all? Did he regret what he had divulged in his delirium? She determined to forget all her current tendency towards such mind meanderings at present. There would be time or reasons enough perhaps in the near future.

Brandon's thoughts were certainly happily centered upon enjoying feeling better enough to eat once more, having the beautiful maiden Ruby near him to gaze upon between bites and sips, hearing her pleasing voice and listening to her kindly words; so much so that he was fairly easily able to leave his pressing hopeful dreams regarding her, aside for a time.

Indeed, it was somewhat surprisingly easy for Brandon and Ruby each to leave the dream that had passed between them secure in the past, presently, for both their focus of thought and deed was prudently put upon getting the recuperating patient fully well. Brandon had recovery work to do. Ruby had her nursing duties. Mrs.

MacLeod and the children were very soon recruited to help in the matter pertaining to lifting the wounded patient's constitution up to full health, and Brandon's convalescing room was once more a place of entertainment and family delights.

That day was full of activity revolving around Brandon, even when he was left to sleep a while; for all in the household exerted every effort to remain silent that the patient might sleep deeply. When Brandon could drift off to sleep, Ruby silently took the children up to their schoolroom to read and draw quietly, and to speak in hushed tones of all the exciting raucous things they would wish to do with their uncle once his health allowed him to be at liberty to play with them like a benevolent ruffian once more.

That night, after all the household was put to bed, Ruby laid awake staring upwards, under her own canopy of mahogany, trying to escape her true thoughts and feelings that slumber might find her, but finding no comfort other than giving way to her mind and heart. She had run herself ragged and kept ahead of such musings all the day long, but now in the quiet stillness of the late evening, she could outrun such thoughts no longer and was caught by what she had eluded all those hours of sunlight. With every fiber of her being she wished to confront Brandon fully with her own honest feelings relative to his words of love and marriage regarding her, whether hinted at previously or delivered so forcefully in his so recent interesting state of delirium. Brandon's desire for marriage to her seemed almost a dream too good to be true to an orphan-turned-governess, yet she knew what her ears had heard him say to her that night before, and she still could feel the strength of his hand holding hers. She dare not ask Brandon about such a subject in all candor, though she passionately wished to. She could not breathe a hint of a word regarding. Ruby felt assuredly that the broaching of this subject was within his own dominion, as a man; and more particularly, as the one who had offered his hand and proclaimed his love to her in the first place. She would have to wait. All such dreams of marriage must be up in the air until and unless Brandon should bring up the subject before her again, in full consciousness this time.

If he would but put forth that effort, Ruby would accept him for life (and beyond, which was her own belief in possibilities following mortal existence).

Brandon indulged his fancies relative to his prior night's dream that night, before he drifted off again towards greater healing in a depth and length of sleep. He had almost thoroughly convinced himself that he had only dreamt of confessing his love to Ruby, and begging for an answer from her to his question of marriage with him. He determined that once he had fully recovered, he should bring himself to finally bravely ask the woman he loved to marry him: in a proper way and perhaps with permission from either his sister or the pastor, a sort of attempt at complete propriety. He preferred to do all things rightly by Ruby. She deserved no less. He wished to start marriage off with her on the right footing. He desired to give Ruby every due that would be expected from even the richest and highest lady of society in either these still wildish western frontier parts or out east. Indeed, Brandon did not wish to give Ruby any less respect than a European princess might demand or expect to receive from any man who was offering a life of marriage with and to her; for what woman could be more virtuous or lovely than Ruby was? She deserved every goodly attention due her.

As the days proceeded, even as Brandon rallied in health and strength, Ruby felt a certain kind of sadness overtaking her. At first, she did not admit to herself what her melancholy spirits might be owing to, but then, some nights, when alone and still (after retiring), she allowed that she felt injured to the heart that Brandon had said nothing to her akin to his delirious addresses of love towards her during the depth of his illness. She could not make sense of it. Why had he professed sincerest love and firmly begged for her hand in marriage whilst so sick and feverish, and yet showed no true hints again of such thing once well again and since? Was love for her only a silly dream to him? Her heart broke at the thought of such a sad possibility.

Ruby's generally depressed inward state was temporarily diverted and relieved somewhat by happy cascading letters from her old friends

Scarlet and Patsy. Scarlet was full of joyous news of her betrothal to a most worthy and handsome young man who had been her favorite neighbor, friend and beau for quite some time. Patsy had written to announce that she had finally left the drudgery of the oppressive orphanage and the horrid Miss Mortimer forever, and had gone to work for the newly married Scarlet! While Ruby was so very happy for both her friends in their new lives that put them contentedly together in such a way, the news of Scarlet's marriage could only remind her of her own breaking heart due to Brandon's seeming indifference regarding his past dreamy declaration of love to her and his feverish offer of marriage. Ruby seemed to love Brandon all the more, even as he seemed to absolutely forget what was once as if in a dream between them.

Most fortunately, more diversion was fated for Ruby, for she was suddenly treated to an overdue visit from her two favorite cooks in all the world. Mrs. Hanratty and Miss Rhodes had come journeying together to visit their freckled redheaded friend. The visit was a delightful one, as the children entertained Brandon far enough away from the parlor that only muffled sounds of the women laughing and chatting could be heard in the distance. Miss Rhodes had managed to leave her assistant cook fully caring for her kitchen and hungry subjects at Horizon House school ,while Mrs. Hanratty was enjoying a small vacation between jobs, for she had left the ungrateful Biggsley wretches' to work for an excessively kind family for far higher wages. Mrs. Biggsley would need to find herself another cook to flog, and would likely have to pay a far higher price to do it, for the wages of late in and surrounding all that town had been climbing quite nicely. All this joyful visiting from her dear old friends was a good medicine to Ruby's soul, but did serve to keenly remind her of what she had left in and near Horizon House school.

Once her friends were gone home to the territory of that happy school, Ruby gradually became overtaken with a homesickness of the heart and mind. She found excuses not to attend personally to Brandon's needs, preferring to send the children or Mrs. MacLeod to serve the patient while she attended to almost anything else.

Soon, though the physician finally gave Brandon permission to go to his own house, being that he was well out of harm's way (near completely healed) and recovered enough to return home; Brandon was subconsciously finding excuses to stay. He thought that his nieces and nephews needed their uncle in the house until their mother and new father returned home from their wedding journey. Brandon also hoped that he could find the exact moment to speak to Ruby, though the opportunities to steal her away for a private audience seemed strangely lacking to the utmost degree. He finally began to painfully sense her desired distance from him. He wondered if she had only been a ministering angel (a goodly nurse) but did not harbor any feelings of marital love towards him. Was her growing distance of attitude and behavior, her outward sign to him that he should leave the happy fantastical dreams about her relative to him in his past? Did she only think of him as a brother? He did not know what to think of Ruby and what she might think of or feel for him. Brandon soon took himself home to his own house in a state of wondering confusion and general wretchedness.

In several days' time, Mr. and his new Mrs. Massey were finally arrived home from their wedding journey. The children were all elation to see their mother, as well as the numerous brightly packaged gifts in her and her husband's arms. Dancing and jumping about like steady rain on a roof, the children were required to be hushed at least several times by their governess before they could be calmed and brought to a near proper level of reasonable decorum.

The new blissfully glowing couple had decided that Mr. Massey would now live at his wife's home and his own grand house could be sold off to the highest bidder. Being a highly successful man of business, Mr. Winchester Massey enjoyed many contacts which were sure to bring him a lucrative deal on his great old place. His heart was no longer there, back at his own house, and thus he wished to invest solely in his dear Cynthia, her life, home and most particularly her children. Never having become a father in his first marriage, Winchester Massey was only too delighted, charmed and joyful to know that he would in time become a true father to the children of his lovely wife. It had been exclusively his idea to return bearing gifts for the children, and had not Cynthia held back the reins on her Winchester, he would have spent a mighty fortune spoiling her children with treasures.

Brandon was noticeably absent in the ensuing days, away protecting his ailing heart even all the while that Ruby was every daily moment preparing to protect her own heart should Brandon come calling as he was entirely expected to do. Cynthia Massey wondered aloud many times over, 'where could Brandon be?', so much so that her gallant husband took himself out and over to find the missing brother.

Brandon was all surprise to see his new brother-in-law at his own door that sunny morning, "Well, well… my new dear brother! What brings you to my door?"

"I am come to bid you to your sister's place. She is all concern over you. Have you been unwell?"

Brandon adeptly guided Winchester Massey into his front sitting room even as he awkwardly answered, "Oh… I… yes… I suppose I should have come calling upon you both long since. It is terribly remiss of me to put off a visit to my sister and her husband so very long, since I did know of your return… but… I have been much engaged in business and…"

"And what business could have kept you from your sister, I pray? You know of how she depends upon you. She is quite dejected for your neglect, I tell you!"

"Well, I…"

"I have been required to calm my wife as she has wondered and worried about you, sir. Ruby and Mrs. MacLeod have assured us that you were well when you left them, but, having been told of your severe illness, Cynthia has been inclined to think you ill once more. Thus, I determined to make my way over to you instantly and demand that you relieve your sister's worries regarding you."

"Tell her to worry not, for…"

"Tell her yourself, I beg you! Why can you not come call upon your dear sister?"

"I…"

"And… if I may be so bold… your Ruby seems quite dreary for your loss as well."

"*My*… Ruby?"

"Yes… man, I have *eyes*, you know. All the while I was watching your sister; I caught glimpses of you watching your sister's governess. I am no fool. I could plainly see that you were in love with Ruby long before I was so fortunate as to win Cynthia for myself."

In a sudden desperately heart-rending move, Brandon decided to bow to his new brother: his face fell as his shoulders drooped, "Yes… I do love Ruby… but it is of no use. She does not love me. I have been avoiding a visit in order to protect my aching heart from her."

"Protect your heart from Ruby?! My word, man! She is as much in love with *you* as you are with her! I saw her watching you as well… yes… all the while she did her utmost to fend off all those other fellows, she obviously secretly hoped that she would be pursued by you, my dear boy."

"Oh, no… I do think you must be wrong…"

"Brandon, boy… even now… every time your name is mentioned by your sister or anyone else, I see it in Ruby's face. She is pained. I am convinced she thinks that you do not love her."

"Oh, no… I think she is pained because she only cares for me as a sister or a friend, and she knows that I love her… and so she feels discomfort at the prospect of rejecting me. She fears my proposal. She is *so* good. She does not wish to crush my spirit and…"

Winchester was shaking his head vehemently, "Brandon, m'boy, this line of thinking is *pure* folly. You could not be more wrong, I am certain of it."

"I cannot attempt… I do not wish to put Ruby in such a position… she is *too* good to be discomfited…"

"Let me speak with her then…"

"No!"

"Then I will speak to Cynthia and she will speak to Ruby for you."

"No… no… it is of no use…"

"Of no use!? Brandon! Think, man! *Think* what you are doing! You are quite likely throwing away your best chance at love! Or, at least you are causing yourself and that dear beauty to suffer while you take *forever* to boost your courage enough to ask her to be yours."

"I can find courage enough… I only fear to harm an angel of perfection…"

"Oh, Brandon… dare to try, won't you?"

"I have tried to follow her lead…"

"I too waited to follow your sister's lead… I should not have done so… I regret that I waited so long to finally pursue Cynthia… do not wait much longer and risk losing the one you love… as a man, it is your own *duty* to lead… and she will follow if you do so."

When Winchester Massey returned to his beloved bride, he took her aside for a private conference. None in the house heard a word.

That evening, once alone in her room, Ruby sat down to write to her dear friend and mentor, Iris Fenton. All the talk of Brandon had been tearing at her heart. She could suffer no longer. She determined that it was finally time for her to leave her position of governess forever. With her beloved husband at her side, the new Mrs. Massey could manage her children well enough herself or she could find another more suitable governess. Ruby began to believe that she needed to concern herself upon her own needs, for she must put at least her aching heart first, this once and finally. In her quickly scrawled letter to Miss Iris Fenton, Ruby begged a position again as teacher at Horizon House. Ruby believed her sadness might never abate if she stayed near Brandon, for she could not bear to see him toy with her or marry another and thus Ruby wished to move away from him before that would most inevitably happen.

When Ruby came down for breakfast the following morning (her letter to Iris Fenton in her pocket, awaiting her first opportunity to send it off with the post), she was uncomfortably shocked within to see Brandon unexpectedly sitting at table with his sister. They had obviously been deep in quiet, private conversation when Ruby silently arrived to accidently interrupt them. Both Brandon and Cynthia stopped short, not wishing Ruby to hear a word of what they had been saying. The poor governess felt a hint of having been talked of and felt horribly awkward regarding. She stood in the doorway, attempting in her thoughts, what way she might invent an excuse to leave; that Cynthia and Brandon might continue speaking again as they had been doing prior. The three all stared at one another, suspended in time briefly, though it felt to each of them to last a temporary eternity.

Before Ruby could bring her mouth to speak something of going back to her room (retreating) to fetch something (or some other excuse) to give her legs permission to take her away to anywhere but there with Cynthia and especially Brandon, Ruby was suddenly mortified to hear and see Cynthia speak of, and then abruptly leaving herself. In that moment, Ruby was transparently alone with Brandon, with no seeming way to leave him with polite impunity within her reach. Brandon's mouth opened, his mind extending itself hopefully at length whilst he appeared rather silly, gaping at the beauty he so heartbreakingly longed for. Brandon sat still. Ruby still stood.

Though Mr. Brandon Wallace was an excessively successful man of business and for quite some years had been adept at speaking with all manner of men in order to further his own financial achievements; he was at a general loss in the realm of speaking with his Ruby. It is true that the redhead, being a woman, was no man as Brandon was accustomed to dealing with. It is also fact that Brandon was younger than his new brother-in-law, Mr. Winchester Massey; and perhaps therefore possessed less in the way of maturity, experience and wisdom, particularly in the ways and thoughts of women. He was also somewhat younger than his sister, Cynthia, yet, he was enough older than Ruby that one would think him quite fully capable of speaking to her of what was pressing upon his mind and encouraged by his heart. Though, even with all his accomplishments and triumphs in the world of business around him, with Ruby standing so breathtakingly before his eyes, he was soundly made as if a little boy, stutteringly halting and faltering in his wish to speak his own mind clearly and forcefully enough to capture this young woman to become his own.

Suddenly, Brandon stood up (remembering manners and propriety relative to a man and a woman, standing and sitting and so forth) and begged that Ruby would take a seat, "That I might speak to you a moment?"

Brandon's tongue had swiftly recovered itself for etiquette's sake, at least. The stillness and silence being broken between them, he gained in courage, "Ruby. Please do sit down here with me. I must speak with you. I have something… something pressing upon my mind that I must say to you."

Ruby had not sat down as yet. She put her hand in her pocket to hold onto the letter that she had written to Iris Fenton, as a sort of symbolic measure and private gesture to give herself a kind of strength. She politely complied with Brandon's request, acquiescing to his gentle command, almost calmly setting herself on a chair that held Brandon at a safe distance, leaving a number of chairs betwixt them both.

A complete surprise to Ruby, Brandon boldly brought himself over to sit next to her. She shifted her chair slightly away from him to ease her discomfort, for her heart was beating rapidly and her tears were welling, her eyes readied for such a rush of water against her will. She held tightly to her letter to Iris. Ruby determined to remain composed, blinking down all dogged tears, painfully looking forward to when she would away to safety within Horizon House. She would force herself to listen to this man, and then, she would escape from him and the pains he seemed to bring to her. She could not imagine what he might have to say to her. Why would he toy with her? Why would he playfully dance about with her heart? Could not he leave her alone to her misery? She wished to be away from him forevermore. She could not chance a moment's glance at him, for her heart might break altogether and a waterfall of tears would surely follow.

Abruptly, Ruby's free hand (the hand not firmly holding the letter in her pocket), was seized most forcefully by Brandon's two. Ruby's smallish soft and smooth hand peaked out amid Brandon's clasping tanned gentlemanly hands.

Gazing intently at her, he falteringly spoke, hushed though energetic, "Ruby. I have long wished to beg… to beg for your hand… in marriage."

Ruby blinked twice. She frowned in an attempt to think what she thought she had heard him say to her. Did he truly ask her to marry him? Was he in earnest?

Looking down, away, and then back at her, "I know I am not worthy of you… I know that you do not love me as I do you… but… if you will only give me a chance… an opportunity to win your heart…"

Ruby dared to look into Brandon's gaze. He was truly sincere. He was indeed asking her to marry him. He was professing his love for her. She could not entirely believe what she heard and saw of this Brandon. Ruby was surely stunned. The letter in her pocket was summarily crushed.

"I near took myself away for a goodly length of time to spare you from my courting impulses towards you… for I know you could find a better man… you surely deserve more than I can give you… perhaps you could never love me… but, my sister and her husband convinced me that I would never forgive myself if I did not try to win you. Forgive me, but, I had to ask."

Brandon pulled his hands away. He looked away. He sighed. He shifted his chair a little away. Pain was written on the man.

The still silence was broken by Ruby's voice as she impulsively reached out to swiftly grasp the one hand of Brandon's which was still within reach of the both of hers, "Brandon. Can it be true? Do you truly wish me to marry you?"

He looked back at her, his eyes wet. He rose above his lumped throat and answered hoarsely, "Yes. If *only*…"

"If only I *loved* you?"

"Yes."

"Oh, Brandon… the thing is done. Long done. I have loved you since I barely knew you. I have fought loving you. How I have fought it. I thought I should never wish to marry… until I found you. You turned my heart upside down... and I did not think that you truly loved or wished to marry me."

Brandon could not save more than the one tear from falling own his whiskered cheek. Ruby's blinking sent several salty fluid drops cascading down her own freckled cheeks. Brandon brought his other hand to envelop both of Ruby's, most tenderly.

Once again, the young besotted fellow inquired of his beloved, "Ruby, will you marry me? Will you marry me as soon as may be?"

Ruby delighted, "Yes! Oh, please, let us wed... tomorrow if it be at all possible!"

The household was abuzz and aflutter. Preparations were sent into full swing. Even the pastor's wife was in a tizzy trying to make everything perfect for dear Ruby's wedding. Cynthia was so elated at the prospect of her brother marrying her darling Ruby that she had no thought to worrying over losing the world's very best governess, or whether or not and when she might consider searching out for a new one. Mrs. Cynthia Massey took great pleasure and pride in taking her soon-to-be new sister to the shops in town to choose all needful wedding clothing, as well as jewelry and any other sort of fancy or feminine thing a beautiful young bride might need for her wedding and her wedding journey. Cynthia delighted in throwing her money about. Ruby was all caution in the matter of letting coins be spent so frivolously upon herself, though Cynthia overrode her in every little detail and thing. Cynthia wished for Ruby to be exceedingly spoiled beyond all joyful measure.

Ruby mournfully expressed, "Oh, Cynthia... you are *too* excessively kind to me! I am embarrassingly obliged to you, though I... well, I think you far too generous, and I wish to curtail your expenditures upon me..."

"Let me pay half of my due to you! Will you please? And don't forget that I am now richer than ever. Indeed, my dear husband expects and even begs me to spend freely of his coins, as he lives in my house and sits uncomfortably upon his mountain of money since selling his own home! Please allow me to spend only a little on you. I owe you a debt of gratitude for what you have done for my family, for me in my marriage to my wonderful Winchester, and now you are giving my brother the very best women for a wife he could ever have hoped to stumble across and win to be his own!"

"I am terribly humbled..."

"Oh, dear Ruby... if only you realized *half* your worth. I will always be eternally grateful to Iris Fenton for sending you to me in the first place. I have half a mind to set her up in her own marriage!"

"Oh? And who do you have in mind? Anyone?"

"Anyone, indeed! A Mr. Browning! He is an attractive, kindly, rich and lonely business associate of my husband. I think he might just suit Iris perfectly."

"Oh, truly?"

"Oh, yes... I have told my Winchester all about lovely Iris, he has told me all about his Kenneth Browning fellow, and we both are certain that we might have a match in the making. I have met the man and thoroughly approve of him for Iris, though I cannot believe that you have not been introduced to him as yet! I am delinquent in my duties. He should have come to dine many a time already! Anyhow, we will see what we can do with the pair of them when Iris comes for your wedding festivities! I am determined to give them a true chance at wedded bliss!"

"Yes, do give Iris a chance at a happy marriage! Hopefully, he will suit her... for I cannot imagine her not suiting any appropriate man."

"Well, to own the entire truth of things, I wrote to Iris all about Kenneth Browning, even including a small likeness of him; she gave me leave to give him permission to write to her, and they have been corresponding happily ever since! From all I understand, there is a match already in the making! They seem to be lovebirds from afar!"

"You have both been withholding secrets from me! Neither you nor she breathed a word or a hint of it! This is too much! What happiness for her if it turns out to be!"

"Well, well... would it not be something if we made a perfect marriage for Iris as well in all this happiness we are enjoying ourselves? What interesting twists fate sets before us. You were sent to me to save my children and then because of you, my brother and I find the best fortunes in marriage, and now, perhaps Iris will finally find a worthy match as well… And to think that I thought my chance at true love was wasted on a beast of a man… may he rest in peace, regardless… she and you thought yourselves happy to remain lifelong spinsters… and now… we are all to be so very happily married. Who would have thought any of such things would have come to pass… before you came to be with me, dear Ruby?"

Ruby smiled, eyes shining towards her dear sister, "I have shared in much joy here."

Cynthia returned the warm smile and then her face turned quite serious, "Well, I always thought it a sort of blasphemy that women as fine as you and Iris could go through this life without worthy husbands."

"And it is also a true blasphemy that you should ever have suffered with other than someone as worthy of you, as your Mr. Massey."

"Oh, I must teach you to call him Winchester. He would not mind it, m'dear. Truly. He will be as your brother, do not forget!"

"I will try… if he truly does not mind it."

"Well, well… Iris should arrive by tomorrow. I called her here early on pretext that we need her help with wedding plans… all that I might get her and Kenneth together for as many days as possible. I wish to get the thing done and settled before she has a chance to go back… you know… unengaged! I must have my old friend engaged to her beau even before you are sent off on your wedding journey!"

Ruby delighted, "Would that not be grand?"

"Oh, yes… and so… speaking of your wedding journey… I understand that you will visit old dear friends out east before you set off for your European tour?"

"Yes, I do have a few friends that I will be overjoyed to see again… though, going out east would have been wedding journey enough for me. I tried to convince Brandon that I did not expect anything so grand as Europe!"

"Oh, Ruby, but you must allow Brandon to show you Europe… even if only to set the hoity-toity Miss Rochelle Behr in her place. I have heard already that the hussy is beside herself in frustration and blazes that you have caught the prize she had protractedly attempted to win once more."

"Oh, please… do not mention her…"

"I'll say no more save that I thank heavens that my brother saw clear to choosing you. Anyway, you will adore Europe!"

The following day brought Miss Iris Fenton, who was thrown into the midst of the wedding preparations and plans. She, Cynthia and Ruby were as cheerful as ever they were together, speaking of any related subject that their minds drifted to.

Cynthia could not resist, "Iris, do not forget to tell those Biggsley women that Ruby is marrying a wonderfully perfect and handsome young man!"

Ruby added, with specific clarity in order to ignore the Biggsley womenfolk, "I will not argue with anyone on such a point regarding your brother."

Iris Fenton smiled with raised eyebrows, "I fear that there will be some jealously in that quarter."

Cynthia turned fully to Iris, "And make certain that you tell Mrs. Biggsley that Ruby has caught herself one of the richest men in these parts!"

Ruby suddenly counseled, "Do not tell her to spread any falsehoods!"

Cynthia laughed, "Oh, Ruby, but you do not know that my brother is far richer than I ever was! Brandon is always so reservedly secretive!"

Iris smilingly lamented, "Oh, dear, the Biggsley women will be green with envy… that is certain!"

Cynthia and Iris enjoyed the thought whilst Ruby wished to think elsewhere. Her mind happily drifted to settle upon her sweet Brandon.

Suddenly, Cynthia's mind set her mouth in an interesting direction, "Iris, my dearest friend! Who could have known your act of providence when you sent Ruby to become my governess? Did you ever speculate for a moment that my brother might fall in love with her?"

Iris turned on her broadest and most mischievous smile, "I confess… I confess that I thought once, or perhaps twice, that your Brandon might find my Ruby irresistible. I knew that he could do no better, as I knew that Ruby would find him worthy of herself. Yes, I confess that I was not terribly surprised when it all finally unfolded as it should."

Both Cynthia and Ruby stared at Iris in shocked disbelief. Cynthia was the first to regain her tongue, "Iris! You sent Ruby for Brandon? You were matchmaking from afar? You planned all this from the beginning? I am in shock!"

Iris defended herself, "I suspected that a match might end in the making, and I knew that it would do them both good; though in the meantime, I knew I was sending you the best governess you could ever deserve. In the very least, you were gaining Ruby as governess. I knew that you needed her all the more than I suspected that she and Brandon needed each other."

Cynthia got over her shocked state, "Well, you were right on both counts. Ruby saved me and my children and then my brother, after all. I suppose I should begin my endless thanks to you…"

Iris diverted, "Oh, no… thank the heavens above… for that is where the idea truly came from in the first place. I shall take no credit for the hand of providence… only in doing my duty in obeying a higher command by following the little persistent feeling I was given to send Ruby to you."

The happy three ladies continued in pleasant lively conversation, and more pointedly, in finalizing all coming wedding plans.

And so, Ruby was wed to her darling Brandon in a beautiful ceremony and they settled into married bliss quite nicely in his lovely home after their extended European tour. Marcia, Camile, Albert, Arthur and Jemma were each and all very soon excited to know that at least one Wallace cousin was expected to arrive to earth from heaven above. Ruby and Cynthia were thrilled beyond measure to shortly thereafter greet the new Mrs. Iris Browning as their intimate neighbor and dearest friend, after she returned from her own wedding journey with her dear darling Kenneth. The Masseys, the Brownings and the Wallaces oft met together in true happy company in their firm friendships together. Any of the three grand houses would do, every time they each wished to gather: to feast, to sing, to laugh and to dance; all together, like unto one grand extended happy family.

Elsewhere, quite near on the western frontier, the Biggsleys continued in their greedy ways, gradually found out for their true natures, and generally shunned by all fine folks. Mr. Biggsley began to find business successes evading him, so much so, that Mrs. Biggsley became so very poor as to become beholding to her daughters' husbands, who, being men of *some* sense, did not like their mother-in-law at all whatsoever, and thus Mrs. Biggsley did find herself in a position of having to cook and clean for herself. Though the Biggsley girls were married to men of general sense, they were each miserable in their matches nonetheless, wanting what they did not possess, and never appreciating what they had. The Biggsley boy became a no-account fool, freely wasting any money that his father might give him: he was in a fast way towards a miserable marriage himself, as he only generally found himself matching up with girls that would likely become very much like unto his mother. Mrs. Hanratty and Miss Rhodes enjoyed fond friendships together and with many other goodly folk in the parts surrounding where they still lived. Horizon House continued to bloom as it always had, being guided by women who had been well mentored by their beloved Miss Fenton.

Out east, Patsy joyfully served her benevolent Scarlet in comfortable surroundings and peaceful circumstances. Miss Mortimer was caught in her growing habit of stealing from Mr. Graver and was then summarily thrown out, to become a lowly maid, forced to work very hard all the remaining days of her miserable inconsequential life. Mr. Graver soon tired of his part in the running of Humble House Orphanage and sold it off quickly to a kindly old couple who took the place and all the children under their gentle wings, to turn it into quite the opposite of what it had long since been. No longer was any poor orphan *doomed* to go there, but the name of the institution was changed to Heaven's House, and entirely reflected the spirit of the home and the treatment and outcomes that befell any child fortunate enough to enter therein.

Author of numerous books, Kerri Bennett Williamson has also worked many years as a freelance artist. Deeply connected to her pioneer, early and Native American ancestors, and greatly inspired by favorite classic English literature (such as the works of Jane Austen, the Brontë sisters and Elizabeth Gaskell); Kerri has found her niche in romantic historical-setting fiction.

Made in the USA
San Bernardino, CA
13 August 2015